MASTERS & MATES

The Master's Pet
Dream Mate

D1795872

Stormy Glenn

EROTIC ROMANCE

Siren Publishing, Inc.
www.SirenPublishing.com

A SIREN PUBLISHING BOOK
IMPRINT: Erotic Romance

MASTERS & MATES
The Master's Pet
Dream Mate
Copyright © 2010 by Stormy Glenn

ISBN-10: 1-60601-790-X
ISBN-13: 978-1-60601-790-6

First Printing: March 2010

Cover design by Jinger Heaston
All cover art and logo copyright © 2010 by Siren Publishing, Inc.

Printed in the U.S.A.

PUBLISHER
Siren Publishing, Inc.
www.SirenPublishing.com

DEDICATION

To Pooky, maybe one day you'll master your own pet.

SIREN PUBLISHING *Classic*

THE MASTER'S PET

Stormy Glenn

THE MASTER'S PET

STORMY GLENN

Chapter 1

The end of the world as we knew it did not come as everyone expected. There were no wars, no conflicts, no great battles. Instead, it started with a simple virus. Before anyone knew what happened, millions were infected and had died.

The world had never seen a sickness like this. Most died within a few hours of contracting it, but not all. Some became the monsters seen only in Hollywood movies. It seemed their sole purpose in life was to create death and mayhem.

Some became carriers of the disease, infecting others with their blood. They looked normal, behaved normally, but they were deadly. Still others seemed to be immune to the disease, not getting infected no matter what. For all of those that survived, life was changed forever.

Chaos and destruction reigned over the earth until almost nothing was left. Cities were destroyed, entire cultures erased as governments tried to eradicate the virus, but to no avail.

The orderly societies of the early twenty-first century were no more. Those who survived banded together in small groups littered throughout the world and tried to survive as best as they could. But everything had changed...

A loud thud outside of his room woke Jiri from his troubled sleep. He sat up, hanging his legs over the side of his small cot. Wiping a hand down his face, Jiri tried to remember what day it was, but nothing came to mind.

He wasn't even sure if it was day or night. There were no windows in the small room he inhabited. Just a door, a small army cot, a crate Jiri used as a nightstand, a lamp, a cardboard box that housed what clothes he had, and a sink with a mirror. It wasn't much, but it was his.

Jiri stood up and walked to the small sink in the corner. He turned on the cold water and cupped some in his hands, bringing it up over his face. Turning off the water, he looked at himself in the mirror above the sink.

Lifting his hand, Jiri gently touched the soft purple color around his left eye. Well, at least the swelling had gone down a little. His lower lip was another matter. It was cracked and swollen, dried blood on the corner.

He'd looked worse, but that didn't mean it hurt any less. He was tired of getting beaten up. Of course, he was also getting used to it. Maybe that's what he had such a problem with. He was getting used to being knocked around by his stepfather and his buddies.

If that didn't say how sad his life was, Jiri didn't know what did. A person should never get used to being beaten up. Jiri just didn't know what other choice he had. He had nowhere to go and no money to get there. Larry had taken all his money last night, right before he and his buddies beat the crap out of Jiri.

He was stuck living in hell with Larry. He lived in what was once a storage closet in Larry's auto repair shop. He worked from the time the sun came up until it went down, repairing cars and working the gas station out front.

Jiri didn't intend to be here forever. He'd run the first chance he got. He had even been saving up his tips until last night. He had to because Larry didn't pay him anything for the work he did. Oh, Larry provided just enough food and personal supplies to keep Jiri alive, but just that.

Shaking his head at the sad condition he was in, Jiri reached into his cardboard box and pulled out the cleanest shirt he had to wear and pulled it on. He buttoned up his pants and pulled his shoes on.

He was just reaching for the door handle of his small room when he heard another loud thud outside of his room. Turning the handle slowly, Jiri eased the door open and peered out. He really hoped Larry and his buddies weren't still around. He so didn't need to run into them again, at least not until he healed up from the last little party they threw for him.

Peering out, Jiri couldn't see anything. The garage was unusually dark. Maybe it was nighttime? Jiri was a little confused by that. If it was night, Larry must have let him sleep in and Larry never let him sleep in.

Jiri looked around the door, but he still couldn't see anything. A small shaft of light was coming from Larry's office, which meant Larry was still around. Just perfect. Jiri hoped he could avoid him, but knew he probably couldn't.

Closing the door behind him, Jiri made his way toward the far door. To get to it, he would have to pass by Larry's office, but if he were really quiet, he might be able to make it without Larry hearing him.

As Jiri inched his way past the smoky glass window of Larry's office, he saw shadows move out of the corner of his eye. Jiri froze, trying to even out the breath that was rushing rapidly in and out of his chest.

It was only when Jiri heard the voices coming from Larry's office that he realized the people in Larry's office were not Larry's buddies. He didn't recognize their voices, but he knew that they were angry.

"You cheated me, you son of a bitch," someone yelled.

"I didn't mean to, honest, Zane. It was a mistake!" That was Larry. Jiri would recognize that simpering voice anywhere.

"You're damn right it was a mistake!" the other voice shouted. "Now, how do you plan to rectify it?"

"Rectify?" Larry asked. He sounded confused, the moron. Jiri seriously doubted Larry even knew what the word meant. He was big and beefy and as dumb as the day was long. "Rectify" would be a word he wouldn't understand.

"Fix it, you dumbass. You owe me, and if you don't pay up, I'm going to let Slash here take it out of your hide."

Jiri quickly covered his mouth with his hand as a giggle threatened to escape. He would love to have a ringside seat to someone handing Larry his ass. He'd even pay for seats, if he had any money.

"I don't have anything, I swear," Larry cried out.

Jiri could see enough shadow coming through the smoky glass to know that Larry was cowering back in his chair. A much larger man bent over him. Several more shadows moved throughout the small office.

"I don't believe you, Larry," the large man replied. "I want what's mine!"

Jiri's eyes widened as the man picked Larry right up out of his chair by a hand at Larry's throat. He barely had time to scramble out of the way before Larry flew through the window to land on the floor at Jiri's feet, glass spraying everywhere.

Jiri stood there, stunned to see his stepfather, the man who had made his life a living hell, lying on the floor covered in blood and broken glass. Jiri's eyes slowly made the track back up the wall to the shattered window.

Shock held Jiri immobile as his eyes landed on the biggest man he had ever seen. He leaned out the broken window, staring down at the floor where Larry lay groaning. Jiri could just make out several more large men standing behind him.

Jiri knew that the shadows he stood in hid him from view. He also knew he hadn't made a sound, not even a whimper, but the man's eyes suddenly moved up to look right at him as if he knew exactly where Jiri stood.

The man's dark green eyes seemed to pierce the darkness and see right into Jiri. It was enough to give Jiri the willies and make him turn and run. His heart beating frantically in his chest, Jiri ran for the side door and what he hoped was freedom.

Pulling at the door, Jiri cried out as a large hand landed on his shoulder, stopping him from leaving. Jiri struggled, hitting out with his hands as large hands lifted him into the air and threw him over the man's shoulder.

"What did you find, Zane?" one of the leather clad men called out, causing the others in the group to laugh.

"Find yourself a toy, Zane?" another man called out.

"Naw, Zane found himself a pet," yet another man said, laughing.

Jiri continued to pound on the back of the man holding him, but it was like hitting at a bulldog with a napkin. The man didn't seem to feel any of it. He didn't even stop his stride across the room.

The air in Jiri's lungs suddenly left him as the man dropped him onto his back on the floor. Jiri took a moment to breathe, his chest rising and falling rapidly. Then he looked up at the man that had caught him.

Just as quickly as he had regained his breath, it left again as Jiri realized how big and menacing the man actually was. He had to be at least six and half feet tall, maybe taller. His shoulders were so broad, Jiri was surprised he could even make it through the doorway without turning sideways.

The man crossed his massive arms over his chest and stared down at Jiri. Jiri gasped, a shiver of panic coursing through his body when he saw the skull tattoo on the large man's arm. He knew that tattoo. Everyone knew it. It was a Death Dealer's tattoo.

The Death Dealer's were the scariest, deadliest motorcycle gang on the West Coast. They made the motorcycle gangs of the 1970s look like a kindergarten class. No one messed with them and lived to tell about it.

Jiri glanced over at his stepfather, still lying on the floor groaning. He wondered how stupid the man could possibly be. Jiri knew the world had gone to hell, but cheating the Death Dealers was just asking for trouble.

"What's your name, boy?"

Jiri looked back up at the large man standing over him. A wave of apprehension swept through him as he realized that the others had moved over to surround him. He sat in a circle of hell and he was about to die. Jiri just knew it.

"J-Ji-Jiri," he stammered.

"Who are you?"

Jiri suddenly felt like every brain cell in his head had left. He couldn't understand what the man was asking. He had just said who he was. Was there some other answer? "Jiri," he repeated.

The man abruptly squatted down next to Jiri, grabbing his chin with strong fingers and tilting Jiri's head up. Jiri quickly lowered his lashes, afraid to look the man in the face directly. He tilted Jiri's face to one side, then the other as if he were appraising him.

"Who gave you these bruises, boy?" he asked.

Jiri couldn't keep his eyes from straying over to his stepfather, but he quickly brought them back when the man grunted harshly. Jiri's eyes widened. He could see anger in the man's eyes. He silently prayed it wasn't directed at him.

Just as suddenly as he had squatted down next to Jiri, he stood up and walked over to stand over Larry. "You cheated me, Larry, and I don't take kindly to being cheated. So, you and I are going to have a little conversation about what you owe me and how you're going to pay me back."

Jiri didn't like the look in the man's eyes as he glanced back over at him. Something was about to happen and Jiri knew he wasn't going to like it one bit.

"Slash, go with Jiri and get his belongings," the man ordered. Before Jiri could even protest, he was hauled to his feet by a large beefy hand on the back of his shirt and propelled out of the room.

"Where do you bunk, boy?" Slash asked.

Jiri pointed to the storage room that had been converted into his living quarters. The man holding his arm pushed him toward the door, pulling it open and shoving Jiri inside. Jiri stumbled forward then stopped, looking over his shoulder at him.

"Well? Get to it, boy. Get your shit together. Zane doesn't like to be kept waiting."

Zane? Was that his name? Wasn't that the name of the leader of the Death Dealers? Jiri's mind was a whirlwind of questions and fear as he grabbed his clothes and shoved them into his pillowcase. What was going to happen to him? Why did Zane want him to gather all of his belongings together?

Jiri grabbed the one picture he had of his mother off the nightstand and pushed it into the bag, then looked around the room to see if he forgot anything. Shaking his head, Jiri realized that everything he owned fit into a standard size pillowcase. *How sad was that?*

"Is that everything, boy?"

Jiri looked up to see Slash leaning against the door frame, his arms crossed over his chest as he watched Jiri. He tightened his grip on the bag in his hand and nodded his head. Yep, this was everything he owned in the world, if he didn't count the money Larry had stolen from him the night before.

"Come on, boy, Zane is waiting," Slash said as he grabbed Jiri by the arm again and escorted him back into the main room.

Jiri quickly noted that Larry now sat in his office chair when he walked back into the room. The man Slash had referred to as Zane leaned back against the wall, his arms crossed over his chest. The moment Jiri stepped into the office, Zane's eyes zoomed in on him.

The way that Zane looked at him made Jiri nervous. It was like Zane could see right into him, know what Jiri was thinking, what he was feeling. Jiri felt naked and exposed under the man's intense gaze.

Leaning forward slightly, Zane motioned with his hand and pointed to the floor. Jiri's eyes drew together in a frown. He didn't understand what Zane wanted. A sudden push to his back made Jiri stumble across the room. The solid body he ran into stopped him.

"Sorry," Jiri whispered as he tried to push himself away from Zane. He wasn't brave enough to look up into the eyes of the man holding him. He just knew if he did, he would see his own death in them.

"Stay," the man simply said.

Then Jiri did look up. Stay? What? Was he a dog or something? Jiri wanted to ask what Zane meant, but the other men in the room captured his attention. They had all started to encircle Larry. They looked very menacing.

"Have we come to an understanding, Larry?" Zane asked.

Larry remained silent for several moments, then reluctantly nodded his head. Jiri knew he wasn't going to like what Larry had to say the moment his stepfather turned to look at him. There was too much enjoyment in his eyes.

"You belong to Zane now, boy," Larry said. "You'll go with him and do what he says."

Jiri tilted his head a little, his eyebrows drawn together in a frown as he tried to make sense of the words that had just come out of his stepfather's mouth. "What?"

"You heard me, Jiri," Larry replied.

"You can't just give me away."

Larry jumped to his feet and started toward Jiri, his hands fisting at his sides. "I can do any damn thing I want, boy."

"No, I won't do this," Jiri said. He knew he wasn't going to like what Larry had to say and he was right. After all the things Larry had done to him, he had never expected this. Larry had given him to the Death Dealers?

"I don't remember asking, you little shit!" Larry spat out. "I owe Zane money. Money I don't have. He's agreed to take you instead."

"You sold me?" Jiri asked in horror. "I'm your son."

"You ain't my son, boy," Larry yelled. "You're just the whelp your mother saddled me with before she died, the stupid bitch. And you've never been good for anything but costing me money. It'll be a relief to finally have you off my hands."

Considering the dire situation he was in, Jiri should have used his head to try and get himself out of trouble. But the anger he felt toward the man who had been his stepfather for nearly fifteen years overcame whatever common sense Jiri had left.

Growling out his anger at Larry's smug face, Jiri dropped his bag on the floor and leapt across the space between them, his hands going toward Larry's neck. He wanted to wring the very last breath out of his slimy body.

Large hands wrapped around Jiri's waist, holding him off the ground and away from Larry. Even if he couldn't reach him, Jiri had the satisfaction of seeing Larry jump back in shock, and maybe just a little fear.

"Whoa, Zane, looks like you have a spitfire on your hands," Slash laughed.

Several of the other men in the room laughed along with Slash. Jiri could feel his face heat up with embarrassment as the chest pressed against his back rumbled with laughter. It was only then that Jiri realized Zane held him.

"I like a little fire," Zane said.

"He owes me money," Jiri ground out between clenched teeth. "He and his buddies took it from me last night before they beat me up, and I want it back."

"That right?" Zane asked, looking over at Larry. "You holding out on me, Larry?"

"No, no, of course not, Zane. The boy's lying, I swear."

"Third drawer down there's a gray lock box. He keeps the key on a string around his neck," Jiri said. He pointed to the drawer.

Jiri was surprised when Zane set him down on the floor and released him. Zane didn't have to say a word. Jiri walked over and pulled the drawer open. He grabbed the little box, setting it on the desk.

He turned to Larry and held out his hand, waiting for Larry to hand the key over. Larry glared at Jiri for several moments before reaching up and pulling a string over his neck and handing it to Jiri.

"You're gonna pay for this, boy, mark my words. You're gonna pay for this," Larry sneered.

"You first, you fat pig!" Jiri said. He reached down and unlocked the box. He could hear several astonished exclamations from those standing around him as he lifted the lid to reveal several stacks of cash.

Jiri counted out the one hundred and eighteen dollars that Larry had stolen from him the night before, all the money he had in the world. Once done, Jiri shoved the money into his pocket. He closed the lid and locked the box.

"I just want what is mine," Jiri said as he glanced up at Zane. "What you do with the rest is up to you." A satisfied smirk on his face, Jiri picked up the box and handed it and the key to Zane.

Jiri pushed past Zane and walked over to stand next to the wall. Grabbing his bag off the floor, he leaned back against the wall, turning to watch what Zane would do with Larry and the remaining money.

Jiri tried to show disinterest, but knew he had been caught looking when Zane chuckled. He could feel his face heat up again and wondered if that was going to be a regular thing in his life now. Zane seemed to have the ability to make him feel very embarrassed.

"Slash, since Larry here was so forthcoming with his finances, you and the boys may divide up what remains in the box between you," Zane said as he set the box down on the table and unlocked it.

"You don't want a cut, Zane?" Slash asked. He was already reaching into the box to pull the money out.

Zane shook his head. He glanced over at Jiri. "I have what I want."

Chapter 2

Zane glanced down at the head resting back against his chest. He shook his head in wonder at all the golden, white blond hair covering Jiri's head. His hair was so light it looked like each strand had been spun in sunlight.

It had captured his attention the moment he spotted Jiri standing in the shadows of Larry's garage. If a sudden stream of light from Larry's office hadn't chosen that exact moment to hit Jiri, Zane wasn't sure he would ever have seen the man, and that would have been a damn shame.

Zane had come to Larry's garage after discovering that Larry had cheated him. The motorcycle parts Larry had sold to the Death Dealers were inferior parts, breaking down before they could use them. No one cheated the Death Dealers and got away with it. Zane had gone to Larry's garage, determined to teach Larry a lesson.

Instead, he had discovered Jiri. Zane couldn't even think about how excited he had been the moment he had learned that Jiri belonged to Larry. Once that had been established, Zane had no guilty feelings about taking Jiri as payment for Larry's debt.

The bruises on Jiri's face alone told Zane that he could offer Jiri a better life than he had with his stepfather, even if it was only as Zane's pet. Jiri could never be anything else. The life that Zane led was a harsh one.

Jiri wasn't strong enough to be a Death Dealer. It took strength, experience, and just a bit of madness to be a Death Dealer. Zane doubted Jiri was even big enough to ride a motorbike by himself.

But Jiri was just perfect for what Zane had in mind for him. Jiri's ethereal beauty had enchanted Zane the moment he had seen him. The golden blond hair and deep sky-blue eyes had only added to Jiri's allure.

What had really sold Zane on the idea of having Jiri was the way the little man had attacked Larry. Jiri had been so fierce even when facing a man that was vastly larger than him and one that had beaten him, probably on numerous occasions.

Jiri hadn't even hesitated. The moment he had realized that Larry had sold him, Jiri had gone crazy. The only reason that Zane hadn't let Jiri attack Larry was because he didn't want Jiri hurt again. But Zane felt strangely proud at how ferocious Jiri behaved toward Larry. It showed that Jiri had a backbone, even if it was a small one.

Jiri was sure to need it in the new life he was about to have. Even though Zane had claimed Jiri and the rest of his gang would protect him, there was always the chance that someone would try to hurt Jiri, or take him.

As pretty as Jiri looked, Zane knew it would be the latter. Jiri could garner a lot of money on the open slave market. The long dark lashes covering Jiri's sky-blue eyes alone could bring a grown man to his knees.

Zane would have to keep on his toes to protect Jiri from the riff raff that inhabited the world around them. There weren't too many places left that were safe for anyone, not since the plague had taken over the world and killed most of the population. What was left almost wasn't worth protecting. After the dust had settled, so to speak, the people who were left in the world had banded together in small groups for safety.

Zane had lost his family long before the plague hit. His mother died from working three jobs, his father from alcoholism. When the plague hit, Zane's life didn't change that much. He joined the Death Dealers, working his way up until he became the leader.

And there were a lot of perks to being the leader of one of the most feared motorcycle gangs on the West Coast, the least of which was being able to claim Jiri as his. Zane was pretty sure that special perk was going to quickly become the most important one.

Zane looked back down at the head resting against his chest. Jiri had his eyes closed as if he didn't even perceive that they were speeding down the highway at nearly a hundred miles an hour. He hadn't said a word since they had left the garage. He hadn't even put up a protest that he now belonged to Zane. Jiri had just gathered up his stuff and followed Zane out of the building.

Turning the bike, Zane pulled onto the main road that ran the length of the little town the Death Dealers claimed as their own. It was nothing more than an old ghost town now, but they had made it theirs. Zane had discovered the old ghost town several years ago. When he had become the leader of the Death Dealers, he had moved them from the big city to this little plot of land.

Zane was proud of the fact that his little town had a grocery store, schoolhouse, barber shop, bike repair shop, mercantile store, a small café, and even a jail. The biggest building in town was the hotel. It also doubled as his headquarters.

As the leader of the Death Dealers, he had the largest accommodations in the hotel. His quarters were on the second floor of the hotel, taking up the entire front of the building. From his balcony Zane could oversee the entire town. He also had a large office on the main floor with a walk-in safe.

Zane pulled into his reserved parking spot in front of the hotel. He looked down at Jiri. He hoped Jiri liked it here because he wasn't leaving any time soon. Zane also hoped that Jiri would adjust to being Zane's pet.

It wouldn't be easy, not for either of them. Zane lived in what was essentially a master/slave world. Those who were stronger protected those who were weaker, but that protection came at a price.

The masters protected and cared for the slaves. In exchange, the slaves provided the masters with comfort and entertainment, including seeing to their sexual needs. In the world they now lived in, it was an equal trade.

Zane had resisted taking a pet in the past. He didn't want the added responsibility. He already had an entire gang and town full of people to care for. But there was just something about Jiri that called to Zane. He had to have him.

"Hey, little one, you ready to go in and see your new home?" Zane asked.

Jiri shrugged his shoulders.

Zane reached down and tipped Jiri's head back so that he could look down into his sky-blue eyes. "It's going to be okay, Jiri. I won't let anyone hurt you anymore. You belong to me now, and no one messes with what's mine."

Jiri didn't look like he believed Zane. He had a sudden desire to feel Jiri's soft, pink lips against his and leaned down to kiss him. It was everything Zane had hoped for and more. Jiri's lips were so soft and lush. Zane couldn't contain his deep growl as he pulled Jiri closer.

When Zane finally lifted his head, Jiri's face was flushed. He watched Jiri's eyes dart up to his, then fall down just as quickly. Jiri clearly looked embarrassed, but the hard bulge in his pants told Zane Jiri had enjoyed their kiss.

"What's wrong, little one?" Zane asked softly. He rubbed his thumb down the side of Jiri's face that wasn't bruised. When Jiri shrugged his shoulders again, Zane chuckled. "Uh uh, little one. That won't do. I asked you a question and I want an answer. What's wrong?"

Jiri's eyes came back up to meet Zane's. "I'm not supposed to like that."

"Like what?"

"Whe–when you kissed me. It's wrong and I'm not supposed to do it."

Zane's brows drew together as he frowned. "Who told you that?"

"La–Larry," Jiri replied.

"And you believe him?" Zane chuckled. "This is the same man who beat you to a pulp and took all of your money, then sold you to me. Somehow, little one, I don't think Larry is the authority on anything. Besides, now that you belong to me, what I say is what matters, not Larry."

Zane was thrilled when Jiri let out a small laugh. "I guess," Jiri said.

Zane tilted Jiri's face back up to his. "No *I guess* about it, Jiri. Would you rather believe me or your stepfather?"

Jiri was so quiet that Zane was almost afraid that he wasn't going to answer him. When he did, though, it wasn't the answer Zane was expecting, but it thrilled him just the same.

"It's okay to like kissing you?"

Zane laughed. "It's very okay. In fact, I prefer it. Just as long as you remember that you're only allowed to kiss me. I catch you kissing anyone else and what Larry did to you will be a cakewalk. Got it?"

Jiri quickly nodded. Zane watched several emotions move across Jiri's face, wishing he could read the little man's mind. He seemed to want to ask something, but Jiri was either afraid to or embarrassed.

"What do you want to ask?" Zane asked, trying to set Jiri at ease.

"When I was with Larry I worked in the repair shop. I fixed whatever cars Larry told me to fix, cleaned up the shop, and stayed out of Larry's way." Jiri glanced up at Zane. "What do you want me to do? Am I supposed to fix your bikes?"

Zane shook his head. "No, Jiri." He realized that Jiri really had no clue about what was expected of him. While Zane hoped that Jiri wouldn't fight him too much when he found out what his duties were, Zane wasn't going to give him up.

"Your only duty is to me," Zane said. "You answer to me and only me. If you behave yourself and do as I tell you, I'll reward you. If you misbehave, though, I will punish you. I'd really prefer not to have to punish you, Jiri, so you need to listen to what I tell you."

Jiri gulped, then nodded. "Yeah, I think I'd prefer that, too."

Zane chuckled. He lifted Jiri to his feet and climbed off his bike. Zane reached down and opened his saddlebag. He pulled out a small leather collar attached to a length of chain. He could see Jiri's eyes widen considerably as he stood back up.

"Until I can get you permanently marked, this will have to do," Zane said as he wrapped the length of black leather around Jiri's neck and clicked the collar closed. "This tells everyone that you belong to me and if they mess with you, they're messing with me."

Jiri's fingers slowly moved down the length of silver chain, then his eyes came up to meet Zane's. "I'm your pet?"

Zane could hear the worry and confusion in Jiri's voice. He could see it in Jiri's trembling fingers. Zane wished that there was an easier way to introduce Jiri to his new life, but there just wasn't time. Jiri had to be wearing Zane's mark before they went inside or someone would try to claim him and then Zane would have to hurt them.

"In a sense, yes." Zane nodded. "Remember, I told you. You belong to me now. You're my possession, my pet. You do what I say when I say it. If I tell you to strip off all of your clothes in a room full of people, I'd expect you to do it without protest."

Zane didn't think it was possible, but Jiri's eyes widened even more. This time, though, a pale face devoid of color framed them. It made the blue of Jiri's eyes stand out even more, making them look huge.

"You–you want me to take all my clothes off in–in a room full of people?" Jiri whispered, the horror thick in his voice.

"If I tell you to, yes. I won't, though. What belongs to me is for my eyes only." Zane reached over and flicked a length of golden white hair off of Jiri's forehead. "You'd do best to remember that, Jiri. I don't share. Ever."

"I don't understand any of this," Jiri murmured.

Zane knew that Jiri had spoken to himself, that he hadn't meant for Zane to hear him. Zane reached over and patted Jiri on the back. "I know you don't, baby. I'll try to make it as easy for you as I can. Just remember to do exactly as I say and you'll be fine."

Jiri didn't even nod. He just clutched his pillowcase closer to his chest and looked at the floor. Zane took a deep breath and let it out slowly. This wasn't going to be easy for either of them. Zane had never had a pet before, and Jiri obviously had no idea what a pet was. They would just have to muddle through.

Zane grabbed his saddlebags off the bike in one hand. In the other, he grabbed the end of the chain attached to Jiri's collar. "Come on, baby, let's go get you settled. I'm sure you could use a hot meal and a warm bath."

Zane pulled Jiri behind him as he led him into the hotel. He could see people staring. He could feel their curiosity about Jiri and see the instant arousal Jiri inspired in nearly everyone that looked at him. He wasn't surprised.

Jiri was beyond beautiful. Zane was almost afraid to see what Jiri would look like after a few good meals and a hot bath. A little more flesh on his fragile bones, some soap and water, and Zane was positive Jiri would be breathtaking.

He couldn't be anything less. The delicate bone structure of Jiri's face alone made him seem elf-like. The golden, white blond hair that fell in waves down to Jiri's small shoulders and the big, blue eyes that dominated his face made Jiri seem unreal.

As much as Zane knew he would have a fight on his hands for possession of Jiri once he cleaned up, Zane still couldn't wait to see him. He also desperately wanted to explore all of the pale flesh hidden behind the baggy jeans and dirty shirt that Jiri wore.

Zane knew he needed to establish his claim to Jiri. He just needed to find the right person to make an example of. He didn't want to take anyone out, just rough them up enough to give everyone the clear knowledge that Jiri belonged to him.

"Nice pet, Zane," someone said as Zane led Jiri into the building. *Yeah, yeah, Zane already knew that.*

"Is he going to dance for us?" someone else yelled out. *Dance? Yes. For everyone? No. For Zane? Definitely.*

"I'll trade you for him, Zane." *Nope. Not going to happen.*

"You gonna share him, Zane? I wouldn't mind getting my hands on his hot little ass," yelled another voice. *Bingo!*

Zane stopped so fast Jiri ran into him. He reached behind him and steadied Jiri with his hand as he turned to look at the offending voice. Pug. He should have known. Zane never liked Pug. The man was a slime ball that enjoyed hurting other people. Zane just couldn't figure out how to kick him out of the gang.

Maybe he could kill two birds with one stone. He could show everyone that Jiri belonged to him and only him. At the same time, he would have an excuse for getting rid of Pug. Everyone who knew Zane knew he wouldn't accept disrespect from anyone. Zane prided himself on it.

"What did you say, Pug?" Zane said quietly. That should have been Pug's first clue. When Zane was truly angry, he became very quiet.

"I asked if you were going to share you little pet, Zane," Pug replied as he took a few steps closer. He peered past Zane's shoulders to where Jiri huddled, a sneer crossing his lips. "I have a nice pet, too. I'll trade you for the night. Billy can give you a good time."

Zane watched with disgust as Pug yanked on the chain in his hand. A small man, just a bit taller than Jiri, stumbled forward to fall at Pug's feet. The fading bruises on the man's face attested to the bad treatment Pug gave his pets.

Some people were like that. They saw their pets as just that, pets. They didn't see them as human beings that were trading themselves for the protection masters offered.

Pug reached down and grabbed a handful of Billy's hair, yanking his head back. "Billy's very obedient and if he's not, you can always punish him."

Zane wasn't surprised when he heard a low growl from behind him. He knew without looking that it had come from Slash. Pug and Slash often fought over Pug's treatment of Billy. Zane suspected that Slash had a thing for Billy even though he had never said anything.

Maybe he could kill one other bird here. Zane reached out for Billy's leash. He could see the glee in Pug's eyes as he quickly handed over the leash to Zane. Before Pug could reach Jiri's leash, Zane handed them both to Slash.

"Hold these, Slash," Zane said. As he turned back to Pug, Zane clenched his fist and shoved it into Pug's face. He had the satisfaction of hearing the cartilage in Pug's nose crunch under the power behind his punch.

Pug was so stunned by the sudden attack that Zane got in three more strikes before Pug began to resist and fight back. Zane felt one punch hit him in the face, but he shook it off, going after Pug with renewed vigor.

Several more hits, a few kicks, and a couple of body slams later, Pug lay on the floor in a pile of blood. Zane stood over the top of him, his chest rising and falling rapidly. His bloody and bruised fists were still clenched at his sides.

Zane lifted his head and let his furious gaze roam over everyone standing in the room. "Jiri belongs to me. He is my pet," Zane bit out harshly. "I don't share. I will kill the next person, man or woman, who even thinks about taking him from me."

There were several nods and few quiet chuckles. Not many people liked Pug. They put up with him because he was here. That was about to end. Zane turned back to Slash and held out his hand for Jiri's leash.

When Slash went to hand Billy's leash to him, Zane shook his head. "Billy belongs to you now, but I expect you to care for him better than Pug did. I don't want to see any more bruises on him. Is that understood?"

Slash's mouth dropped open in surprise, then quickly slammed shut as he nodded. The look Slash cast down at Billy told Zane that Billy was in good hands. Slash would care for him and treat him as a pet should be treated. Zane had an inkling that Billy's life was about to change in a big way.

"You can't do that," Pug yelled as he climbed to his feet. His hand came up to wipe the blood from his lips. "Billy belongs to me. I claimed him fair and square. You don't have the right to take him away from me."

Zane turned back to face Pug, anger filling him and making his muscles tighten as he prepared for the fight he knew was coming. "I have every right. I am the leader of the Death Dealers. I can do any damn thing I want to."

"Then I challenge you for leadership of the Death Dealers."

Big surprise there. Zane reached his hand back behind him, holding Jiri's leash out to Slash. "Slash, take care of Jiri until I'm done with this asshole."

"Zane?"

Zane turned back to look at Jiri. He reached out and caressed the side of Jiri's face. "It's okay, little one. You just do what Slash says until I'm done here, and then we'll go up and have that bath."

Jiri's wide eyes dominated his pale face as he nodded. Clutching his bag of possessions closer to his chest, Jiri stepped over to stand next to Slash. Zane nodded, sending Jiri a small reassuring smile. Jiri learned quickly. That boded well for their future together.

Jiri had a lot to learn about was expected of a pet, especially the pet of the leader of the Death Dealers. Zane was encouraged by Jiri's quick obedience that they could come to an understanding faster than he had initially thought.

Once Zane was confident that Slash would take good care of Jiri, he turned back to face Pug. He wasn't surprised by the smug look on Pug's face. Pug always felt that he was better than everyone else. It was one of the many reasons the others in the gang hated him.

"Once I'm leader, I'm going to have fun with your little toy, Zane."

Zane lifted an eyebrow at Pug's insistence that he was going to win. "Slash," Zane said. He didn't even turn his head to look at him. "If something happens to me, Jiri belongs to you. The moment you think I'm losing, you're to take Jiri and leave. Pug is not to have him. Understood?"

"Yes, Zane," Slash replied.

Zane nodded, grinning at the rage that filled Pug's face. No matter what happened, Pug now knew that he would never get his hands on Jiri. The moment that it looked like Zane might lose, Slash would leave and take Jiri with him.

However, he had no intention of losing. He had too much to look forward to. Zane motioned with his hands for Pug to bring it on. He was gratified when Pug's face burned even redder.

Pug was thoughtless when he was angry. He made stupid moves. He didn't think things out, just reacted. Even before Pug took his first swing, Zane knew the fight was over. Pug was going to lose.

Zane dodged Pug's swing and brought his fist into Pug's ribcage. He winced a little at the force of his knuckles hitting Pug, but he had accomplished what he set out to do. He had heard Pug's ribs crack. Zane landed another punch in Pug's kidneys.

He was just about to swing his legs around behind Pug and push him onto his back when he heard someone yell out and he felt a sudden sharp pain in his side. Before Zane could even step back, he knew that Pug had stabbed him.

Just went to show how unqualified Pug was for leadership. He liked to cheat, especially when he wasn't winning. And no matter how much blood dripped out of the small wound in his side, Zane was still determined to win.

Zane swung around and grabbed the hand holding the long silver knife with one of his. His other hand wrapped around Pug's throat, slowly squeezing. Zane didn't want to actually kill Pug, but he knew he was angry enough right now to do it.

He tried to regain control of his temper even as his fingers continued to tighten around Pug's throat. He was momentarily unsteady when Pug fell back onto the floor. Following him down, Zane straddled Pugs body.

He forced the hand with the knife up toward Pug's throat, grabbing it with both hands. The closer to his throat that the sharp blade got, the wider Pug's eyes became. He started to struggle wildly.

Just as Zane got the blade pressed against Pug's throat, Zane looked down at him. "Do you yield?"

Zane knew it was uncommon for a gang leader to be lenient when challenged for their position. Many people thought Zane was too soft, but he didn't actually like killing. That didn't mean he wouldn't when he had to. What was his, stayed his.

"I'm going to kill you," Pug snarled. "And then I'm going to fuck that little pet of yours until he bleeds."

Well, that tears it, Zane thought. *Pug had to die.* He shoved the knife into Pug's neck. No one threatened his pet and lived. It was as simple as that. Zane watched the light in Pug's eyes slowly fade as blood flowed from the large wound in his neck.

Zane closed his eyes for a moment, taking several deep breaths. The smell of blood overwhelmed Zane and reminded him of his own injuries. He needed to get upstairs and see how bad the damage was. But first…

Standing to his feet, Zane glared out over the crowd surrounding him. "As I said before, no one touches Jiri except me. He belongs to me and I will kill anyone that touches him. Is that understood?"

As soon as everyone had nodded, Zane dropped the knife in his hand to the floor. He stepped away from Pug's body and reached for the leash Slash held out to him. Zane pulled on the leash just enough to get Jiri over next to him.

He started toward the stairs, stopping to glance back over his shoulder at Slash. "Get that out of here," Zane said as he pointed to Pug's body. "And get someone to clean up the mess, then come to my quarters. Jiri is hungry and he needs a hot meal. See to it."

"Sure thing, Zane," Slash said, a slight smile gracing his lips.

Zane hadn't even taken two steps before he heard Slash directing people to clean up the mess and get rid of the body. He knew Slash would take care of things until Zane could. In the meantime, he needed a bath and some rest.

Chapter 3

Jiri followed Zane up the stairs. His eyes kept straying back to the bloody body on the floor. He couldn't believe that Zane had just killed someone right in front of him. It made Jiri wonder what kind of man Zane was.

There just seemed to be so much violence here. It made Jiri shiver. There had been a lot of violence living with Larry, but Jiri was always pretty sure Larry wasn't out to kill him. Larry needed him to work on the vehicles. Here, Jiri had no purpose. There was no reason really to keep him alive.

"You okay, Jiri?"

Jiri looked up at Zane. He wasn't quite sure how to answer that. Technically, yeah, he was probably okay. He felt scared and unsure of what was going to happen. Zane had said that he just needed to do as he said and he would be fine. Jiri hoped that Zane meant that he wouldn't kill him.

Jiri's life might not be perfect, but he didn't want to die. He knew the best thing he could do to ensure his continued survival was to do exactly what Zane told him to do, and nothing else. Maybe that's what being a pet meant.

"I'm okay," Jiri answered carefully. He didn't want to make Zane angry.

"You hungry?" Zane asked as he unlocked the door they stood in front of and opened it. Jiri followed Zane into the room, looking around cautiously.

"I could eat," he replied.

The sheer size of the room amazed Jiri. It was much larger than the little storage closet he lived in. The main room sported a large couch and a couple of overstuffed chairs sitting in front of a fireplace along the wall to his right.

Directly across from the door was a set of double doors. Just beyond them, Jiri could see a wood railing, so he assumed the doors led to a balcony. To the left was a single wooden door. Jiri wondered what was beyond that door, but he was afraid to ask.

"Go ahead and look around if you want, Jiri," Zane said as he walked through the door Jiri was looking at. "This is your home now. You might as well get acquainted with it."

Jiri hesitated just a moment, then followed Zane through the single door. His mouth nearly dropped open the moment he spied the large bed centered against the far wall. Jiri wasn't sure he had ever seen a bed that big.

It made sense, though. Zane was huge. He'd need a bed big enough to accommodate his large body. Still, Jiri was pretty sure at least five people his size could fit into the bed and still have room to move around.

Other than the massive bed, Jiri could see two dressers against the wall, two nightstands on either side of the bed, a large overstuffed chair that could have doubled as a bed for Jiri alone, and a simple desk with a chair. Bookshelves lined the entire wall behind the desk.

Jiri briefly wondered if Zane had actually read any of the books on those bookshelves. Jiri himself had never finished school. He had been needed in the garage too much for Larry to let him finish school. Jiri could barely read.

When Zane walked out the door on the left side of the room, Jiri looked over at him. This time, his mouth did drop open. Zane had taken his shirt off before he came back into the room. Jiri was awed at the sheer masculinity Zane exuded. The bandage he applied to his side didn't even distract from his virile good looks.

Zane had a tight, sculpted chest, tons of definition and muscles from the top of his broad shoulders down to his flat abdomen. In a word, Zane was hot. Even his thick thighs, which were still encased in tight jeans, were hot.

"Well," Zane asked, bringing Jiri back from his drooling, "what do you think?"

Jiri stared at Zane for a moment in confusion. Then it dawned on him. "Oh, it's very nice, much bigger than my room."

"Jiri, this *is* your room now. There's a dresser where you can put your stuff," Zane said as he pointed to one of the dressers against the wall. "Through here is the bathroom." Zane indicated the door behind him.

Jiri just nodded.

"Look, why don't you put your stuff away in the dresser while I make sure our food is coming. Go jump in the shower and clean up. I'll get you something clean to wear. Whatever of yours is dirty just leave in the bag and we'll get it cleaned tomorrow."

"Uh, okay," Jiri replied. He stood there and watched Zane walk out of the bedroom before heading over to the dresser. He wasn't sure anything he had was clean so there didn't seem to be any point in putting anything in the dresser.

He took out the picture of his mother and set it on the back of the dresser leaning up against the wall, then carefully arranged his stuff. There wasn't much, just a couple personal hygiene items and a small black bag.

Pulling the money he had taken from Larry out of his pocket, Jiri pushed it into the bag and tightly closed the opening. He looked around the room, wondering where he could hide the black bag so no one would find it.

Before he could find a place, Zane walked back into the room. "I thought you were going to go take a shower?"

Jiri clutched the small bag tightly to his chest. "I was just…uh…finding a place for my stuff."

"What do you have there?" Zane asked nodding toward the little bag Jiri held in his hands.

Jiri looked at the bag for a moment then up at Zane. Would Zane take his money like Larry had? Jiri didn't want to tell Zane what he had. He hoped that Zane had forgotten about the money. But he also didn't want to make Zane angry.

"My money."

"Oh, well, you should probably keep it in the safe. People don't usually go through my stuff, but you can never be too careful."

Jiri almost cried out when Zane reached over and took the small bag from him. It was all he really had in the world. He had worked hard for every cent. If Zane took it from him, he had nothing.

Jiri watched Zane walk over to the bookshelf and remove a few books. He was surprised to see a small safe built into the back of the bookshelf. He tried to see what Zane was doing when Zane looked up and motioned him closer.

"Come here and I'll show you how this works."

Jiri walked over to stand next to Zane, watching as he turned the dial this way and that until there was a distinct clink and he could turn the handle. He opened the door and put the little black bag inside, then closed the door.

"Did you see how I did that?" Zane asked.

Jiri nodded. Yeah, he had seen it. He wasn't dumb and he resented Zane treating him like he was. Jiri was about to open his mouth and say something, but Zane started speaking again.

"You can't give out the combination to anyone, Jiri. Only you and I know what it is. Slash doesn't even know. Okay?"

Jiri's eyebrows went up in surprise, but he nodded his head anyway.

"If you forget the combination, just ask me. It's 37-44-32," Zane continued. "Also, I know that money is your nest egg and I don't want you to have to use it if you don't have to. If you need any money for anything, you can either ask me or get some out of the safe. Just don't go overboard."

"I can use your money?" Jiri asked, astonished.

"Well, I can't think of anything you need to buy that I won't provide for you but, yeah, if you need money for something, it's here for you to use."

Jiri didn't know what to say. No one had ever offered to share anything with him. Well, there was that one time Larry's buddy, Frank, had offered to share his cot. Jiri had turned him down as fast as he could and locked the door. Frank was just as big a pig as Larry.

"Bath time, baby," Zane said as he unlocked the collar from around Jiri's neck and pulled it off. He pointed toward the bathroom. "I don't mean to be rude, but you stink."

For the first time in a long time Jiri felt like laughing. It was a very unusual feeling for him, one he hadn't experienced a lot. Without a word, just a small smile, Jiri headed into the bathroom.

He quickly took his clothes off and turned on the water. Climbing under the hot spray felt wonderful. Jiri couldn't remember the last time he had bathed in hot water. Larry wouldn't allow it. He said it cost too much money, especially since Jiri was just going to get dirty again working on the cars in the garage.

Jiri just stood there letting the hot water drain the tension from his shoulders. Finally, he lifted his head and reached for the shampoo on the small shelf in the corner. Pouring a good amount into his hand, Jiri washed his hair.

Several moments spent with a washcloth and a bar of soap and Jiri finally felt clean. He rinsed off, then reluctantly turned the water off and climbed from the shower. A folded towel sat on the counter next to a large cotton shirt.

Jiri quickly dried himself off, then his hair, before hanging the towel on the towel bar. He grabbed the shirt and pulled it over his head, laughing when the shirt fell all the way down to his knees. It must be Zane's shirt.

When he was all done, Jiri looked for his dirty clothes, but they were gone. He was pretty sure Zane had been the one to take them, but he wanted to ask anyway. As he had said earlier, he could never be too careful.

It was sad that they lived in a world that was that way now. Jiri still remembered what life had been like before the plague hit. He lived in a nice house with his mother in a quiet neighborhood.

He went to school every day and came home to his mother and a home cooked meal. Life was simple. People were simple. Then the plague hit. Jiri's mother tried to make do to keep them both safe from the evils that roamed the streets.

It hadn't been easy. In desperation, she had married Larry, hoping that he could keep them safe. It had worked until she had had been killed by the Night Dwellers six months later. Then Jiri's hell truly began. He found out what life was like in the real world.

Everyone was out for what they could take, steal, or swindle. People killed over a simple piece of bread. Jiri supposed he had some relative safety living at the garage. He did have food every night, such as it was. He also had a roof over his head when many people didn't.

And then there were the monsters that roamed the streets, the Night Dwellers. Jiri never actually saw one, but he had heard stories. The virus that had taken out most of the world's population didn't kill everyone. There were those that caught the virus and didn't die. Those were the worst.

They killed for the joy of killing. They couldn't infect others with the virus, but they were bloodthirsty monsters that came out at night to kill any and all they could find. They also destroyed anything they could get their hands on.

Jiri lived most of the last few years in fear that the Night Dwellers would attack the garage and kill him. Strangely enough, they seemed to not be interested in the little repair shop, attacking the surrounding area instead.

Larry always said it was because the Night Dwellers knew he was an important person and that attacking him would be paramount to slitting their own throats. Jiri wasn't so sure.

He didn't know why the Night Dwellers didn't attack but he was grateful that they didn't. The stories he heard about what they could do curled his toes.

Jiri truly hoped that he never faced one. He knew he wasn't strong like Zane was. He didn't know if he would even know how to defend himself if he had to. Jiri knew how to fix vehicles. That's it.

Of course, maybe he could be of some use to Zane in that department. There didn't seem to be an engine that didn't purr for him. Larry used to say he had the magic touch where vehicles were concerned. Maybe that was something he could use.

"Jiri? You done yet?"

Jiri hurried out of the bathroom when Zane called, only to come to a halt when he saw Zane lounging on the bed, a tray of food beside him. "I was just cleaning up," Jiri quickly said when Zane looked up at him, one of his dark eyebrows raised in query.

Zane nodded. "Come eat before it gets cold."

Jiri felt self-conscious as he climbed onto the bed to sit next to Zane. Standing up, the shirt he wore fell down to his knees. Sitting down, it was just a bit shorter. Jiri felt like he was on display. The strange look in Zane's eyes as he looked down at Jiri's bare legs didn't help.

When Jiri yanked on the edge of the shirt and tried to pull it farther down his legs, Zane raised his eyes to look at him. Jiri knew his face burned red. He could feel it. Jiri rolled his eyes when Zane just laughed.

"Eat," Zane directed again, holding up a piece of chicken. Jiri took the chicken and bit into it. He was surprised at how good it tasted. Not too dry, not too juicy, and the flavor came right through. Jiri quickly took another bite and chewed it.

"Who cooked this?" he asked before taking another bite, then another.

"Harvey is our resident cook. Why? Don't you like it?"

Jiri shook his head. "No, it's very good. I just wondered. Does Harvey cook everything?"

Zane nodded. "Yeah, Harvey was a chef before the plague hit. I think he loves cooking just for the sake of cooking. He's always coming up with something new for us to eat. If you have anything you won't eat or you'd prefer, just let me know and I'll pass it along to him."

"I can't think of anything I won't eat. Food is food and you eat what's put in front of you." Jiri took the last bite of chicken and laid the bone down on the dish. He eyed Zane for his reaction as he picked up another piece. When Zane didn't protest, Jiri quickly began eating it.

On his third piece of chicken, Jiri heard Zane laugh. He looked over to see Zane smiling at him, a twinkle in his eyes. "What?" Jiri asked.

"It's good to see a strong appetite on you. I'll have to tell Harvey you like his chicken."

Jiri felt his face heat up again. He really wished his skin wasn't so pale. Every time he became embarrassed his face turned beet red. A symptom of having an Irish mother, he supposed. "It's good chicken."

"Is there anything else you like? Steak? Potatoes? Hamburgers?" Zane asked.

Jiri shrugged his shoulders. "I'll eat whatever you give me."

"That's not what I asked, Jiri. Is there anything you'd like to eat?" Zane's voice sounded more severe this time.

Jiri suddenly wasn't so hungry anymore. What if he said the wrong thing? Would Zane punish him? Would he kill him? Jiri set the half-eaten piece of chicken back down on the plate. He picked up a napkin. Using the excuse of wiping his face, he wiped away the tears threatening to seep out of his eyes.

"Jiri? I asked you a question and I want an answer."

"I—I like homemade bread," Jiri quickly said. "My mother used to make it three times a week when I was a child. I remember coming home and the whole house smelled of homemade bread."

Zane nodded. "Anything else?"

Jiri shrugged. "I don't know. Larry used to give me rice." Jiri looked down at his hands as he nervously twisted them together in his lap. "I don't much like rice."

"Okay, so no rice. What do you like then?"

"I'll eat whatever is—" Jiri started only to be interrupted by Zane.

"Put in front of you," Zane finished for Jiri. "Yeah, you said that, Jiri. What I want to know is what you would like to eat. What have you been dreaming about eating? Anything?"

"I don't know. Larry—"

"Jiri!" Zane said loudly making Jiri jump. "Larry is not here. Larry is never going to be here. You need to forget about Larry." Zane scooted up farther in the bed, leaning back against the pillows. "Now, answer my question, Jiri."

Jiri's eyes darted frantically around the room as he tried to think of some food that he could tell Zane he wanted. He knew Zane was angry with him. He wasn't giving Zane the answers he wanted, but Jiri couldn't think of any foods that he wanted. He was just happy to have food.

When Zane reached for him, Jiri cringed. "I don't know," he cried out as he fell sideways onto the bed and closed his eyes. He curled into a fetal position and covered his head with his arms. "Please don't kill me."

When silence reigned in the room for several moments, Jiri opened his eyes and peered through his arms up at Zane. Jiri was stunned by the look of horror on Zane's ashen face. He looked truly troubled by Jiri's words.

"Jiri, what makes you think I'd kill you?" Zane asked quietly.

"You killed that other man when he made you angry," Jiri squeaked. He lifted his arms from his head and pushed himself up, making sure that there was plenty of space between him and Zane. While Zane seemed horrified by what Jiri said, Jiri wasn't taking any chances. He didn't know him.

"Baby, he tried to take you away from me. He challenged my leadership. I didn't want to kill him, but he left me choice. I had to do it."

When Zane sat up more, Jiri scooted away from him, getting a stiff glare from Zane. Jiri didn't know what to do, what to expect. Zane admitted that he was a killer. Jiri knew he had every right to be terrified of him.

But the sad, resigned look on Zane's face made Jiri wonder if Zane was a killer because he had to be, or because he wanted to be. Larry wouldn't have had any guilty feelings about killing someone. Maybe that's what made Zane different from Larry.

"I don't know what I like to eat. Larry gave me rice every day. Once a week, he put gravy over it. If I was really good, he'd add some meat. It's been too long since I had anything else," Jiri said quickly, nearly stumbling over his words. He nervously drew circles in the blanket beneath him with his finger as he waited for Zane's reaction.

"So, I guess rice is definitely out, huh?" Zane chuckled.

"It's really gross," Jiri laughed nervously. His eyes suddenly widened and he looked up at Zane. "But I'll eat it. I'll eat whatever you—"

Zane held up his hand to stop Jiri. "Okay, I get it. You'll eat whatever I put in front of you and you won't complain. But I think that we need to try a few different things and see what you do like. Maybe I can Harvey make a variety of dishes for us to try."

Jiri couldn't help but smile even as his face heated up again. "I'd like that."

Zane was quiet after that. The look on Zane's face as he watched him made Jiri fidget. Jiri wasn't any good at reading the expressions on people's faces. Zane was no different. Jiri had no idea what Zane was thinking. But from the way Zane's mouth opened, then closed, Jiri suspected he was about to find out.

"Jiri, I would never hurt you. I hope you know that," Zane said. His eyes fell down to where Jiri was fidgeting with the blanket, then roamed around the room. "I'm sure that all of this is rather scary to you."

Jiri nodded. Hell yeah, it was scary. His situation wasn't that much different than where he had been before. A different roof over his head, a different set of rules, but he was still under someone's thumb.

"I promise to do everything in my power to make sure you're safe, Jiri."

"Larry always promised things when he wanted something, too," Jiri countered. He wanted to believe Zane, he really did. Jiri just didn't hold much belief in promises. People only made them when they wanted something. Jiri wondered what Zane wanted from him.

"Fair enough," Zane replied. "I guess that trust can only come with time."

Well, that made sense to Jiri. He was just surprised that Zane understood that. Jiri was also surprised that Zane agreed with it. Jiri would have thought that the leader of the Death Dealers would be uncompromising. Guess not.

"So, how about you and I make a deal, hmmm?" Zane asked. "I'll try and prove to you that you can trust me, and you give me a chance to prove it."

"Why?"

"Why what?" Zane asked.

"Why do you even care if I trust you? You're the leader of the Death Dealers," Jiri cried out. "You can have anyone you want, do anything you want. Why me?"

"You're cute."

Jiri's eyebrows shot up to his forehead in stunned amazement. "I'm cute?"

Zane nodded his head.

"You bought me from Larry, then killed a man, because you think I'm cute?"

Zane nodded again, a small smile starting to cross his lips.

"You're out of your fucking mind," Jiri laughed. He couldn't do anything else. Zane was certifiable. Jiri laughed until his sides hurt, tears streaming down his face. When the laughter finally started to fade away, he looked up at Zane. "So, what now?"

"If you'll come up here, I'll explain it to you," Zane said as he gestured to the spot between his legs.

Jiri watched Zane for a moment, then climbed over the breakfast tray and settled down between Zane's legs. He slowly leaned back against Zane's chest until his full weight pressed against Zane's.

Even knowing he was nearly sitting in Zane's lap, Jiri still jumped when Zane wrapped his strong arms around him.

"Shh, it's okay. I'm not going to hurt you," Zane whispered into Jiri's ear. "You're going to have to get used to me touching you, Jiri. I plan on doing a lot more than that. By the time I'm done with you, you won't know where you end and I begin."

"Wha–what do you mean?" Jiri stammered.

"You remember that kiss outside?" Zane asked.

"Yes." Boy, did he. It had made Jiri's toes curl. He was hoping there were a few more like it in his future. No one had ever kissed him like Zane had. Hell, since his mother, no one had ever kissed him, period.

"That's just the beginning of the things I'm going to do to you, Jiri. You're my pet now. My duty is to protect you and provide for you. Your duty is to provide for me as well."

"Provide what? I don't know how to do anything except repair engines," Jiri said, raising his face up to look at Zane in confusion. "You said that wasn't my job anymore."

"It's not. I'll teach you what you need to know. For now, the only thing you need to know is that you belong to me and you need to do exactly as I say. The other stuff will come with time."

"What other stuff? Is Harvey going to teach me to cook or something?" Jiri was totally confused.

"No, baby," Zane chuckled. He ruffled the side of Jiri's head. "Although, if you wanted to learn to cook, I can arrange that."

"Zane, you're really confusing me. I'm really not trying to make you mad or anything, but could you please just explain what you want from me? If you're willing to protect me and provide for me, there has to be something you want in return. People just don't do things like that for free."

Jiri felt Zane take a deep breath and let it out slowly. He knew Zane probably wasn't happy with him right now, but Jiri needed to know what was expected of him. One, he didn't want to be sent back to Larry. Two, he was kind of beginning to like it here. He didn't want to leave.

"Please, Zane?"

"I don't want to scare you, Jiri," Zane admitted.

"You're scaring me more by keeping things from me."

"I protect you and keep you safe. Provide whatever it is you need, like food and shelter."

"And in exchange?" Jiri asked.

"You provide comfort for me," Zane replied quietly.

From his tone of voice, Jiri almost had the impression that Zane was embarrassed, but that couldn't be right. Zane was the leader of the Death Dealers. Nothing could embarrass him...could it?

"Comfort?" Jiri hedged.

"That's what being a pet means, Jiri. You see to my needs while I see to yours. Since you're not big enough or strong enough to protect yourself, I do that for you. In exchange, you provide for me what I can't provide for myself."

"What could I possibly provide you that you can't provide for yourself?"

"Sex, okay!" Zane shouted. "You provide me with sex."

Chapter 4

Zane knew the conversation wasn't going well even before Jiri went still in his arms. It wasn't easy to explain to someone that they had just become a sex slave. Especially to someone like Jiri, who Zane suspected had never been touched like Zane desperately wanted to touch him.

"I'm a sex pet?"

Zane rolled his eyes. "Not exactly how I would put it, but essentially you are correct. I provide you with protection and whatever else you need. You provide me with comfort and companionship, including sex."

Jiri was so quiet, Zane was afraid he had silently freaked out. Zane wondered if Jiri would be able to accept the things he wanted from him. Zane had a large appetite for sex. He liked it a lot. Jiri was very small and delicate compared to him. What if he was asking too much?

"And it's okay for us to do that?"

"For us to have sex?" Zane asked in astonishment. "Yes, of course. Why wouldn't it be?"

"Larry always said it was wrong for two men to be together like that."

"I thought we already discussed this. Larry is off his rocker. He doesn't know anything. Besides, here I am leader. What I say goes. And I say it's okay for two men to be together if that's what they want."

Zane waited while Jiri thought about that. He hoped that given time, Jiri would understand that the things Larry said were wrong. It only mattered what they wanted.

"Zane? I have another question," Jiri murmured.

"Go ahead," Zane replied. He could feel Jiri's fingers plucking at the edge of his shirt. Jiri seemed nervous, anxious even. Zane mentally crossed his fingers, hoping for the best, but expecting the worst.

"Does that mean you'll kiss me like you kissed me before, because I really liked that."

Zane's head fell back against the pillows as he groaned. "Damn, Jiri, you're going to kill me."

"No!" Jiri cried out. He quickly turned and grabbed the front of Zane's shirt pulling on it frantically. "I would never kill you, I swear."

Zane lifted his head as he pulled Jiri down to his chest. He pushed Jiri's head against his neck then wrapped his arms tightly around his shaking body. "No, of course not, Jiri. I never meant to say that you would. You misunderstood me."

"Then what—"

"I meant that sometimes the things you say are very…arousing to me." Zane reached down and grabbed Jiri's hips and pushed them down against his own so that Jiri would feel Zane's hard cock.

"See? This is what your words do to me. This is what being close to you does to me." Zane was gratified to hear Jiri gasp. He wasn't massive, but he felt that he might be somewhat impressive in size. He just hoped he didn't scare Jiri too much.

"Can I see it?"

"Uh…okay," Zane choked out. He reached down between his body and Jiri's to unzip his pants. Grabbing the sides, he pulled them apart and pushed down until his hard cock popped free. Zane tried to keep his eyes on Jiri to see his reaction, but Jiri's head was bent down, his hair falling over his face as he looked down.

"Does it hurt?" Jiri asked, his voice almost a whisper.

"Not like you think," Zane chuckled.

"But it hurts?" Jiri asked, quickly looking up at Zane.

Zane was mystified by the lower lip caught between Jiri's teeth. He looked agitated, worried. "It's okay, Jiri. It doesn't hurt the way you think. It's not painful, exactly. More like, uncomfortable."

A sudden thought came to Zane. His brows drew together as he looked down at Jiri. "Jiri, haven't you ever had a hard on before? Been sexually excited? Masturbated even?"

Jiri shook his head rapidly, his cheeks blossoming red. "Larry said it was wrong. He punished me every time it happened."

"Oh damn, baby, I'm sorry." Zane pulled Jiri back against his body and caressed his back as he wondered what kind of hell Jiri had been living in. Zane had half a mind to go back and beat the crap out of Larry for the things he had done to Jiri. "Having a hard on is not wrong. You can not control the way your body responds. Do you understand that?"

Jiri sat back slowly. His eyes were anxious as he glanced up at Zane. "This isn't wrong?" Jiri asked as he grabbed Zane's hand and pressed it against the hard bulge in his pants.

Zane briefly closed his eyes before opening them and looking back down at Jiri. "No, Jiri, it's not wrong. In fact, I think it's great. I'm hoping it means that you are attracted to me. It will make things between us a lot easier."

Jiri looked so confused that Zane felt the need to explain. He hoped he didn't sound like a complete moron. He was swimming in uncharted waters. Explaining to someone like Jiri about sex wasn't going to be easy. He had been taught that it was wrong.

"When someone is attracted to someone else, as I am to you, our bodies react in certain ways. You make my cock hard and I want to touch you all over, to kiss you. I'm hoping since your body has reacted the way it did that you are just as attracted to me."

Zane nearly laughed when Jiri's face turned red, but refrained. Jiri didn't need Zane laughing right now. He needed reassurance and understanding.

"I like it when you kiss me," Jiri admitted.

"How about when I touch you?" Zane asked as he squeezed his hand around Jiri's cock through his pants. "Do you like that?"

"It feels, it feels really good," Jiri moaned.

"It's supposed to feel good, Jiri. That's why we like to do it." Zane squeezed Jiri again, rubbing his hands up and down a little until Jiri began to fidget. His hand went to the button on Jiri's jeans. "It would feel a lot better if I didn't have to touch you through your clothes, Jiri."

"Okay."

Zane quickly unbuttoned, then unzipped Jiri's pants before he could change his mind. The moment Zane's hand wrapped around Jiri's length and gave it one simple tug, Jiri cried out and spilled himself all over Zane's hand.

Zane continued to stroke Jiri for a few more moments until Jiri's body stopped shuddering and he collapsed against Zane's chest. Zane wiped his hand on a napkin then wrapped it around Jiri's neck.

"See, baby, it feels really good, doesn't it?" Zane whispered against Jiri's hair.

Jiri just nodded. "What happened?"

Zane chuckled. "You had an orgasm, baby. That's what happens when people have sex."

"That's sex?"

"No," Zane laughed as he wondered how anyone could be so naive in this day and age. "That's not exactly sex. That's part of it. There's a lot more to it than that. What you just got was called a hand job. There are also blow jobs, rim jobs, intercourse, making out. A lot of stuff."

"Do they feel just as good?"

"Yeah, some of them feel even better."

"Oh, I want to try those." Jiri tilted his head back to look at Zane. "Can we, Zane?"

Zane groaned. Jiri *was* going to kill him. Maybe it was a plot by Larry to torture him first and then kill him. Zane knew that Jiri had no idea what his words were doing to him and he prayed Jiri never found out. Zane was strangely afraid that if Jiri discovered his power over Zane's body, there'd be no question who was the master and who was the slave.

"Zane?"

"Yeah, Jiri, we can try them."

"Now?" Jiri asked.

Zane nearly jumped out of his skin when he felt tentative fingers wrap around his cock. He couldn't hold back the groan that broke free from his lips. He was sure that Jiri had no idea how good that actually felt.

"Harder, baby, squeeze harder and move your hand up and down," Zane encouraged. The moment Jiri began moving his hand, Zane knew he wouldn't last long. Jiri might not be experienced, but he more than made up for it with enthusiasm.

"I'm going to come in a minute, Jiri," Zane groaned. Hell, he was going to come any second if Jiri kept doing what he was doing. Jiri had one hand wrapped around Zane's cock. The other hand was gently stroking Zane's ball sac.

"Jiri," Zane cried out as his body went stiff and his cock erupted. Like Zane had done to him, Jiri continued to stroke Zane's cock several times as Zane's cock shot out ropes of pearly white cum. He felt Jiri buck against his leg, then warm liquid covered him.

"Enough, Jiri," Zane said as he reached down and grabbed Jiri's wrist. He was very sensitive now. Zane grabbed Jiri around the waist and pulled him up to lay against his chest.

"Is that supposed to happen?" Jiri asked.

"What?"

"You didn't even touch me and I...I..."

Zane chuckled. "It happens, but not all of the time. Personally, I think it's great that you got excited enough to come again. Maybe after we rest we'll see if we can get you to do it again, huh?"

Jiri laughed. "I'd like that, Zane."

"Me, too," Zane said. "I also think we should get out of these wet clothes and get into bed. This stuff gets a little sticky after awhile."

Jiri nodded and climbed off the bed to pull his shirt over his head and drop it on the floor. Zane watched him getting his first good look at Jiri's nude body. Oh hell, he was right. Jiri was breathtaking. *He was so doomed.*

Rolling to the side of the bed, Zane quickly pulled his clothes off before crawling underneath the covers. He held the edge up for Jiri, smiling when Jiri climbed right in and laid down, one leg thrown over Zane's, head tucked under Zane's chin.

Zane wrapped his arms around Jiri and settled back against the pillows. He realized that he was suddenly content, something he hadn't felt in a long time. Maybe having a pet wasn't such a bad thing.

"Zane?"

"Yeah, Jiri?"

"I don't have to do this with anyone else do I? It seems kind of personal and–and–well, I just don't want to do it with anyone else," Jiri explained. "You won't make me, will you?"

"No, Jiri, you only do this with me. You're my pet and I don't share. Remember what happened to Pug when he wanted me to share?"

"You killed him."

"And I'll kill anyone that tries to do this with you. This is only for me, Jiri. I'm the only one that gets to see you like this or touch you like this. I'll be very upset if you do this with anyone else. Got it?"

"Got it, Zane," Jiri laughed.

"Now, close your eyes and go to sleep, Jiri. We are both going to need our rest if I'm going to teach you about sex."

"I'm already asleep."

* * * *

Zane opened his eyes, not quite understanding what the warm body curled around him was doing in his bed. He lifted his head and looked down at the man pressed against his side, gasping as the previous night's events flooded back.

"Jiri," he whispered. Zane let his head fall back against the pillow. It was Jiri in his bed. Not some stranger he had brought home. Not some nameless man that he would never see again. It was Jiri, and Jiri belonged to Zane.

That thought alone had Zane's arms curling around Jiri's body. He pulled him up until Jiri was splayed over his chest, his head nestled in the crook of Zane's neck. A low groan fell from Zane's lips when Jiri's legs separated and fell to the mattress on either side of Zane's body. It pushed Zane's cock right up against the underside of Jiri's soft nut sac.

He reached down with his large hands to palm Jiri's ass cheeks. Damn, such a perfect little ass. Each rounded globe fit neatly into the palms of Zane's hands as if they were made for him. Not an inch wasted.

Zane lifted his hips. He let out another low groan as his hard cock slid up the crease of Jiri's ass. He again briefly thought of his theory that this was all a plot to kill him after slowly torturing him. The more time he spent with Jiri, the more he wondered if he was right. Jiri just seemed too perfect to be real.

Just then, Jiri began to stir. Zane watched with amusement as Jiri rubbed his face with his hand then turned to look down at Zane.

"Morning, baby. Did you sleep well?"

Jiri's eyes darted around as if confused, then came back to Zane's. "Did I sleep on top of you all night?"

"No," Zane chuckled, "but it would have been okay if you did. You hardly weigh anything at all. Besides," Zane said as he pushed his hips up again, "I kind of like this position. It has lots of possibilities."

Zane could barely contain his grin as Jiri's eyes widened. "Za–Zane," Jiri croaked. His hands clenched against Zane's arms, fingernails digging into Zane's flesh. "You–you–your…"

Zane nodded. "My dick is in your ass." Well, it wasn't, not yet, but Zane had every intention of it being there soon. Zane pumped his hips again. His eyebrow went up in surprise at the hiss that slid out of Jiri's mouth, Jiri's eyes closing.

When Jiri's eyes opened back up and looked down at him, Zane was surprised by the arousal burning in their blue depths. "Is this okay? Are we allowed to do this?" Jiri asked hesitantly.

"Yeah, we're allowed to do this," Zane chuckled.

Jiri was silent for a moment, his lower lip caught between his teeth. Zane thought Jiri looked absolutely adorable.

"Is there more?"

Zane grinned. He couldn't help it. On one hand, he was amazed that someone could be so completely sheltered from the realities of life, including sex. On the other hand, he was thrilled that Jiri had been sheltered.

It left the teaching of the intimate relationship between two people up to him. That was a daunting task, but one Zane looked forward to with great enthusiasm. Jiri seemed innocent and naïve, but the curious look on his face told Zane that he might be interested in learning.

Jiri was giving Zane his trust, even if he didn't realize it. Zane had to make sure that he didn't betray that trust by doing anything that Jiri might object to. And he wouldn't know what that might be until he tried.

"Get the bottle of lube out of the nightstand drawer and I'll show you."

Zane watched as Jiri climbed over him to reach the nightstand. He pulled the drawer open and searched around until he found the bottle of lube, holding it up in his hand and looking over his shoulder at Zane.

"This?"

Zane nodded, his eyes already straying down Jiri's naked body with great interest. He held out his hand for the bottle, taking it from Jiri and dropping it on the mattress beside him before reaching up for Jiri.

"Climb back on, baby," Zane directed.

Jiri climbed back on Zane, straddling his body. Zane grabbed Jiri, one hand around his neck, the other hand grazing his ass. He pulled Jiri down and took his lips. Zane explored, took and gave, as he kissed Jiri until Jiri squirmed against him, kissing back.

Zane pulled Jiri further up his body, then grabbed the bottle off the mattress beside him. Popping the lid, he poured some out on his fingers and dropped the bottle back onto the mattress. As Zane started spreading the lube between Jiri's ass cheeks, Zane saw his eyes widen and his face flush.

With a little grin of knowledge about what was to come, Zane pressed his finger against Jiri's tight entrance. Jiri was so tight Zane wondered if he was going to be able to loosen him up at all. He didn't want to do anything that would hurt Jiri.

"Relax, Jiri. Take a couple of deep breaths and relax. We won't do anything you don't want to do."

"It just feels weird," Jiri whispered.

"Yeah, now it does, but wait until I have you loosened up a bit. I promise you, it's worth it," Zane replied.

"You've done this before?"

Zane nodded. "Many times. It gets better, I swear," he chuckled.

Finally, after several deep breaths from Jiri, Zane was able to press one finger in. He moved it up and down, side to side, and in and out. After a few minutes, Zane felt Jiri relax even more.

"Ready for another one, baby?"

"Another one?" Jiri squeaked. "You're putting in another one? How many are you going to put in there?"

Zane chuckled. "No less than three, baby. I have to stretch you out enough to take me without hurting you."

"Okay," Jiri said. He squeezed his eyes closed and stiffened his body as if he was bracing himself.

"Jiri, we don't have to do this if you don't want to," Zane said.

Jiri popped one eye open and looked down at Zane, then the other. "No, I want to do this. I'm just—I guess I'm scared. I'm afraid this is going to hurt."

"That's why I'm preparing you first, so that it doesn't hurt. Although, it would be better if you were on your hands and knees."

Jiri shook his head rapidly. "No, I like it where I am."

"Jiri, it really would be easier if you were on your hands and knees, or even your back. This position," Zane explained as he slapped Jiri on the hip, "is not the best position for your first time."

Jiri shook his head again. "No, I don't want to be on my hands or knees or my back. I need to be able to see you."

"Jiri, you can still see me if you're on your back," Zane reasoned.

"No!" Jiri nearly shouted.

When Jiri started to pull away, to climb off of him, Zane wrapped his arms around Jiri and pulled him back down to lay against his chest. "It's okay, Jiri. If it's that important for you to be on top, we can do that."

Jiri was silent. Zane could feel Jiri's chest moving rapidly against his own. Zane smoothed Jiri's golden hair back from his face. He ran his hands down Jiri's back and over his ass, then back up. His intent was to soothe Jiri, but he felt another reaction pressing against his abdomen.

"You ready to try this again?" Zane asked.

Jiri was slow to nod, but a small smile played across his lips. Zane took that as a good sign and moved his hands back down to Jiri's ass.

He reached down and grabbed the bottle of lube again, pouring more onto his fingers before dropping the bottle on the bed.

Spreading Jiri's ass cheeks, Zane pressed his fingers into him again. Zane could only assume Jiri felt more at ease because he didn't have far to stretch Jiri before he could get a third finger in.

Zane spent a few minutes stretching Jiri, moving his fingers around. He couldn't tell if Jiri was enjoying what he was doing because Jiri's face was buried in his neck. Zane just hoped that the soft mewling sounds he made were good ones.

"You ready for me now, baby?"

Jiri lifted his head to look down at Zane in confusion. "Ready for what?"

"Remember? I told you I was going to have my dick in your ass?" Zane watched Jiri gulp, then nod. He looked like he was starting to tense up again, bracing himself. Zane couldn't have that. "Kiss me, Jiri," Zane demanded.

Jiri immediately leaned down and pressed his lips against Zane's. Once Jiri was occupied kissing him, Zane grabbed Jiri's legs and spread them further apart, pulling them up until Jiri was kneeling over the top of him. Jiri's knees hugged Zane's chest, his ass hovered over Zane's thick cock, right where Zane wanted him.

Zane grabbed Jiri's ass and pulled the cheeks apart. Slowly, he lowered Jiri down, pushing his body back a little. As Jiri's body began to take him, inch by slow, aching inch, Zane pressed his hands down on Jiri's hips.

By the time Jiri was fully impaled on his cock, Zane was in heaven. Jiri was so tight, so perfect. And Zane didn't think Jiri even realized that it happened. But, he could be wrong, Zane realized a moment later when Jiri reared back into a full sitting position, taking even more of Zane's cock into him.

"That's–that's unbelievable," Jiri stammered. "I can feel you in me."

Zane chuckled. "It gets better."

The astonished look on Jiri's face said that Jiri didn't believe him, but Zane was determined to prove it. Grabbing Jiri's hips, Zane began pushing himself up into Jiri. Over and over again, he thrust.

He watched Jiri the entire time. A kaleidoscope of emotions crossed Jiri's face, everything from wonder to desire to complete fascination. Zane thought he might have created a monster.

Jiri's hands had moved to rest on Zane's chest. His fingers clenched against Zane's pec muscles. Once again, Jiri's lower lip was caught between his teeth. Zane absently noted that Jiri seemed to do that a lot. It was still adorable. "Lean back, baby," Zane ordered.

As Jiri leaned back, Zane grabbed Jiri's hard cock and began stroking it to the rhythm he was creating with his hips. Within seconds, Jiri's head had dropped back, his neck arching, as he cried out.

Zane felt Jiri's muscles tighten around him at the same moment that warm seed shot out of Jiri's cock. Zane continued to stroke Jiri even as he roared out, light flashing in his eyes as the world around him exploded.

When Zane came back to his senses, he realized that Jiri had collapsed down onto him. Jiri murmured softly against Zane's neck. His hands gently kneaded the muscles on Zane's chest.

Zane also realized that he still had Jiri's cock in his hands. Giving it one last stroke, Zane released Jiri and brought his wet hand up, licking the seed off of it. Damn! Even that was good. Shaking his head at his folly, Zane tilted his head down to look at Jiri.

"You okay, baby?"

Chapter 5

Okay? Was he okay? Jiri lifted his head to look up at Zane, wondering if Zane had lost his mind. Of course he wasn't okay. He had just had sex for the very first time in his life. And he liked it a lot.

No wonder Larry had kept him sheltered from this. If Jiri had known this delight was out there waiting for him, he would have left Larry ages ago. He had no idea it could be this way between two people.

Jiri wanted more. "So, how often can we do that?"

Jiri smiled at the deep chuckle that came out of Zane's mouth. "We can do that as much as we want. However, my little sex maniac, we need food first. Not enough food means not enough fuel. Not enough fuel…"

"Yeah, yeah, I get it. No fuel, no go," Jiri replied as he sat back up. "I am a mechanic, you know."

"Not anymore you're not. Now you're my pet," Zane reminded Jiri as he carefully pulled out of Jiri and rolled them onto their sides.

"Put sex in front of that and I might agree to it."

Jiri grinned when Zane's eyebrows shot up. Jiri was realistic. He knew he now belonged to Zane. There wasn't much he could do about it, even if he wanted to. He just didn't see the need to protest.

He was in a good position with Zane and he knew it. Zane was big enough and strong enough to protect him from just about everyone and everything. If all he wanted in return was someone to take care of him and give him *comfort*, Jiri was all for it.

That didn't mean he was going to be a mindless slave, however. Zane needed to learn that right from the beginning. Oh, Jiri had no doubt he'd be as obedient as he could. He still had misgivings about Zane killing the man downstairs.

"You might agree?" Zane asked.

Jiri shrugged. "I think sex pet sounds better. Gives me a definite designation, don't you think? I mean, anyone can be a pet. If I'm a sex pet, I'm more than just a regular pet," Jiri reasoned. It sounded plausible to him.

Zane stared down at him, silent for so long, Jiri wondered if he had overstepped his bounds. He was kind of joking around. Jiri did want to mean more to Zane than just a pet, but he wasn't totally serious about being called a sex pet. Maybe Zane didn't have a sense of humor.

"Sex pet, huh?" Zane said as he rolled to the side of the bed and swung his legs over the side.

Jiri pushed himself up to his elbow as he watched Zane sit up. "You don't have to call me a sex pet if you don't want to. I just thought—" Jiri stopped speaking as Zane stood to his feet and walked into the bathroom, leaving Jiri by himself without a word.

Okay, so Zane didn't have a sense of humor. And obviously, Jiri was going to remain a pet and not be elevated to sex pet. Maybe he hadn't earned the right to be considered Zane's sex pet.

And maybe Zane hadn't been satisfied with him. Why should he be? What did Jiri know about sex? Everything he knew he had learned in the last few hours from Zane. That wasn't nearly long enough to learn how to please the leader of the Death Dealers.

As Jiri rolled himself to the side of the bed and sat up, he really wished he had kept his mouth shut. He shouldn't have said anything at all. It was obvious Zane was upset with him. Zane might not be outright angry, but he didn't seem pleased, either.

"Get dressed and I'll take you downstairs to meet Harvey."

Jiri looked up to see Zane walk back into the bedroom. He watched him cross the room to his dresser, grabbing a black shirt and pulling it over his head. Then he grabbed a clean pair of black jeans and some socks.

"Yes, Zane," Jiri replied quietly as he got up and walked over to his bag of dirty clothes. Reaching into the bag, Jiri pulled one item out at a time, smelling each to see which was the cleanest. Finally settling on a dark brown shirt and a pair of faded jeans, Jiri got dressed.

Jiri turned to look at Zane, his eyes instantly falling to the collar and leash Zane held in his hand. He didn't want to wear it. They were heading downstairs where everyone would see him, everyone would know what he was.

"You don't need that," Jiri said quickly. "I won't run."

"I'm not worried about you running, Jiri. Until I can have you permanently marked, you have to wear the collar when we leave the room."

Jiri rolled his shoulder a little. He eyed the collar and leash with distaste. "Can I just wear the collar?" Maybe that wouldn't be too bad. Jiri's spirits fell when Zane shook his head. He closed his eyes briefly, praying for the courage to get through his new life with some dignity.

Opening his eyes, Jiri stepped over to Zane and turned around so that the collar could be attached to his neck. The black leather felt cold against his skin as Zane wrapped it around his throat and clicked the latch closed.

Jiri ran his hands along the edge of the collar, pulling it away from his neck a little. He felt ridiculous. He wore a collar and leash like a dog. Maybe that was the interpretation of *pet*. Jiri had thought it meant companion or something.

As Zane pulled the leash and led Jiri from the room, Jiri realized that he had been wrong. He wasn't Zane's companion. He wouldn't be sharing stolen moments with him, or companionship, or anything else Jiri might have fantasized about. He was a pet. He was Zane's possession, like Zane's motorcycle.

Jiri even doubted that he would have any say in his future from now on. Jiri felt tears prickle the edges of his eyes as he realized that once again he was at the mercy of someone else, and there didn't seem to be any way out.

His life, his wellbeing, even his ability to breathe, were all in Zane's hands. Jiri wondered what would happen if he misbehaved. Would Jiri be punished for not pleasing Zane? Killed like the man from the night before?

Jiri suddenly felt miserable. He dropped his head down, watching as he put one foot in front of the other. He didn't look up to see where they were going. He didn't really care. He just followed behind Zane, stopping when Zane did, walking when Zane did.

"Harvey," Zane said, bringing Jiri out of his gloomy thoughts. "This is Jiri. We need to get a little more meat on his bones. He's been eating nothing but rice and gravy for quite a while. I'm hoping you might be able to interest him with your fine cooking."

Jiri looked up when a short, thick, bald man walked up to him. He stood several inches shorter than Zane, almost as short as Jiri, but he seemed very intimidating. Jiri took a step back, closer to Zane.

"What do you like to eat, boy?" Harvey asked.

"Oh, you don't even want to go there, Harvey," Zane chuckled. "I can tell you right now, the answer would only drive you batty. Just provide him with a variety of dishes until we figure out what he does or doesn't like."

Harvey reached over and grabbed Jiri's chin, tilting Jiri's head from one side to the other. He dropped Jiri's chin and grabbed his arms, squeezing his hands around Jiri from wrist to shoulder.

"Uh huh," he murmured. He turned to look at Zane, nodding his head. "Well, it may take a while, but I can get him fattened up for you."

"I just want him healthy, Harvey," Zane replied.

"I can do that, too," Harvey said as he walked back over to his stove and picked up a spatula. "You can start him out on breakfast."

Harvey waved the spatula in his hand toward the doorway. "Go sit down and I'll bring you out something."

Zane chuckled as he led Jiri into the dining room. Jiri followed slowly behind, pulled along by the leash attached to the collar around his neck. The noise level in the room they walked into stunned him enough to look up. What Jiri saw surprised him.

It seemed to be just like a regular restaurant. Tables and booths littered the room. The level of noise in the room came from the multitude of people sitting here and there. Some chatted, others ate. Everyone seemed to be enjoying themselves immensely.

What truly stunned Jiri and made him very uncomfortable were the men and women sitting on the floor. The collars and leashes they wore looked similar to his and they all seemed to be sitting at the feet of others. Jiri knew instantly that they were pets, just like him.

With that thought in mind, Jiri followed Zane across the room to a large half-circle booth sitting close to the back wall. When Zane stopped next to the booth, Jiri glanced around the room again, then at the floor next to Zane's feet. He knew what was expected of him.

With a great deal of trepidation, Jiri started to kneel at Zane's feet only to feel a hand grab him around the arm. Halfway down to the floor, Jiri looked up at Zane.

"No, Jiri, you sit up at the table with me."

"But," Jiri waved his hand around the room at the other pets sitting on the floor, "the other pets are sitting on the floor."

Zane pulled Jiri up and pointed to the booth. "Regular pets sit on the floor, Jiri. Sexy little men who have been elevated to the status of sex pet sit at the table."

"Sex pet? Really?" Jiri whispered.

Jiri couldn't keep the grin off his face when Zane nodded. His previous sullen mood suddenly flew away, replaced with delight. He stepped over to the booth and scooted in to sit down, making room for Zane to sit next to him.

He felt like jumping up and down with joy. Zane had heard him and had agreed to consider Jiri a sex pet. Yes, he was still a pet. Yes, he was still a possession. But now, he was more than that, too.

"Hungry?" Zane asked.

Jiri nodded. He suddenly felt ravenous. He folded his hands together in his lap as he waited, anxious for their food to arrive. He found it hard to sit still.

"I thought after breakfast we'd go talk to DJ about your mark," Zane said. "How does that sound?"

"My mark?" Jiri asked curiously.

He felt Zane's hand brush against his neck. "Yes. When a protector claims a pet, the pet is given a permanent mark, like a tattoo, that says you belong to that protector. Each protector's mark is different, unique."

Jiri's eyes roamed around the room. He began to notice what he had missed before. Several pets wore collars and leashes but even more had just marks on their necks. Some wore all three.

"How come not everyone has a mark?"

Zane shrugged. "Pets usually aren't marked until the master has decided to keep the pet permanently. Until then, they wear the collar and leash."

"You're going to keep me permanently?" Jiri asked in surprise, and a great deal of delight.

Zane smiled. He reached over and caressed the side of Jiri's face. "I'm definitely keeping you, Jiri."

Jiri couldn't help ginning. He knew he must look like a fool but Zane's words thrilled him all of the way down to his toes. "Will I still have to wear the collar and leash if I get this mark?"

"Sometimes, but not usually. My mark should be enough of a deterrent to most to stay away from you." Zane looked a little sheepish, which Jiri found endearing. "There will be times when you will have to wear the leash and collar, Jiri, for your own safety. I'm sorry."

For some reason that Jiri could not fathom, he believed Zane. "Okay."

Zane looked surprised. "Okay? That's it? You're not going to argue with me?"

"What good would that do me? I'm a pet, remember?" Jiri wished he could take the words back the moment they left his mouth. A blank wall fell down over Zane's face as he turned away from Jiri.

Jiri scooted over until his body pressed against Zane's. He leaned up a little to whisper into Zane's ear. "I'm sorry, Zane. That didn't come out like I wanted it to."

Zane turned to look back at Jiri, his face still guarded. "Then how did you mean it?"

Jiri shrugged. "I just meant that I understand. There will be times that I have to behave like a pet, even if it means I have to wear a collar and a leash." Jiri waved his hand over the table they sat at. "Other times, I get to be a sex pet."

Zane stared at Jiri for several moments as if trying to gauge Jiri's truthfulness. Finally, he wrapped an arm around Jiri's shoulders and pressed him close. He tucked Jiri's head under his chin.

"This is not always going to be easy, Jiri. I know how to have a pet about as much as you know how to be a pet." Zane chuckled quietly. "I suspect that we're going to have to muddle through this together."

Jiri smiled against Zane's neck. He reached behind him and grabbed Zane's hand, then tilted his head back to look up at him. "As long as we do it together, right?"

Zane grinned. "Right."

Jiri jumped as a loud clank sounded behind him. He turned to see a slim man setting several dishes of food down on the table beside him. Jiri felt disappointed when Zane dropped his arms from around him, but turned anyway to look over the food.

It all looked so delicious and the smells alone made Jiri almost groan. Harvey seemed to have cooked a lot of food. Jiri wondered if there was anything left in the kitchen, but he wasn't about to complain. He had never seen so much food in his life.

"What looks good, little one?"

Jiri shook his head. "Everything?"

Zane chuckled. "How about we start off with one thing and go from there?"

Jiri nodded, still eyeing the food set out before him. He wasn't even sure what everything was.

"What would you like to try first?" Zane asked as he grabbed an empty plate.

Jiri shook his head again. "I don't know. It all smells so good," he replied getting another chuckle from Zane. Jiri could feel his face heat up.

"How about you just sit back and relax. The food is not going anywhere. We'll try a little bite of everything and see what you like, okay?"

Jiri nodded, letting out a relieved breath. That sounded like a good plan to him. With so much food before him, he couldn't decide what to try first. He couldn't remember the last time he had so many choices.

Jiri watched with great anticipation as Zane pulled a plate closer and cut a small bite with his fork. His mouth was already open when Zane turned and offered him the bite. A moment later, Jiri's eyes closed in ecstasy.

He chewed slowly, savoring the sweet tastes cascading over his tongue. When he was done, he opened his mouth again, hoping for another bite. He heard Zane chuckle as he cut another bite with the fork.

"Well, I guess it's safe to say that you like waffles."

"Waffles?"

Zane nodded as he placed another bite in Jiri's mouth. "Harvey's specialty breakfast, waffles with strawberry compote and whipped cream. The side dishes are fried eggs, hash browns, sausage, and toast."

Jiri had no idea what those things were, but they sounded wonderful. If they tasted anything like the waffles, Jiri felt positive he would love them. Jiri opened his mouth for another fork full of food.

Twenty minutes later, Jiri sat back in his seat and rubbed his stomach. He groaned. He felt so full he could burst. He couldn't ever remember eating so much. Zane must think he was a complete glutton.

"Get enough to eat?"

Jiri turned wide eyes to look at Zane. "Seriously? If I eat another bite I might burst."

Zane reached over and patted Jiri's thigh. "Good. Let's hope you like lunch as much as you did breakfast." Zane scooted out of the booth and stood up. He reached a hand back for Jiri. "Now, it's time to get down to business."

"Business?" Jiri asked curiously as he grabbed Zane's hand and scooted out of the booth. He felt his leash drop down behind him. Knowing that he had to be tethered right now, he reached back and pulled the leash around to the front of his collar, then held the long length out to Zane.

Zane grimaced as he took the length of leash. "Yes, we need to go see about your mark."

Jiri nodded. "What type of mark will I have?" Jiri asked as he followed Zane out of the dining room. Suddenly, he stopped. He saw Zane pause to look back at him.

"Jiri?"

"Can we—is it okay if we go thank Harvey for breakfast?"

Zane stared at Jiri long enough to make him feel anxious then nodded his head. "I suppose that would be okay."

Jiri clenched his hands together nervously as he followed Zane into the busy kitchen. He probably should have kept his mouth shut. Jiri was pretty sure that thanking someone for something instead of just taking what you wanted would be seen as a weakness by just about everyone here.

He couldn't help it. His mother had drilled into his head that he should have good manners, no matter what the situation. Good manners and a kind heart separated the men from the monsters, even the human monsters.

"Harvey? My pet has something he wants to say to you," Zane said as he stepped back, his arms crossed over his chest. He had a strange sort of smirk on his face as if he knew something that Jiri didn't.

Jiri glanced over at the cook, wondering if he was once again going to make an ass out of himself. He usually did when he tried to be polite to people. They all thought he was out of his mind, especially in this day and age.

Gathering together all of his courage Jiri smiled over at Harvey. "I wanted to thank you for breakfast. I haven't tasted anything so delicious since before my mother died when I was a small child."

Harvey just stared at Jiri for several moments then nodded his head. "You're welcome, boy. Now, get out of my kitchen so that I can cook your lunch. You'll be having hot roast beef sandwiches with dipping sauce and homemade potato salad." Harvey shook his spatula at Jiri. "And I expect you to eat every last bite. I'll make you something special for dessert if you do."

"Yes, sir," Jiri said. "I will."

Jiri turned back to follow Zane out of the kitchen only to find him staring over his head at Harvey with his mouth hanging open in shock. Jiri glanced back over his shoulder to Harvey. He was surprised to find a small smile on Harvey's rugged face. Jiri was pretty sure that Harvey didn't smile often.

"Good manners are always appreciated, Zane. You might want to remember that," Harvey said as he turned back to his stove. "You're little pet might be able to teach you a thing or two about that."

Jiri felt a small thrill shoot through him at Harvey's compliment, at least until he looked up into Zane's face. He didn't look happy. It was only then that Jiri realized that by complimenting Jiri, Harvey had insulted Zane.

"Zane works really hard to take care of everyone," Jiri tried to say to Harvey as he turned to face him. "He doesn't need to have good manners if he—"

"No, Jiri," Zane said as he settled his hands on Jiri's shoulders, "Harvey is right. I haven't thanked him enough for all that he does for us. He was just reminding me of that, weren't you, Harvey?"

"Of course." Harvey chuckled. "Zane is a good leader, boy. You'd do good to listen to him. He takes good care of us, but sometimes he forgets the little things. I think you also might do well to remind him of what he forgets."

"Oh, no, I couldn't—" Jiri stammered.

"He protects you well, Zane. That is a rare quality in a pet."

Jiri had no idea what Harvey meant by that statement. He couldn't protect Zane from a stiff wind. He briefly wondered if Harvey had lost his marbles. He seemed to talk in riddles that Jiri didn't understand.

"Come along, Jiri. Harvey needs to get back to work, and you and I need to go see about getting you marked."

Jiri nodded, a little dazed and totally confused as he turned and followed Zane out of the kitchen. He still felt confused about what had just happened and he certainly didn't like the strange little looks Zane kept giving him. He didn't know what they meant.

"Zane?" Jiri asked when they came to a room that looked as much like an office as Jiri had ever seen. There was a large wooden desk in the middle of the room with chairs in front of it. Bookshelves lined one wall and a couch sat against the other. This was where they were going to get his marking done?

Zane simply closed and locked the door behind them, then turned to look at Jiri. The gleam in Zane's eyes made Jiri nervous. He felt like prey before a hunter. Jiri took a couple of steps back until the desk bit into his thigh.

"I thought we were going to go see about my mark?" Jiri asked as Zane advanced on him.

"We are but we have something else to do first," Zane drawled just before his hand wrapped around Jiri's neck and he lowered his mouth to press his lips against Jiri's.

Jiri whimpered as his body melted against Zane's. Oh, he really loved it when Zane kissed him. He loved it when Zane did anything to him. He felt like his body went from okay to hot and bothered in seconds.

As Zane's lips moved to his neck, Jiri let his head drop back on his shoulders. His hands clenched around Zane's arms. "Oh, Zane," he whispered. Jiri was so intent on Zane's lips on his neck that he didn't realize Zane had unzipped his pants and pushed them out of the way until he felt the cold air pass over him.

Before Jiri could say anything, Zane had turned him around and pressed his body down over the desk. Jiri felt the hard wood bite into the palms of his hand as he tried to grip the edge of the desk, his breath coming out in great gasps.

"I'm going to fuck you now, Jiri," Zane growled into Jiri's ear.

Yeah, Jiri had kind of gotten that idea just about the time Zane had thrown him down on the desk. He wasn't complaining. He just wished Zane would hurry up and do it. A long moan fell from Jiri's lips when he felt Zane's lubed fingers press into him, stretching him.

A moment later, Zane replaced his fingers with his hard cock. Jiri grunted as Zane thrust into him, sinking all of the way in. Zane had been so careful with him the last time they had done this. Jiri hadn't been aware that it could be so...so...so animalistic.

He released his grip on the desk and tried to reach for his own aching cock, but every time Zane rammed into him, it shoved Jiri further across the desk. Jiri just had to hold on for the ride, but it was killing him. He could feel his hard cock pulsing, aching for one small touch.

Suddenly, it was there as Zane leaned close over Jiri's back and wrapped his large hand around Jiri. He began stroking Jiri's cock to the same rhythm he thrust into his tight ass. Jiri went out of his mind with sensation.

"You going to come for me, baby?" Zane whispered heavily into Jiri's ear as he rubbed his thumb over the small slit at the top of Jiri's cock.

"Yes! Oh, God, yes!" Jiri wailed. His hands dug into the hard wood of the desk as the tingle at the base of his spine wrapped around his body and spiked in his cock. Jiri's cock throbbed, then seed shot from him as he let out a loud cry.

Even as his vision swam before him, Jiri felt Zane's body stiffen behind him, then warm shots of liquid filled him. Zane continued to thrust into him for several moments before collapsing down over Jiri, holding his larger body up by his arms.

Jiri panted heavily, his breath coming rapidly from his chest. He was quickly coming to like this sex thing. Zane could throw him over a desk anytime he wanted as far as Jiri was concerned.

When Zane sat up and pulled his softening cock from him, Jiri groaned in disappointment. He liked the feeling he got from being connected so intimately with Zane. It made him feel special, as if Zane might really care about him.

"You okay, little man?" Zane asked as he handed Jiri a napkin to clean up. "I didn't hurt you, did I?"

Jiri laughed, shaking his head as he stood up. "No."

Zane turned Jiri and cupped his face. "You'll tell me if I do?"

Jiri could feel his face heat up even as he nodded his head. He dropped his eyes down, embarrassed to be talking so openly about what they had just been doing. He wasn't used to being so matter of fact about sex. Hell, he wasn't used to talking about sex at all.

"I'm serious, Jiri," Zane said as he pulled his pants up and zipped them. "I'm a lot more experienced than you are. I also have very big appetites."

Jiri zipped his pants. He looked over at Zane in confusion. "Appetites?"

"That means I like to have sex a lot."

Jiri nodded his head. Okay, that made sense. Jiri couldn't really blame Zane. The feeling he got from Zane when they had sex was amazing. If it was like that all of the time, he'd have a large appetite for sex, too.

"I'm not sure that's going to be a problem," Jiri said, laughing.

"Oh? You don't, huh?" Zane chuckled. He walked over to the door, waiting for Jiri to join him.

Jiri cursed his pale skin again as he felt his face heat up again. "No, I don't."

Zane grabbed for Jiri's leash, chuckling. He unlocked the door and opened it. "Ready to go get your mark now?"

Jiri nodded. Well, he was pretty sure, anyway.

Chapter 6

Zane chuckled as he walked out of his office. Jiri was a constant surprise to him. He took to sex like a duck to water. Zane felt a little leery about that, though. It concerned him that Jiri might want to try sex with someone else.

If Jiri became too interested in sex, he might want to know what sex with someone else felt like. Zane already knew he couldn't allow that. He had known it last night the moment his lips had met Jiri's.

He wasn't going to share. Anyone who tried to touch Jiri would seriously be taking their life into their hands. Zane wasn't known for playing well with others, but Jiri put a whole new spin on that.

The mere thought of Jiri with anyone else made Zane's muscles tense as if he was getting ready for a fight. He didn't realize he broadcasted his feeling so much until he felt Jiri's hand on his back.

"Zane?"

Zane reached behind him and grabbed Jiri, pulling him closer to his side. "It's okay, little one. I was just thinking of some stuff."

"Anything I can help with?" Jiri asked as he smoothed his hand down Zane's chest. Zane knew Jiri was just trying to soothe him, but all it did was make him want to drag Jiri into the nearest room and fuck him again.

Zane knew he had to get over this obsession he had with Jiri before he couldn't function properly. It wouldn't do for the leader of the Death Dealers to be so wrapped up in his little *sex pet* that he couldn't think of anything else.

The best thing he could do would be to get his mark on Jiri, then leave him in their quarters. At least if he didn't have Jiri following him around constantly, he might be able to get some things done.

"Zane?" Jiri asked, reminding Zane that Jiri had asked a question.

"No, there's nothing you can do, Jiri. I just have some stuff I need to do around here. We'll go get your mark done, then you can go back to the room for a nap while I do what needs to be done."

Zane could see the disappointed look on Jiri's face before he nodded. He felt like a heel, but he couldn't think of anything else that he could do. Being too intrigued with Jiri was dangerous to both of them.

If his attention centered on Jiri, he couldn't be an adequate leader for his people. Besides, someone might try to take over while he wasn't looking. The other problem was that someone might think they could get to him by hurting Jiri.

They'd be right, and Zane couldn't chance it. He was becoming too attached to Jiri in just the few hours that they had known each other. He liked having him around too much, liked the sex too much. No, he needed distance from his little sex pet.

With that thought in mind, Zane led Jiri out of the hotel and down the street to the tattoo parlor operated by DJ. He walked in and waited for DJ to look up, smiling when DJ just shook his head and gestured to a seat.

"Go sit down in that chair, Jiri," Zane ordered as he unclasped the collar from around Jiri's neck. Jiri looked hesitant, but went to sit down, anyway. Zane walked over to stand next to him.

"So," DJ said as he reached for his tattoo gun, "what sort of tattoo are we getting today?"

"Mine," was all Zane said. He crossed his arms over his chest and stared at DJ when DJ looked up at him in surprise.

"Seriously, man? You've taken a pet?" DJ asked.

Zane just raised an eyebrow at him.

"Okay, okay, don't get your panties in a bunch." DJ leaned over Jiri, his eyes intent on Jiri's skin. "Where you want it?"

"Where do pets usually get their marking tattoos?"

DJ shrugged. "Depends on the master, really. Some get them on the arm, some on the neck. I even had one master get his mark tattooed on his pet's forehead. Pretty much anywhere you want it."

Zane saw Jiri's eyes shoot to his in panic when DJ mentioned the forehead tattoo. As much as he would like to have a visible tattoo for anyone to see, he would never do that to Jiri. It just seemed too cruel.

"The neck, I think," Zane said as he leaned down and brushed his fingers at the bottom of Jiri's throat, "just here."

DJ nodded. "Okay. Color or old fashioned?"

"Color, I think," Zane replied. "It will fit Jiri's personality more than black and white."

"Okay, dude," DJ replied as he reached for a marking pen. "This shouldn't take more than a couple of hours."

Zane nodded as he stepped back to let DJ get to work. He watched for a while to see how Jiri would handle it. When Jiri seemed to be okay, Zane decided to head out and get some work done.

"I'll be back in an hour or so. If you finish before I get back, just send Jiri over to the hotel," Zane said. "He's to go back to the room and take a nap."

"Sure thing, Zane," DJ replied.

Zane heard a small whimper behind him as he turned and walked toward the door. He chose to ignore it, leaving and shutting the door behind him. The quicker he became less attached to his little pet, the better for both of them.

* * * *

Jiri couldn't believe Zane was leaving him here alone to get a tattoo. Hell, it wasn't even a tattoo. It was Zane's mark. And Zane was just leaving him here all alone with some stranger.

He knew something was wrong. Things had seemed so perfect when they had been inside the office, but the moment they had left, Zane had changed. Jiri couldn't put his finger on what had changed, exactly, but something had.

It was like Zane couldn't wait to get away from him. Jiri had no idea what he had done wrong, but it was obvious that he had done something. Maybe Zane really had been mad at him for what Harvey said.

Or maybe it had been the way he had reacted when they had sex in the office. Jiri didn't know the proper etiquette for sex between a master and his pet. Zane had said it was supposed to feel good and they were supposed to enjoy it. Jiri certainly had.

But there was so much he didn't know. He had just lain there and taken what Zane had done to him. Maybe that's where he had gone wrong? Jiri knew he was there to provide entertainment and comfort to Zane, not the other way around. Maybe that was the problem? Jiri hadn't been doing his job and Zane was disappointed in him. That had to be it.

Jiri resolved to try better. He would take better care of Zane so that Zane wasn't disappointed in him again. Jiri winced as the inking pen moved over his skin. He hoped this didn't take long. He had a master to care for.

It took longer than Jiri expected to finish the tattoo, but it hurt just as much as he thought it would. Jiri wished that Zane had stuck around for moral support, if nothing else. Jiri would have preferred to be holding Zane's hand during the procedure, but he knew that would be seen as weak.

He couldn't help it. He hated pain. He always had. If he had to go through a needle sticking into his skin like a million times, Jiri wished that he could have at least been able to hold Zane's hand so that he had something else to concentrate on.

Jiri felt like a wimp, but he was grateful when DJ finally sat up. "Okay, pet, you're done. Do you want to see it?"

Jiri nodded. He climbed out of the seat he sat in and walked over to the mirror hanging on the wall that DJ pointed to. His hand moved up to slowly stroke over the colored tattoo that was forever embedded in his skin.

It didn't look so bad. In the middle was a whitish cream colored skull with red eyes. Just in front, and a little below the skull, were two playing cards. One was the king of hearts, the other the ace of hearts. Both were in color. Below that was Zane's name in big bright red letters. Light blue lightening bolts ghosted out from each side of the skull giving the entire tattoo an eerie, not quite real feel to it. Jiri was impressed.

DJ had given the tattoo a three-dimensional look. Jiri wasn't sure how that had been done, but Jiri felt like he could see the letters moving every time he swallowed. There would be no mistaking the mark. Everyone who saw the tattoo would know that Jiri belonged to Zane.

"Well, what do you think, pet?"

"Jiri."

"Huh?"

"My name is Jiri."

"Uh huh, whatever." DJ nodded toward the door. "Zane expects you to go back to the hotel and take a nap, remember?"

Jiri rolled his eyes. "Yeah, I remember."

"Then I suggest you get to it, pet, before Zane gets mad."

Jiri knew there was nothing he could do. He took the small tube of ointment that DJ handed him, listened to the directions DJ gave on caring for his tattoo, then left. He could feel people looking at him as he made his way back to the hotel.

As Jiri made his way up the front steps of the hotel, he wished that Zane were with him. The looks he received from people gave him the creeps. He couldn't remember feeling like this since Frank tried to share his cot.

Jiri quickly made his way inside the hotel and up the stairs. He wanted to get away from prying eyes as fast as he could. As soon as he shut the door to his new quarters, Jiri leaned back against it. He took several deep breaths, trying to calm his rapid heartbeat.

A knock on the door a moment later made Jiri nearly jumping out of his skin. He turned around, one hand flat on the door, the other grabbing the door handle. "Yes?"

"I have your lunch for you."

Jiri's eyebrows drew together in a frown. His lunch? Jiri opened the door to see a young man from the kitchen standing there, a tray of food in his hands. The young man pushed past Jiri and walked into the room. He set the tray down on the side table and promptly left.

Jiri shut the door and walked over to the tray. He lifted the lid to find just what Harvey had said he would make. A hot roast beef sandwich, dipping sauce, and potato salad. There was also a soda and a glass of cold milk.

But there was only enough for one. Jiri knew at that point that Zane would not be joining him for lunch. He was still alone. Jiri suddenly didn't feel much like eating. In fact, his stomach felt kind of queasy.

Jiri placed the lid back on the tray and made his way into the bedroom. He pulled his clothes off and folded them neatly before placing them on a chair near the bed. Pulling back the covers, Jiri climbed in.

There didn't seem much else for him to do but take a nap like Zane had ordered. Jiri closed his eyes and snuggled deeply into the covers. He tried to pretend that someone, somewhere, cared about him and wanted him. It was obvious Zane didn't.

It was a fantasy that had gotten him through many long nights while he lived with Larry. Jiri thought he had been done with that fantasy when Zane came into his life. He now knew that he was wrong.

* * * *

Zane felt exhausted by the time he let himself into his quarters. Darkness had already fallen outside. Glancing at the clock on the wall as he closed the door, Zane realized that he had been gone a lot longer than he had anticipated.

He planned on being back in the room to see Jiri several hours ago. He hoped Jiri wouldn't be too upset with him. Zane started to make his way through the room when he spotted the tray on the sideboard.

He walked over and lifted the lid, frowning when he saw the uneaten food. Jiri hadn't eaten. Zane didn't like that. It was his duty to provide for Jiri. If Jiri didn't eat, he wasn't doing his job properly. Besides, Jiri needed the nutrition.

Zane dropped the lid back down on the tray and made his way into the bedroom. At first, he didn't see Jiri. He started to get concerned until he heard a small whimper come from the bed and noticed the small lump under the covers.

He reached down and pulled the edge of the cover back until he could see Jiri's face. Zane's breath caught in his throat. A shaft of moonlight streamed through the open window casting light right down on Jiri's face.

The moonlight illuminated Jiri's face, highlighting his ethereal beauty, his delicate features. The moonlight also shone on the tearstains on Jiri's face. Zane knew he was the cause of those tears.

Zane's heart felt heavy as he pulled the covers back up over Jiri. He wasn't doing this right and he knew it. Every turn he made he seemed to mess up where Jiri was concerned. Zane wondered why anything couldn't ever seem to be simple.

It seemed that the harder he tried, the worse he made things. If he didn't try at all, he still made things worse. Maybe he needed to give up on the idea of having a pet at all and just let Jiri go, but the very thought made him sick to his stomach.

Zane walked back into the main room and went toward the liquor cabinet. It most likely wouldn't help his situation any, but at least it might make him feel a little better. Zane poured himself a small glass of whiskey.

Grabbing the glass, he made his way over to the balcony that overlooked the front of the hotel. He easily pushed open the double doors and stepped out onto the wooden planks of the balcony.

He liked it out here, especially late in the evening after almost everyone had gone to bed. It was quiet, peaceful. A man could really think sitting out here. Zane made his way over to his favorite chair and sat down. He could hear the occasional voice down below, see the occasional shooting star up above. Mostly, though, it was quiet and dark.

Except for a few lights here and there, the town was dark, as their main source of energy was solar powered. That had been one of the things he had brought into the town after he founded it, electricity.

During the day, it provided what they needed to survive. At night, the stored electricity kept food cold and lights going, even if there was a limit on how much people could use. But, it ensured that their little town functioned.

Still, on nights like this, Zane was glad that there was a limit as to how much power could be used to light the town. He preferred the darkness at night when he came out to the balcony for some peace. It just wouldn't have been the same if the town had been lit up.

"Zane?"

Zane turned when he heard a small whisper at the door to see Jiri standing there wrapped in a blanket. He held out his hand to him, gesturing to Jiri to come over. "Hey, baby, did you have a good nap?"

Jiri seemed hesitant as he walked over and knelt down on the floor at Zane's feet. He nodded his head.

"You didn't eat."

"I fell asleep."

"Guess you needed your rest, huh?" Zane asked. He reached down and ran his hand through Jiri's hair. Zane was amazed by how soft and silky Jiri's blond locks felt.

"It's so quiet out here," Jiri said.

Zane looked around. "Yeah, I like it. I come out here by myself a lot in the evenings after everyone has gone home or to bed. It gives me time to think."

"You want me to go back inside?"

Zane shook his head. "No, little one. You can stay."

Jiri was silent for several moments. Zane knew he was thinking hard. He could almost hear the wheels turning in Jiri's mind. Zane just waited, letting Jiri gather his thoughts and speak when he was ready.

"I read a book today," Jiri finally said.

"You read a book?" Zane asked. He thought Jiri couldn't read very well.

"Well, I looked at the pictures," Jiri said. "Want to know what I read about?"

Zane leaned his head back against the side of the building, smiling to himself. "Sure, Jiri, tell me about this book you read."

"I'd rather show you what I learned."

"Okay," Zane replied, a little confused. A moment later, Zane nearly jumped out of his chair when Jiri scooted over to kneel between his legs and reached for his zipper. Before Zane knew it, Jiri had his pants undone and his cock pulled out of his pants.

"Jiri!" Zane exclaimed as Jiri's lips closed over the head of his cock. "Oh, God!" Zane's hands clenched in Jiri's hair as Jiri's mouth and tongue began to torture him.

His mind reeled. Zane had his share of blow jobs in his time, but never one like this. He didn't know if it was due to Jiri's enthusiasm or his inexperienced touch, but Zane was going out of his mind.

When Jiri pushed against his thighs, Zane spread his legs wider, allowing Jiri to move closer to him. Hesitant fingers pushed into his pants and brushed against his balls, dragging a deep moan from Zane's throat.

When Jiri sucked him all of the way in, his nose settling in Zane's pubic hair, Zane felt his balls draw up tightly against his body. He knew he was mere seconds away from blowing his load. Jiri's mouth felt like heaven.

"Jiri," Zane groaned, tugging on Jiri's hair, "I'm going to come, baby."

He tried to hold off too, to give Jiri the time to pull back, but the feel of Jiri's tongue brushing over the top head of his cock blew Zane's control away. His hands tightened in Jiri's hair as he thrust himself deep into the warm, wet haven surrounding his aching cock.

"Aaahhh," Zane cried out as he came, shooting stream after stream of hot seed into Jiri's mouth. Zane's mind fuzzed as lights danced in front of his eyes. His entire body seemed to stiffen, every muscle tense, as Jiri continued to suck at his hard flesh until Zane wasn't sure he would ever breathe again.

Finally, the air returned to Zane's lungs and his mind came out of the haze of lust it had sunk into. Zane realized that his hands were still clenched in Jiri's hair holding him in place. Feeling like a heel once again, Zane let Jiri go.

"Sorry," he whispered when Jiri dropped his cock and looked up at him. "I didn't hurt you, did I?"

Jiri grinned, shaking his head. "Nope."

"Where in the hell did you learn to do that, Jiri?" Zane asked. He tried not to growl as he thought about where Jiri might have learned to give blow jobs. He had been under the impression since meeting him that Jiri had no sexual experience at all. Had he been wrong?

"I told you. I read it in a book."

"What book?" Zane shouted.

He regretted it as soon as the color drained out of Jiri's face. His head slumped forward and he ran his hand down his face. Great! Now he had made Jiri upset. He heard Jiri moving, then the slight padding of his feet as he left the balcony, but he didn't raise his head.

A moment later, Jiri came back. Zane tried to rein in his precarious emotions. He had loved the blow job. It had been wonderful. He just couldn't help be suspicious of where Jiri had learned it. The thought of Jiri with anyone else made Zane so angry he could feel the heat moving into his clenched fists.

"Zane?" Jiri whispered softly.

Zane took a deep breath and released it slowly, then looked up at Jiri. He was surprised to find Jiri standing before him holding a book in his hands. When Jiri held it out to him, Zane took it, looking at Jiri in confusion.

"Page twenty three," Jiri instructed. The soft blush that filled Jiri's face intrigued Zane. Interesting. He opened the book and flipped it to page twenty-three. Zane's mouth dropped open at the pictures he saw.

A man was lying on his back on a nondescript bed. A blonde woman knelt between his legs. One picture had her leaning toward him. The next had her taking the man's penis into her mouth. Close up pictures showed the woman's mouth moving over the man's penis. There were nine pictures in all, each one more descriptive than the last one.

"I know it's a man and woman, but I figured the mechanics were pretty much the same," Jiri said quickly.

Zane glanced up to see Jiri standing before him, twisting his hands together. His eyes kept darting around as if he were afraid to look Zane in the eyes. Jiri's face burned red. He looked so nervous, so uncertain.

"This book was on my bookshelf?" Zane asked as he looked back down at the pictures.

"Yes," Jiri whispered. "I know you didn't say I could read them, but I got bored and—"

"It's fine, Jiri," Zane said. He closed the book and handed it back to Jiri. "Go put it back on the bookshelf now and then we need to talk."

Jiri hesitated for a moment, shifting from one foot to the other. Zane could see his hands gripping the book so hard that his fingers where white. "Did I do something wrong?"

"Go put the book back, Jiri," Zane said again. He needed a moment to compose himself. He had been so worried that Jiri had been with someone else that he had never considered that Jiri might have learned something from a book, especially since Jiri could barely read.

Zane knew he should have had more faith in his pet, but what did he actually know about him? They had known each other all of twenty-four hours. Granted, they had lived a lot in those twenty-four hours, but still…

Hearing a soft sniffle next to him, Zane turned to see Jiri standing in the doorway of the balcony. What light came from their quarters shined behind him, illuminating Jiri's slim form. Zane still couldn't see Jiri's face.

Zane held out his hand to Jiri. "Come here, little one."

* * * *

Jiri took the hand Zane held out to him. He didn't want to. He wanted to run and hide. He knew when he had looked at the pictures that it was wrong. The pictures showed a man and a woman, not two men.

He had just wanted to please Zane, to make him feel good. Zane had done so much for him. He had taken Jiri away from his horrible stepfather and given him a whole new life. Zane had taught him about being intimate with someone. He provided food, safety, and companionship.

Jiri had just wanted to repay Zane and make him feel good. Now, he had fucked it all up. Jiri let Zane pull him down onto his lap. He curled himself up and rested his head on Zane's chest.

"Okay, first things first," Zane said. "Thank you."

Thank you? "Huh?" Jiri mumbled.

"For the blow job?" Zane chuckled. "Thank you. It felt wonderful."

"Really? You're not mad?"

Zane shook his head. "No, I'm not mad."

"But you—" Jiri stopped speaking when Zane placed a finger over his mouth. He lifted his head and looked up at Zane.

"You need to understand, Jiri, I've never had a pet before. I'm learning through this thing as much as you are. I'm going to make mistakes."

Jiri didn't say anything, just watched as Zane seemed to be gathering his thoughts. He didn't know what to say at this point. Zane had said he wasn't mad that Jiri had given him a blow job, but Jiri knew that wasn't all that was going on.

"I told you early on that I don't share well, Jiri, and I meant it. Just the thought of you being with anyone else makes me want to kill something."

"But I wouldn't...I'd never—" Jiri stammered. He felt Zane pat him on the back.

"I know, baby. But when you did what you did, and knowing that you don't have a lot of sexual experience, well, you can see where my mind went."

"You thought..." Jiri suddenly realized that Zane thought he had been with someone else. He was so shocked that for a moment, he couldn't move. His shock was quickly followed by hurt that Zane would think he would ever want to be with anyone except him.

That quickly rolled into hot, uncontrollable anger. Jiri was incensed. How dare Zane assume he had been unfaithful because he had tried to show Zane a little pleasure. He had thought that the mark on his neck meant something.

Jiri pushed himself away from Zane and jumped to his feet. His hands landed on his hips as he glared down at Zane. He couldn't ever remember being this angry before, not even with Larry.

"I thought you were different, but you're not. You're just like the rest of the assholes out there. You just want to take from me and not give back. When I don't do what you want, you get angry with me. You don't remember that I'm a person. I'm just a thing to you."

"Jiri!" Zane exclaimed.

"Oh, that's right, I'd better not make the big bad leader of the Death Dealers angry. I might be punished or killed," Jiri yelled. He leaned over to get closer to Zane. "Well, go ahead. Punish me. Kill me. It won't be any worse than what you're doing to me right now."

Jiri refused to step back when Zane stood to his feet. He just tilted his head back and glared up at him.

"That's enough, Jiri."

"No, it's not." Jiri pointed to the tattoo on his neck. "I thought this meant something, that I was special."

He finally stepped back, his emotions overwhelming him. Jiri shook his head and spoke almost to himself. "I thought I was more than a pet to you, that maybe you would start to care for me."

Jiri swallowed to get past the tears clogging his throat. "I should have known. You didn't even stay around while it was done. You just left me there to be branded as your possession."

Suddenly, the fight went out of Jiri. What was the point? Zane would never understand. He was big and strong. He could have whatever he wanted with a crook of his finger. He didn't have to fight for every scrap of food, for every kind gesture. He didn't need a protector just to keep from being assaulted and used.

Jiri had felt such hope when Zane had begun to explain their relationship to him. When Zane had agreed that Jiri was a sex pet and not just a regular pet, Jiri had been elated. He had even looked forward to wearing Zane's mark.

"I—" Jiri stopped speaking. He wanted something that wasn't meant to be his. He needed to resign himself to being just Zane's pet. That's all he would ever be.

"I apologize for yelling at you," Jiri whispered. He stared at Zane's feet not quite able to look him in the eyes. "It won't happen again."

"Jiri—"

"May I go to bed now?"

Zane was silent for a moment before answering. "Yeah, go ahead."

Jiri refused to look at Zane as he walked past him into their quarters. He made his way to the bedroom and climbed into bed. He grabbed the covers and pulled them up over his head, wishing that today would just go away and tomorrow would never come.

* * * *

Zane watched Jiri walk away, not quite sure what had just happened but knowing something had. The life had seemed to drain right out of Jiri. Zane could swear Jiri's golden hair wasn't even as shiny as it had been.

He knew he wasn't an easy man to understand. He never had been. After losing his family so many years ago, Zane learned to keep his emotions close, to not let anyone in. He just didn't realize how good he had gotten at it.

His position in the Death Dealers didn't leave much room for tender emotion and it wasn't like he had experienced it much growing up. His mother was always working and his father was always drunk and off screwing one of his floozies.

Zane had quickly learned that he could only rely on himself for anything. He wasn't sure if he could open up enough to let Jiri in and he knew that was exactly what Jiri wanted.

Shaking his head at his own misgivings, Zane walked into the room, shutting the balcony doors behind him. He made sure they were locked, then shut off the lights before heading toward the bedroom and Jiri.

He dropped his clothes on the floor and crawled into bed, snuggling up to Jiri's back. He didn't think Jiri was asleep. His body was too tense. Zane rubbed his hand up and down Jiri's side until he began to relax.

Once Jiri started snoring softly, Zane cuddled him closer and closed his eyes. He hoped that sleep would take him soon and he could forget that today had ever happened.

Chapter 7

Zane slammed the bedroom door and stalked across the room to the balcony. If he didn't get away from Jiri he didn't know what he was going to do. The man was driving him nuts.

The last two weeks had been hell for Zane. Jiri seemed to be doing every damn thing he could to drive Zane out of his mind. And it was working. Zane was going nuts.

Nothing he did seemed to make Jiri happy. Zane had tried everything he could think of. He had taken Jiri out for rides on his motorcycle. He had arranged special dinners for them. He had even tried to get Jiri involved in the running of the town.

Nothing worked. It was like Jiri was in a continuous depression. Oh, he smiled whenever Zane looked at him. He smiled so much Zane was afraid Jiri's face might freeze that way. It just wasn't a real smile.

Jiri did whatever Zane asked immediately when he asked. He never protested anything Zane wanted him to do. As much as he had protested when they first met, Zane was pretty sure he could order Jiri to strip off his clothes in a room full of people and he would do it.

Jiri did everything Zane asked of him. He just no longer asked for anything in return. He didn't protest anything. He never told Zane no. He had even eaten a bowl of rice Zane had given him without protest. Zane had been sure that at least would get a rise out of Jiri. It didn't.

Zane was at a loss about what to do. He wanted his Jiri back, the arguing, protesting, questioning Jiri. While Zane wanted Jiri to be agreeable, the way Jiri acted now, it was like he had no mind or thoughts of his own. He was just a vessel.

Zane was deeply afraid he had created the Jiri he now had and he wasn't sure how to change it. Jiri wanted something from him that Zane wasn't sure he had to give.

It wasn't that he didn't care about Jiri because he did, a lot in fact. The little man had wormed his way into Zane's affections without Zane even being aware of it until it had already happened. Zane just didn't know how to show Jiri that he cared.

Zane pushed his hand through his hair and tried to regulate his rapid breathing. He needed to go back into the bedroom and talk with Jiri, to get this thing between them settled so that he could have his Jiri back. Before that happened, Zane needed to get his raging emotions under control. He didn't want to say the wrong thing and send Jiri even further away from him than the man already was.

Zane turned when he heard the bedroom door open to find Jiri standing there. He watched him for a moment, once again stunned by the sheer beauty the man was. Zane wasn't sure he would ever get used to the way Jiri looked. Jiri took Zane's breath away each time he saw him.

"Did you need something, Jiri?" Zane finally asked to break the silence in the room. Jiri shook his head but Zane could have predicted that. Jiri never seemed to need anything from him anymore. Zane was beginning to wonder if Jiri ever did.

"Are you feeling okay?"

Jiri smiled and nodded. It infuriated Zane. He hated that stupid little smile. It wasn't real. Jiri didn't mean it.

"Stop smiling, damn it!"

Jiri looked confused, his eyebrows drawing together in a frown. "You don't want me to smile?"

Zane rolled his eyes. He counted to ten before answering. "Yes, I want you to smile but I want it to be a real smile. Not this fabricated shit you've been giving me for the last two weeks. You don't mean it, so why do it?"

Jiri looked flustered. "I don't—"

Zane walked across the room toward Jiri, his fists clenching at his sides. "Don't give me that shit, Jiri. You know exactly what I'm talking about," he shouted. He came to a stop directly in front of Jiri, his fists landing on his hips as he glared down at the smaller man.

"No one is as happy as you've tried to pretend to be, no one. I swear your face is going to freeze like that. You never do anything but smile, smile, smile."

"You don't want me to be happy?" Jiri asked.

"Christ!" Zane shouted. "Yes, I want you to be happy but this isn't happy, Jiri. This is sad. I've tried every damn thing I can think of to make you happy but nothing seems to work."

A sudden thought came to Zane, a thought that brought a great pain to Zane's chest. "Would you be happy if I let you go, Jiri?" Zane asked quietly.

"You don't want me anymore?" Jiri's voice was low, almost a whisper. His face had drained of all color and he looked like he was about to fall down.

Zane reached over and cupped the side of Jiri's face, softly caressing Jiri's cheek with his thumb. "I'll always want you, Jiri, but I want you to be happy too. If being free is what will make you happy, I'll let you go. You just have to say the word."

Zane watched Jiri's fingers move over the tattoo on his neck. He tried not to let on how much Jiri's answer meant to him. He didn't want Jiri influenced in any way. But Jiri had the power to break him or make him the happiest man on earth.

Zane found it somewhat amusing that his happiness lay in the hands of a man considered by most to be a pet, a possession. Zane knew differently. Jiri was everything Zane has always needed but didn't know he did.

"Do you want me to go?" Jiri finally asked.

Oh, how to answer that one, Zane thought. If he told Jiri he wanted him to stay, would Jiri stay because Zane wanted him to or because that was what Jiri wanted? If he didn't answer, would Jiri take it as a rejection? Zane was torn by either choice.

"I want you to stay if that's what you want, Jiri," Zane said. "I don't want you to stay if you're doing it because you think you have to or for any reason other than because you want to."

Jiri frowned. "Well, that's not an answer."

Zane chuckled. That sentence was the first real thing Jiri had said in days. He was elated. "No, I suppose not, little one, but it's the only one I have for you right now."

"I feel funny telling you what I want when I don't know what you want," Jiri said, his face flushing red.

"Kind of a catch-22, huh?"

Jiri nodded.

Zane wrapped his arms around Jiri and pulled him into a hug. He rested his cheek on Jiri's head. "I don't think either of us are very good at showing what we really want, Jiri. While that can be a plus in my line of work, it doesn't work so much with someone I care about."

"You care about me?" Jiri whispered.

"I do, Jiri," Zane replied. "I know I'm not very good at showing that. I pretty much suck at it. I warned you in the very beginning that I wasn't any good at this master/pet thing."

"Oh, no," Jiri corrected, "you're very good at the master/pet thing. It's the Zane/Jiri thing that I'm interested in."

Jiri's words were a balm to Zane's tired soul. He closed his eyes, hugging Jiri closer. "I'm pretty sure that I suck at that even more, little one. Maybe you can show me how to do better."

"If I decide to stay, you mean?"

Zane flinched and opened his eyes to stare down at the top of Jiri's head. He blinked back the sudden tears that had appeared in his eyes. "Yeah," he murmured, "if you decide to stay."

* * * *

Jiri started to tell Zane that he wanted to stay but a loud alarm sounded making Jiri jump. Jiri glanced around wildly as the alarm blared. He could hear voices yelling suddenly, coming from several directions.

"Zane?"

"I want you to go inside the bedroom and lock the door, Jiri. Don't come out until I come for you," Zane said. He grabbed Jiri by the arms, giving him a little shake. "Do you understand me?"

"What's going on?"

"The Night Dwellers have breached the perimeter," Zane replied.

"Night Dwellers?" Jiri asked frantically as Zane pulled him off the balcony and toward the bedroom. "There are Night Dwellers here?"

Night Dwellers were bad. They were monsters. It seemed their sole purpose in life was to create death and mayhem. They weren't even human anymore, but twisted, scarred monsters with deep fanged teeth and yellow tinted skin.

Jiri stumbled as Zane pushed him into the bedroom. He turned to see Zane pulling the bedroom door closed. His heart clenched in his chest. "Zane! Wait, Zane," Jiri cried out.

Jiri ran to the door and pulled until Zane opened it up again. Jiri reached up and wrapped an arm around Zane's neck and pulled his head down for a quick kiss. He tried to convey to Zane how he felt. Yes, he was still unsure of things, but in the face of the danger outside, he was also worried.

"Be careful, Zane," Jiri whispered as he stepped back. "I'd be very upset if anything happened to you."

Zane cocked his head to one side, giving Jiri a strange look, then nodded his head. He pointed his finger at Jiri. "You remember what I said. Don't leave this room or open this door until I come for you. And lock the balcony doors, too."

Jiri nodded, his eyes staying on Zane until the door closed behind him. Jiri ran forward and locked the door, then ran and locked the balcony doors. Coming back to the bedroom door, he pressed his ear against it and listened. The alarm still blared in the background, but Jiri could hear Zane talking and someone replying.

"Jiri, open the door," Zane said.

Jiri quickly opened the door to find Zane standing there. Slash and his pet, Billy, stood behind him. Zane turned and motioned to Billy, who quickly came forward. Jiri lifted an eyebrow in curiosity when Billy walked into the bedroom.

"Billy is going to stay here with you while Slash comes with me. Slash is worried about Billy being on his own." Zane reached over and ran his knuckles down the side of Jiri's face. "You're in charge until I get back."

Jiri nodded, overjoyed that Zane had confidence in him. "Yes, Zane."

Once again, Jiri watched Zane until the door closed, then leaned forward and locked the door. Turning back to look at Billy, Jiri was surprised to see Billy sitting on the floor next to the bed, his eyes glued to the door.

"Billy? Are you okay?" Jiri asked softly.

Billy nodded his head, but he eyes never wavered from the door. He had his knees pulled up to his chest, his arms wrapped around his legs. Jiri could see small tremors rocking his small-framed body.

Jiri could see that Billy wasn't okay, no matter what he said. He walked over and sat down next to him. Jiri looked toward the door, watching just as Billy did. Billy was looking at it so intently, Jiri wondered if the door was going to pop open.

After several moments, Jiri could still feel Billy trembling next to him. The cold from the hardwood floor began to seep into his butt. Jiri stood to his feet, reaching his hand down to Billy.

"Come on, Billy, this floor is cold. At least come wait up on the bed."

When Billy looked up at him, Jiri had the feeling that Billy hadn't even realized he was in the room. Jiri smiled down at him. "Come on, you'll be more comfortable up on the bed."

Jiri held his hand out until Billy took it and climbed to his feet. Jiri led him over to the bed and climbed on. He settled back against the pillows, then gestured to the spot next to him. Billy climbed onto the bed and sat down. The moment he leaned back, his eyes went to the door again.

"Does this happen often?" Jiri asked after a few moments of silence between them. He could still hear the alarm blaring outside. A few shouts here and there. Inside the room, however, the only sound was his and Billy's breathing.

"What?" Billy asked.

Jiri waved his hand around. "The alarm, the Night Dwellers?"

Billy shook his head. "We haven't had any problems with them in months. Slash says that they're getting braver, though. He thinks we're going to see a lot more of them. He said the pickings are getting slim out there and the Night Dwellers are getting hungry."

Jiri was mildly surprised. That was the most he had heard from Billy since he had met the other man. Billy seemed more like the quiet type. He also seemed nervous as hell, which made Jiri nervous as well.

Living with Larry, he had never really been bothered by the Night Dwellers. Jiri wasn't exactly sure why not, though. They seemed to attack humans almost anywhere that they congregated.

"Have you ever seen one?"

Billy nodded. "They killed my family before the Death Dealers rescued me. I was the only one that survived."

Jiri laid his hand on Billy's arm. "Oh God, Billy, I'm sorry."

Billy just nodded again.

Jiri pulled his hand back. He pulled his legs up to his chest and wrapped his arms around them, resting his chin on his knees. "My father died before I was born. My mother died from the plague."

"No other family?" Billy asked, looking over at him.

"Besides Zane?" Jiri asked. "I have a stepfather out there. He's the one that sold me to Zane. He owed Zane money."

"You really consider Zane your family?"

Jiri smiled. He could hear the doubt in Billy's voice. "Sure. Zane belongs to me as much as I belong to him." He turned and looked at Billy. "Isn't it that way with you and Slash?"

Billy was quiet for a moment, then shook his head. "I want it to be, but ever since Zane took me from Pug and gave me to Slash, he barely talks to me. Hell, he barely acknowledges that I'm alive."

"Do you want him to?"

Billy's face flushed as he dipped his head. "Yeah," he murmured.

Jiri laughed. "Then have I got a book for you." Jiri quickly crawled from the bed and walked to the bookshelf. He instantly found the book he was looking for and brought it back to the bed, crawling on.

"I found this book a while back," Jiri explained as he started leafing through the pages. "I can't read much, but the pictures kind of tell the story. Zane really liked this one." Jiri pointed to page twenty-three and tilted the book toward Billy.

Billy's face flushed even redder and he pushed the book away.

"What's wrong, Billy?"

"Pug made me do those things. It was horrible."

"Oh." Jiri thought about it for a moment. He didn't exactly know how Billy felt, but he could imagine it. If anyone had forced him to do the things he did with Zane, he'd be horrified, too.

"Have you ever done any of that with Slash?"

"Once. Pug traded me to Slash for the night when he lost a bet." *Double oh!*

"Did you like it? With Slash, I mean?" Jiri didn't think it was possible, but Billy's face got even redder. He did, however, see a small smile move across Billy's lips.

"Yeah."

"Well, then," Jiri chuckled, "there you go. Pug's dead, so he can never hurt you again and since Zane gave you to Slash, and you liked doing those things with Slash, you should have nothing to worry about."

"That's assuming I can ever get Slash to touch me."

"So, tease him."

"Tease him? How?" Billy looked totally confused. Jiri knew how he felt.

Jiri shrugged. "I'm probably not the one to ask about that. Until Zane showed me, I wasn't very knowledgeable about these things. However, I've seen the way Zane watches me. If I wanted to get his attention, I'd walk around naked in front of him, or at least in something really skimpy, like one of his shirts."

Suddenly, Billy chuckled. "I see where you're going with this."

"Thought you might."

"Let me see that damn book again."

Jiri laughed as he handed over the book. He started flipping through the pages again. "I haven't tried this yet, but the stuff on page forty-five looked interesting."

"Oh my God! Is that even possible?" Billy whispered in awe as Jiri showed him page forty-five.

Jiri laughed, feeling his face heat up. "I have no idea. But it sure would be fun to find out."

* * * *

Jiri jerked awake. He opened his eyes and glanced around the room, trying to figure out what had woken him. The room was nearly pitch black. It took him a moment for his eyes to adjust to the darkness.

He could feel the press of Billy's body next to his. Billy's soft snores filled the silence in the room. Jiri wondered how late it was. He couldn't hear the alarm anymore, but it was still dark outside.

A faint squeak of boards sounded to the right of him. Jiri's eyes swung to the right side of the room. His heart suddenly beat faster in his chest. Jiri could just make out a dark figure moving past the balcony doors.

Moving as quietly as he could, Jiri rolled over and covered Billy's mouth with his hand. "Billy," Jiri whispered as quietly as he could into Billy's ear. "Billy, wake up. There's something outside."

Jiri felt Billy jerk awake. For a moment, there was panic in Billy's eyes until he realized that Jiri was next to him. Jiri instantly felt Billy's body relax, but his eyes shot around the room, still panicked.

Jiri pointed to the far side of the room close to the bathroom. "Go," he whispered almost silently. Billy rolled to the side of the bed and lowered himself to the floor. Jiri watched as he quickly crawled across the floor and curled into a ball on the corner next to the dresser.

Satisfied that Billy was sufficiently hidden, Jiri rolled to the opposite side of the bed. His eyes glanced around the room as he tried to find something to defend himself with. Zane had told him that he needed to care for Billy. That's exactly what he was going to do.

Spotting a fireplace poker, Jiri crossed the floor to the fireplace and grabbed it. He weighed it in his hand. Hard, uncompromising, lethal, the long, round iron would do perfectly. With the poker in one hand, Jiri grabbed the iron fireplace tongs and carried them over to Billy. They wouldn't do much, but they were better than nothing.

After handing the tongs to Billy, Jiri held his hand up, gesturing for Billy to stay put. Once Billy nodded, Jiri made his way over to the double doors that led to the balcony. He positioned himself to one side, poker raised to strike, and waited.

Jiri's heart pounded. He prayed that whoever was outside of his door wouldn't hear it. Taking slow, even breaths, Jiri tried to slow his heart rate down. It wouldn't do to give his position away. He needed the element of surprise in order to overcome whatever opponent stood outside the door.

Jiri glanced once more across the room to Billy. He held his finger up across his lips for Billy to be silent. Looking back at the door, he was surprised to see the handle begin to turn. Jiri could have sworn he had locked the door when he had come in. He'd have to ask Zane about that later, much later.

Right now, he needed to defend himself and Billy from whoever was opening the door. Jiri held the poker over his head as the door inched open, ready to bring it down on the head of the person sneaking into the room.

The moment a head appeared, Jiri swung with every bit of strength he had. He heard a loud grunt as he swung. Even as the body began to fall to the floor, Jiri swung again. He wasn't letting anyone get to him or Billy.

The body dropped to the floor, not moving. Jiri stepped forward, the poker raised over his head as he waited to see if the body would move again. When it didn't, he motioned for Billy to come over.

"Hold this," Jiri said as he handed the poker to Billy. He grabbed the fallen body by the arms and pulled it into the room, then stepped over it to lock the door again. Turning back to the unconscious man, and he could tell it was a man due to the size, he wondered what to do with it.

He knew that the smartest thing would be to tie the man up until Zane returned and then Zane could do whatever he wanted with the intruder.

"We need something to tie him up, Billy."

Jiri and Billy both looked around the room. Jiri spotted the curtain strings. He hoped Zane wouldn't get mad at him as he ripped them off of their rods. Coming back to the body, he tied the man's hands together behind his back, then tied his feet.

Once he was all done, and feeling a whole lot safer, Jiri rolled the man over. He didn't need any light to tell him who he was looking at. He'd know that face anywhere. It was his stepfather, Larry.

Chapter 8

Zane's body hurt so much he was surprised he could even walk. He had felt exhausted before the alarm had gone off. The adrenaline that shot through his body carried him for the next several hours, but now that battle was over, he could feel his bones ache. He wanted nothing more than to crawl into bed with Jiri and sleep for a week.

As Zane thought about his little pet, he prayed that he had remained safe. The battle had been a bloody one. They had lost three fighters, even more had been injured. Zane still couldn't figure out why they had attacked the town.

They hadn't had trouble with the Night Dwellers in several months. It wasn't that the Night Dwellers didn't want to attack them, but rather that they were afraid to. Zane had made it his business after taking over the Death Dealers to make sure that everyone knew not to attack them.

What was his remained his, and Zane was merciless to those who tried to take anything from him. Zane considered every member of his gang, master and pet alike, as his. That included every inch of the safe zone that they had established as their haven from the world.

Zane walked into the hotel. He grimaced at the injured bodies lying everywhere. It looked like most of the injuries were superficial. A few, though, seemed life threatening. He hoped that everyone pulled through.

"Hey, boss, you need to get that looked at."

Zane turned to see Slash standing beside him. Slash looked as bad as Zane felt. Blood caked the side of his shirt. There was a small cut on his face near his right eye, which was swollen and purple.

"Have you been looked at?" Zane asked as he gestured to Slash's wounds.

Slash chuckled. "Oh, this?" he asked as he gestured to his face. "It's not too bad. Nothing that a soft bed and a cold beer won't fix. How about you? That's a pretty nasty-looking cut on your side."

Zane glanced down at the cut on his ribcage. Acknowledging that it was there seemed to make it hurt more. It was a small cut in comparison to others, just a couple of inches long, but it was deep enough to still bleed.

"I guess I could use a needle and thread."

"Come on over here and let me fix you up real quick, and then we can go upstairs and reclaim our boys."

Zane sat down in the chair Slash pointed to and held his arm over his head. He could hear the worry in Slash's voice when he mentioned Jiri and Billy. Zane felt pretty much the same. He was concerned for their safety, as well.

"Slash, can you think of any reason that the Night Dwellers might attack us now? We haven't had any trouble with them in months," Zane asked as Slash went to work on his side. He hissed, his body jerking as Slash sewed him up. *Damn, that hurt!*

"Not really, but it's not like these things really need a reason to attack anyone. They live for that shit," Slash replied.

"I think we need to double the guard for a while. Maybe they attacked because we've become too complacent."

"Maybe," Slash said. "And maybe they attacked because that's what they do. Don't try and second-guess yourself, Zane. They're pretty much mindless monsters. They kill and they destroy. You didn't do this."

"No, but I'm still responsible. These people trust me to protect them. I let them down."

"Fuck man, no you didn't. If it wasn't for you, a lot more of us would be dead right now. You gave us a home here, a place where we could have families and live in peace. Try to remember that."

Zane scoffed. "Tell that to the families of the three men who died tonight."

"Get over yourself already," Slash chuckled. "You're a man, Zane. You're not God. There's only so much you can do, and you do it. The Night Dwellers are going to attack, whether you like it or not. And no matter how hard you train us or try to protect us, some of us will die. It's a fact of life now."

"Well, it sucks!"

"True, it does. Unfortunately, it's our reality now." Slash patted Zane on the shoulder. "Okay, you're done. Try not to do anything that might rip the stitches out, no matter how much Jiri wants you to."

Zane chuckled. "Yeah, you wouldn't believe what he showed me just before the alarm went off. Damned if he didn't see it in a book, too."

"Oh, yeah?" Slash looked intrigued.

Zane just shook his head. No way was he going to tell Slash about the blow job Jiri had given him. There were just some things he didn't share with anyone. He might share the book with Billy, however. "Come on, let's go see our boys."

Zane and Slash made their way up the stairs. Each step brought Zane closer to where he wanted to be. By the time he reached the top, he practically had a spring in his step. He raced down the hallway and opened the door to his quarters.

All looked good, he thought as he glanced around the room. Zane made his way over to the bedroom door and tapped lightly. "Jiri? Open the door, baby, it's me."

He heard footsteps pad across the room, then the lock clicked. Zane had a wide smile on his face for Jiri as the door slowly opened, only to be surprised by Billy's face. "Oh, hey, Billy. Where's Jiri?"

Billy pointed over his shoulder before pushing past Zane to wrap his arms around Slash's waist. Zane heard Billy say something to Slash, but it was muffled. Zane ignored it and made his way into the room.

"Jiri?" he called out when he didn't immediately see his pet.

"Zane?" Jiri called out. "Oh, thank God you came back."

Zane turned to see Jiri racing across the room. He barely had time to catch him as Jiri threw himself into Zane's arms. He wrapped his arms around Jiri, holding him close to his chest, closing his eyes briefly as a strange calmness overtook him.

It felt so good to hold Jiri in his arms, to know that someone cared about his wellbeing, for him and not because he was the leader of the Death Dealers. Zane knew that Jiri really couldn't care less what Zane was in charge of. He just seemed to want Zane for himself. That thought gave Zane a warm feeling deep inside.

Zane opened his eyes and leaned back a bit from Jiri. He wanted to look down into his face, to assure himself that Jiri was safe. It was only as he looked up that he noticed the bound man lying on the floor by the balcony doors. "Jiri?"

"It's Larry," Jiri explained as he turned to glare across the room. "He tried to break in here when you were out fighting the Night Dwellers."

Zane glanced down at Jiri in surprise, raising one eyebrow at him. "Larry? Your stepfather, Larry?"

Jiri nodded. "I hit him with this," Jiri said as he held up the fireplace poker. "Then Billy and I tied him up."

"Slash?" Zane called out. "You better get your ass in here."

Zane heard the bedroom door slam against the wall, then Slash stood beside him. Glancing sideways, Zane could see the shock on Slash's face.

"Isn't that—"

Zane nodded. "Jiri's stepfather. Seems he tried to break in here while we were busy elsewhere. Jiri and Billy beat him up, then tied him up."

"How in the hell did he get inside the town, let alone the hotel balcony?"

"My thoughts exactly," Zane said as he crossed to room to glare down at Larry. He could see Larry's hands tighten into fists even though his eyes were closed. "I know you're not asleep, Larry, so you might as well open your eyes."

Zane watched as Larry opened his eyes, turning his head to glare up at him. "Want to explain to me why you broke in, Larry?" he asked as he squatted down next to Larry.

"I didn't break in."

"Then how did you get in?"

"I wasn't doing anything. I just…I heard that the Night Dwellers were headed this way and I wanted to make sure that my son was okay. When I saw everyone fighting, I came here to check on him."

"Uh huh, and how did you know where Jiri was?" Zane asked. He could see the lie shining in Larry's eyes. The man was sweating so much it dripped down his face to puddle on the floor.

"I didn't. I was just hoping that I had the right room."

"He's lying through his teeth," Jiri said as he came to stand beside Zane.

"Jiri," Zane admonished.

"Oh, I'm sorry." Jiri crossed his arms over his chest and smirked. "He's lying through his tooth. My bad."

Zane smothered a chuckle. Jiri didn't look the least bit sorry. In fact, he looked pretty pissed. This side of Jiri intrigued Zane. It didn't come out often. Usually, Jiri was compliant and obedient, never even raising his voice.

Every once in a while, however, this *alternate personality* of Jiri's came out to play. Actually, it usually seemed to come out when Jiri was pissed. Zane wouldn't mind seeing this side of Jiri a little more often. It could be interesting. Right now, however…

"Jiri, please, let me do this."

Jiri rolled his eyes. "Fine."

Zane watched Jiri walk back across the room to stand by Billy. He shook his head in wonder. Jiri really was something. Zane knew he needed to show Jiri how much the little man was coming to mean to him, but first he had to deal with Larry.

"So, Larry," Zane said as he stood to his feet, "why should I believe you? Jiri obviously thinks you're lying, and he's known you a lot longer than I have."

Zane reached down and pulled Larry to his feet. He chuckled when Larry went to take a step and tripped over his tied feet. Zane pulled a knife out of the sheath at his side and leaned down to cut the ties holding Larry's legs together.

Standing up, he glanced over to find Jiri glaring at him. He gave Jiri a slight shake of his head, then looked back over at Larry. "So, Larry, I asked you a question. Why should I believe you over Jiri?"

"He's lying."

Zane felt a little nonplused. *He's lying* was all Larry could come up with? "You have to do better than that, Larry."

"Well, of course he's lying," Larry stammered quickly. "I sold him to you. He had a pretty good setup where he was at. He's angry at me for ending that."

Zane's eyebrows shot up. Larry thought Jiri had a pretty good setup? Seriously? "Go on."

"He pretty much had free run of my place. He could come and go whenever he wanted," Larry explained. "I'm sure here he can't do that."

"True." Zane reached down and grabbed Larry's bound wrists. He felt Larry jump just a little as he brought the knife down and cut through the rope tying his wrists together. "I'm listening," Zane said as he put the knife back into the sheath at his hip.

"That money you found on him?" Larry continued as he rubbed his wrists. "He made that by selling himself to customers. He was always selling himself. I tried to stop it, Zane, I swear I did, but that damn mother of his put it into his head that he could make money that way and there wasn't anything I could do about it."

Zane heard Jiri growl even as he tried to control the one fighting to get out of his own mouth. He couldn't believe what he was hearing from Larry. "Are you telling me that Jiri had sex with strangers for money?"

"All the time, Zane. Sometimes he did it with two or three people at the same time." Larry glanced over at Jiri. "He's just like his whoring mother."

Zane quickly turned when he heard a cry from across the room to see Slash's arms wrapped around Jiri, holding him back. Jiri's hands curled into claws and he looked like he wanted to rip Larry's face off.

"So, if all of this is true, why would you feel the need to come check on Jiri? Obviously you're better off without him."

Larry turned to look at Zane, shock on his face. "Well, I…I…" he stammered.

Zane shook his head. "Somehow, Larry, what you're telling me just isn't ringing true."

Zane watched as Larry's face paled. His eyes shot around the room as if looking for a means of escape. Larry took several steps back until his back hit the wall behind him. He looked terrified, and justly so.

Zane could tell he was lying and Larry knew that Zane knew. Zane could see it in Larry's face. Larry had come onto his land and had tried to attack what belonged to him. Larry knew that he faced his death. Zane was not a merciful man.

Zane turned to tell Slash to get some men to come take Larry away. He saw Jiri cry out and break away from Slash. Before he knew what happened, Jiri had thrown himself in front of Zane, his arms tightening around him as the loud shot of a gun reverberated through the room.

Zane looked into Jiri's eyes. He could see the shocked surprise in their sky-blue depths. Unimaginable pain filled Zane as Jiri gave him a shaky smile. "Zane," he murmured quietly just before his eyelids slowly fell down over his eyes and Jiri's body slumped against him.

"Jiri," Zane whispered. He heard a loud sound, a struggle, breaking glass, someone screaming, and a thud. He didn't care. The only thing that mattered to Zane was the unconscious man in his arms. His mind tried to comprehend what had happened to Jiri, but it just didn't seem to want to make the connection.

If he made the connection, if he understood that Larry had shot Jiri, then it would be real, and it couldn't be real. Jiri couldn't be hurt. It just wasn't possible. Nothing bad could happen to his little sex pet. Zane wouldn't let it.

"Zane? Come on, man, we need to get Jiri over to the bed."

Zane lifted his head to look over at Slash in confusion. Bed?

"Come on, buddy," Slash encouraged. His hand pushed against Zane's back ushering him toward the bed. "Jiri would feel much better if he could lie down, I promise."

Zane carried Jiri over to the bed and carefully laid him down. He crawled up beside him. His hand went to Jiri's face, softly caressing his cheek. Zane could hear voices in the room. He knew that someone left, then a few people came back a few moments later. He still didn't care.

"Jiri? Open your eyes, little one," Zane whispered near his ear. "Come on, baby, open your eyes for me. I want to find out what you read in your book while I was gone."

For long moments, Zane stared down at Jiri waiting for him to open his sky-blue eyes and laugh at him for being worried. At this point, Zane wouldn't even be mad at Jiri. He promised.

"Zane?"

Zane turned to see Billy sitting on the bed on the other side of Jiri. "Hey, Billy."

Billy smiled. "Zane, you need to let the doctor look at Jiri and make sure he's okay. Can he do that?"

Zane thought about it for a moment, then nodded his head. He should have had the doctor look at Jiri the moment he brought him home. Jiri's health was very important.

"Slash needs you in the other room. He needs to talk to you about doubling the guard." Billy glanced down at Jiri then back up at him. "I promise I'll stay with Jiri."

Zane nodded. He leaned down and kissed Jiri on the forehead. "I'll be right back, little one. Billy's going to stay with you, okay?"

Zane leaned back and watched Jiri for a response. When none came, he hesitated to leave. Maybe he should stay. Jiri needed him.

"Zane? I need to speak with you. It's really important, man," Slash said.

Zane took a moment longer to stare down at Jiri, then rolled to the side of the bed. He got up and walked out of the bedroom to talk with Slash. The moment he passed through the door, it slammed shut behind him.

Zane twirled around to stare at the door in shock. He rushed toward it, trying to open it, but it was locked. Zane pounded on the door. "Open this damn door right now," he shouted as his fists hit the hard wood.

Jiri was on the other side of the door and someone was keeping Zane from him. Zane felt tears well in his eyes as he pounded on the door. He had to get to Jiri, to protect him. Jiri needed him. He needed Jiri.

"Zane, man, calm the fuck down," someone shouted. Zane felt arms grab at him, pulling on him. "You're going to scare Jiri. Calm down."

"Jiri!" Zane yelled, ignoring the people behind him. He didn't care if he was making a fool of himself, if people saw him losing his mind, because he was. If he didn't get to Jiri, he knew he would go mad.

Suddenly, the door flew open. Zane looked down to see Billy standing in the doorway. Billy glared at him for just a moment, then stepped out of the way, his arm waving toward Jiri. Zane rushed into the room and over to the bed.

The moment he sat down on the mattress, Jiri reached his hand out for him. Zane gratefully took it, holding it tight in his. "Jiri."

"You're being very rude right now, Zane," Jiri whispered without opening his eyes. "You shouldn't shout so much."

Zane cocked his head to one side as he stared down at Jiri's closed eyes. He suddenly realized that everyone in the room watched him, waiting for his reaction to Jiri's words. Zane felt his face flush.

"Sorry, Jiri," he said quietly. Jiri grunted, but he did give Zane's hand a small squeeze. Zane looked over at the man hovering on the other side of the bed. "Well? What are you waiting for?"

The doctor smirked, then sat down on the side of the bed. "Pull him over onto his stomach, please. I need to see his injury."

Zane grabbed Jiri around the waist and rolled him over onto his stomach. He could feel Jiri's body tense. A small groan of pain escaped from his lips. Zane glared at the doctor.

The doctor just shook his head and grabbed a set of scissors. He cut the edge of Jiri's shirt, then up the middle of his back, parting the material to reveal a red, puckered, and bloody wound in Jiri's back.

Zane inhaled deeply. It was real.

Chapter 9

Jiri rolled his eyes as Zane held up another forkful of food for him. Zane was really starting to drive him crazy. It had been almost two weeks since Larry had shot him. In all that time, Zane refused to let Jiri lift a finger. He wasn't even allowed to feed himself.

Another week of this, hell another day, and Jiri just might strangle Zane. It wasn't Zane's fault that Jiri had gotten shot. That responsibility sat squarely on Jiri's shoulders. He should have searched Larry after knocking him out.

By not doing so, Jiri had endangered Zane's life. Jiri could still feel the terror he felt when he had looked across the room and saw Larry pointing a gun at Zane. He had been so sure he wouldn't reach Zane in time to save him.

Thankfully, he had. In the process, he had also gotten himself shot. No, the sole responsibility for getting shot lay with Jiri. He just wished it had hurt a little less. Jiri's shoulder still ached. He hated pain.

"One last bite, baby, I promise," Zane said when Jiri turned his head away from the next forkful of food. "Please?"

Jiri turned and took the last bite of food, chewing it carefully even as he glared at Zane. He watched Zane set the plate down on the table, giving Jiri a little sigh. Jiri smirked. Zane was pretty good at giving Jiri the guilty treatment to get what he wanted.

Jiri reached for Zane's hand with his, only to let it fall back to his lap when Zane turned away from him and began cleaning up. Zane seemed to be doing that a lot lately.

"How about we go outside today? Maybe go for a walk?" Zane asked.

Jiri shrugged. He would much rather stay inside with Zane and fool around, but Zane hadn't been near him since before the shooting. He could think of nothing he'd rather do than to curl up with Zane and while away the afternoon in bed with him.

As far as he could tell, though, Zane didn't seem to be interested. No matter what he did, Zane only touched him to help him. Jiri had started to wonder if Zane would ever touch him sexually again.

Jiri had even tried walking around in just a shirt. When that hadn't worked, Jiri had walked around naked. Zane had just told Jiri to get dressed and left the room. Jiri was close to giving up. He didn't want to beg for Zane's affections if Zane didn't want to give them.

The only thing Jiri could figure is that Zane believed the words Larry had said to him about Jiri sleeping with strangers for money. Zane had always said that he wouldn't share Jiri. Maybe he meant before they had met, too.

It wasn't like anything that Larry said was the truth, but Jiri didn't think Zane would believe him if he tried to defend himself. And maybe there wasn't much point in defending himself.

If Zane had so little faith in him that he believed someone like Larry over him, there wasn't much hope for their relationship, whatever it might be. Jiri could hear Zane droning on about the weather outside and how nice it was. The weather, yeah, like he cared about that when his world was falling apart.

Jiri got up from the table and walked over to stare out the window. He could see people coming and going from his vantage point. Men, women, children, they all seemed to be having a good time.

He wished he could be down there with everyone, enjoying himself. He wished he were anywhere enjoying himself. He was tired of not knowing where he stood with Zane, of not knowing if they had something together or not. He wanted answers.

"Zane?"

"Yeah, Jiri," Zane replied from across the room.

"Am I still your pet?"

"Of course you're still my pet. That will never change."

"Am I still your sex pet?" Jiri held his breath while he waited for Zane to answer. How Zane replied could make or break him. When Zane didn't answer, Jiri's heart sank. He turned around to face Zane. "Well?"

"Oh, Jiri, how could you…"

Jiri knew what Zane was going to say before he said it. Shock and disbelief were written all over Zane's face. Jiri braced himself as he felt his heart begin to crack. Zane didn't want him anymore.

"…want me after what I did to you?"

What? Jiri stared at Zane in confusion as his words sank in. "What are you talking about? You didn't do anything to me." He waved his hands in the air in an exasperated gesture. "Hell, you haven't done anything to me in days."

"Jiri, you got shot because of me."

Jiri's head shot back in surprise. "What?"

Zane sank down to his knees. His head dropped into his hands. "I'm supposed to protect you, take care of you. Instead, you almost lost your life because of me."

Jiri was shocked to see tears in Zane's eyes as he looked up at him. "How could you want me to touch you after that?" Zane said.

Jiri crossed the room to stand in front of Zane. He had no idea that Zane had been avoiding him out of some misplaced sense of guilt. It explained so much and at the same time didn't explain a thing.

He wrapped his hands around Zane's face and tilted his head back so that he could look down into his moss-green eyes. "Zane, you didn't do this. Larry did. You did everything you could to protect me."

"But you—"

Jiri quickly covered Zane's lips with his finger. He shook his head. "No, you didn't do this. If anyone is at fault, it's me for not searching Larry when he was tied up. Besides, I'm fine, almost as good as new, in fact."

Zane leaned forward and buried his face in Jiri's stomach. His arms wrapped around Jiri in a near death grip. "You never should have been shot in the first place."

"I agree. That still doesn't mean it was your fault. You were doing what you are supposed to do. You were out protecting me from the Night Dwellers, as well as everyone else. Isn't that what you're supposed to do?"

Zane nodded. "Yes, but—"

Jiri continued as if Zane hadn't spoken. "Did you know at the time that Larry had made a deal with the Night Dwellers?"

Zane shook his head.

"Did you know that the Night Dwellers were supposed to keep you occupied so that he could get to me?"

Zane shook his head.

"Did you know that Larry knew which room was ours?"

Zane shook his head.

"Did you know that Larry had a gun?"

Zane shook his head.

"Did you know that if you don't kiss me in the next five seconds I'm going to kick your ass?"

Zane started to shake his head again then stopped, looking up at Jiri in surprise. "What?"

"Kiss me, Zane," Jiri whispered as he leaned down toward Zane. "I've missed your kisses."

"Jiri," Zane groaned.

Jiri didn't give Zane a choice. He pressed his lips against Zane's even as he pushed his body back against the floor. The moment Zane's back hit the floor, Jiri threw his legs over him, straddling Zane's waist.

Even with his lips plastered to Zane's, Jiri wasted no time before pulling Zane's shirt up to his neck, then going to work on Zane's jeans. He had every intention of having both of them out of their clothes as fast as possible.

"Jiri," Zane whispered as he pulled his mouth away from Jiri's. He grabbed his hands. "Slow down, little one."

Jiri shook his head. "Don't want to slow down. Want to feel you inside of me."

Zane looked at Jiri for the longest moment. "Are you sure, Jiri?"

"Oh, yeah." Jiri grinned. He was more than sure. He was ecstatic!

"Then get up."

"What? No," Jiri cried out as Zane pushed him up. Jiri thought Zane was rejecting him again so he was surprised when Zane got to his feet and picked Jiri up in his arms, carrying him into the bedroom.

Zane set Jiri on his feet, grinning down at him. "First one naked gets to be on top."

Jiri's eyes widened. His hands quickly reached for the hem of his shirt. He pulled it over his head and tossed it across the room before reaching for his jeans. He started laughing as he watched Zane peeling off his own clothes just as quickly.

Jiri was dressed in jeans and a shirt. Zane had on a shirt, jeans, socks, and boots. Jiri was sure he would be the first one naked. At least, until he saw Zane push his jeans down his legs, his hard cock bouncing as it was freed from his pants.

The long lost sight froze Jiri in place, his jeans halfway down his legs. He could only stand there and stare, licking his lips. He so wanted to feel that cock in his mouth again. Dropping to his knees, Jiri leaned forward and wrapped his lips around Zane's jutting flesh.

Oh, damn. It was as good as Jiri remembered. Zane tasted like heaven, rough, dominant, and all male. Jiri groaned. He smirked around the cock in his mouth when Zane's groan immediately followed his.

"That's cheating, Jiri."

Jiri pulled back long enough to look up at Zane. "Want me to stop?"

"Hell no!"

Jiri grinned, then wrapped his lips around Zane again. He lavished Zane with his tongue, licked and caressed him. He sucked until Zane's hands tightened in his hair, holding him still. Jiri glanced up. Zane's jaw was clenched, his eyes closed, as air hissed out between his teeth.

"Enough, Jiri," Zane growled. "I want to be inside of you when I come."

Jiri was all for that. He quickly got to his feet and pushed his jeans the rest of the way off of his legs, then climbed onto the bed and rolled over onto his back. He watched eagerly as Zane pulled the rest of his clothes off and climbed onto the bed to kneel between his legs.

"You were naked first, Jiri. That means you get to be on top."

Jiri shook his head. "We did that already. I want to try it another way."

Zane chuckled. "Get the lube."

Jiri rolled over and reached into the nightstand drawer to grab the lube. He handed it to Zane and started to roll back onto his bed when a hand in the middle of his back stopped him. Jiri looked at Zane in query.

Zane winked. "On your hands and knees, little one. I want to play."

That plan was fine with Jiri. He climbed back into the middle of the bed and positioned himself on his hands and knees, burying his head in his hands.

He could hear Zane squirting lube out. His body trembled in anticipation. It had been so long since he had been with Zane and he had been so afraid he would never feel it again. The waiting was almost more than Jiri could take.

"Zane," he pleaded.

"Slowly, baby," Zane chuckled. "I don't want to hurt you."

"You won't, I swear."

"We're going to do this at my pace, Jiri, or not at all."

"Fine," Jiri huffed. "Just—oh, God!" Jiri nearly came there and then as he felt Zane press a lubed finger into him. Oh yeah, this was what he had been missing. Only a couple of times with Zane and he was hooked for life. But he couldn't imagine being this way with anyone else.

Jiri thought he might go out of his mind when Zane pressed another finger in. It seemed like weeks since Zane had touched him this way. He would never go without again if he had anything to say about it.

"Zane," Jiri groaned. He pushed his hips back against Zane, impaling himself on Zane's fingers. He could feel the tip of his cock brushing against the comforter. Each pass teased him, aroused him.

Jiri didn't know what to do. He wanted to push down and hump against the comforter, but if he did that he couldn't push back against Zane. The indecision was killing him. Jiri whimpered.

"I've got you, baby," Zane crooned. Suddenly, fingers were replaced with a long, thick cock. Jiri groaned again as Zane sank all of the way in. This was what he needed, what he wanted.

"Hold on, baby, this is going to be quick and rough. It's been too long," Zane said as he grabbed Jiri by the hips and thrust into him.

"And whose fault is that?" Jiri spat out, softening his words by grinning at Zane over his shoulder.

"Yeah, yeah, now shut the fuck up." Zane chuckled. "I'm trying to concentrate here."

"Far be it for me to interrupt you," Jiri said

"Jiri!"

Jiri laughed. He turned back to face the front of the bed and grabbed onto the comforter. It felt like Zane was trying to pound him into the headboard. Each thrust was filled with all of Zane's strength.

If Jiri didn't know better, he would think Zane was trying to push his cock so far into Jiri it would never come out. Jiri knew he would at least be feeling this tomorrow. He couldn't be more thrilled with the prospect.

A sudden smack to his hip made Jiri jerk He looked over his shoulder at Zane in surprise. "What'd you do that for?"

"Roll over, baby. I want to see you touch yourself," Zane replied as he pulled free of Jiri's body, much to Jiri's regret.

Okay, Jiri could do that. He quickly rolled over to his back and spread his legs wide. He grinned up at Zane, one hand moving down his body to grab his hard cock and stroke it several times. His other hand moved up to tug at his nipple. "Is this what you wanted?"

Jiri felt delight spiral through him as he watched Zane's eyes glaze over. A small tic throbbed in his square jaw as he growled down at Jiri. He loved knowing that he could arouse Zane to this point.

Jiri yelped in surprise, realizing that he had unleashed a monster, when Zane grabbed his legs and pushed them up to his chest. A moment later, Zane's cock thrust back into him, filling him to the brim.

Zane began a rapid pace, thrusting into Jiri, then pulling out. Each movement jarred Jiri's body until Jiri had to let go of his cock and grab onto Zane's arms just to keep from being moved up the length of the bed.

"Close, baby, I'm so close," Zane growled.

Jiri let go of Zane's arm to grab his cock. He wanted to come with Zane. But the force of Zane's thrusts instantly pushed him up the bed. Jiri quickly grabbed onto Zane again. His eyes shot up to Zane's in desperation.

"You're going to come with me, Jiri," Zane spat out through gritted teeth as if he understood Jiri's dilemma. "You're my sex pet. You belong to me. I am your master. You do as I say and I say that you're going to come with me."

Well, there was no arguing with that logic. Besides, Zane's forceful words seemed to be having the desired effect. Jiri could feel his cock start to throb, drops of pre-cum dripping from the top. A tingle began at the base of his spine and slowly worked its way up until it wrapped around Jiri's cock and held him, suspended, as if waiting for Zane's permission to erupt.

Zane's hands tightened around Jiri's thighs as he thrust into him once more, his body stiffening over the top of Jiri's. Zane's eyes bored into Jiri's.

"Come for me, my Jiri," Zane demanded.

As if that was all his cock had been waiting for, Jiri cried out, his head falling back against the mattress as an orgasm shot through his body unlike any he had ever experienced before. It hit every nerve ending in Jiri's body, then shot out the top of his cock.

"Zane!" Jiri screamed as his power to breathe, to think, to feel anything but the press of Zane's body against his dwindled down to the powerful green eyes gazing down at him. He was mesmerized, captured by the intense emotions on Zane's face.

"Zane," Jiri whispered, in awe over the love he hoped he was seeing in Zane's eyes. He reached his hand up to caress the side of Zane's face. Zane captured Jiri's hand and pressed a kiss against the palm.

Dropping Jiri's hand, Zane leaned down, pressing his body against his. His hands captured Jiri's face, holding him still. Jiri's breath caught in his throat as Zane lowered his head and kissed him.

He felt the kiss all of the way down to his toes. Zane devoured him. Jiri's hands clenched against Zane's waist as Zane's tongue brushed against his, hard lips nipping at him. When Zane finally lifted his head to stare down at him again, Jiri let out a groan of protest. He didn't want the kiss to end.

"Guess you're keeping me, huh?" Jiri asked after a moment.

Zane chuckled. He brushed a blond curl back from Jiri's face. "Yeah, I'm keeping you."

"No more thinking that my injury was your fault?"

"Jiri—"

"No more thinking my injury was your fault, right?" Jiri repeated as he tapped Zane on the chest with his finger.

Zane chuckled. "Okay, no more thinking it was my fault, but only if you promise me not to get shot again."

"Well, I sure as hell am going to try not to. That sucked."

Zane pulled away from Jiri and rolled to the side of the bed. He reached back and patted Jiri's leg. "You still want to go out for that walk?"

"Yes!" Jiri exclaimed as he quickly rolled to the side of the bed to join Zane. "I've been cooped up in this damn place forever. I'm going out of my mind."

"You know you still can't go outside unescorted, right?"

Jiri shrugged. He had figured as much. He hated the rules that he had to follow to belong to Zane but if that's what he had to do, he'd do it.

Jiri leaned into the hand Zane cupped around his cheek. He loved it when Zane touched him, even if it wasn't sexual.

"I'd let you go outside if the Night Dwellers weren't such a problem, Jiri, I swear I would. I just can't let anything happen to you, and until we know that we won't have any more dealings with them, I can't take that chance."

Jiri smiled. He could see worry in Zane's eyes. He patted the man's cheek. "I get it, Zane. I won't ask to go outside without an escort until you give me the all clear."

Zane let out a heavy sigh. "I'm sorry, baby."

"I'm not," Jiri said. "While this whole situation has been horrible, besides finding you, I mean, we've learned a few things."

Zane grinned. "What have learned then?"

"Well, for one, no matter how safe we think we are from the Night Dwellers, we're not. We always have to be on guard. While that is a horrible way to live, it beats being dead."

"True," Zane replied.

"We also learned that there are some people that may seem harmless but in reality they are the ones we need to be the most watchful of."

"Larry?"

Jiri nodded. "I knew he was a slime ball, but I never thought he would sink low enough to make a deal with the Night Dwellers." Jiri shuddered. "He was giving up other people to keep himself safe. It was disgusting."

"Now, Jiri, we don't know that for sure. We're just guessing."

Jiri shook his head rapidly. "No, I know he was. It just makes sense. The Night Dwellers never attacked us, ever. But they attacked everyone around us. I always thought it was because we didn't have anything they were interested in."

"Baby, they don't rob people. The Night Dwellers kill people. That's all they do. If Larry made a deal with them it was to save his own skin and nothing else."

"That's what I'm saying," Jiri said. "Larry made a deal with the Night Dwellers, not only to leave him alone but to get at you and me. Think about it, if the Night Dwellers could get into your compound they had all sorts of things to go after."

"All sorts of people, Jiri, people."

Jiri grimaced. "Yeah, that too."

"Come on, little one, wipe the sad look off your face and go get cleaned up," Zane said. "We have a walk outside to go and enjoy."

* * * *

Zane shook his head, chuckling, as he watched Jiri race into the bathroom to clean up. Jiri practically bounced with anticipation. Zane thought he looked cute. If taking Jiri outside for a walk made him that happy, Zane was all for it.

He was still a little hesitant to take Jiri anywhere. After Jiri had been shot by Larry, it had been all Zane could do to hold onto his sanity until Jiri healed. Zane wasn't so sure he hadn't lost it somewhere along the way.

When he met Jiri, Zane had no idea that Jiri would come to mean so much to him. Zane would gladly give up leadership of the Death Dealers for his little man. Hell, he'd even give up his own life if it meant Jiri remained safe.

He still couldn't believe that Larry had made a deal with the Night Dwellers so he could get to Jiri. If Jiri hadn't made the connection that the Night Dwellers never attacked Larry's garage but everything around them, Zane never would have figured out that Larry was in cahoots with them. Zane figured Larry hated him for humiliating him and saw killing Jiri as a way to get rid of his stepson and have his revenge on Zane at the same time. It would have worked, too, if Jiri hadn't fought back.

Larry was dead, his neck breaking when he landed on the ground after being thrown off the balcony. The Night Dwellers had disappeared as quickly as they appeared, leaving behind a lot of mayhem. Jiri was alive and safe and for Zane, that was all that mattered.

Zane stood up and reached for his clothes. His mind reeled with thoughts of Jiri's near-death experience as he got dressed. He never wanted to go through anything like that again. If that meant he doubled the guard or kept Jiri by his side every second of every day, so be it.

Jiri was his to protect, and no matter how much he bitched, Zane would do everything he could to ensure that Jiri was protected. In the small amount of time Zane had known him, Jiri had become the center of his world.

"Hey, are you done in there yet?" Zane called out when Jiri didn't come out of the bathroom for several moments.

"I'm coming," Jiri said as he walked out of the bathroom.

Zane's breathing stuttered as his eyes landed on Jiri. He didn't understand it but every time he saw Jiri, his beauty awed Zane. Jiri was without a doubt, the most beautiful man he had ever seen.

Jiri wasn't merely pretty or handsome. He was breathtakingly beautiful. And he was all Zane's. He had no more doubts that Jiri was his and always would be. Jiri had put down any doubts Zane might have had when he had jumped in front of Larry's bullet to protect him.

No one that had designs on someone else, let alone thoughts of being with someone else, would try to protect someone by throwing themselves in front of a bullet as Jiri had done. And, while Zane wasn't happy about Jiri being hurt, he would forever be grateful that Jiri cared about him enough to want to save him from harm.

"Ready?"

"Just a minute," Jiri replied as he hurried across the room to the small table by the bedroom door. "I need to get my collar and leash."

"Jiri," Zane said softly.

"Yeah?" Jiri asked as he pulled open the drawer and searched for the leather collar and leash.

"You don't need them."

"Of course I do. I want to go outside." Jiri opened another drawer and searched through it.

"Jiri."

"Uh huh?"

"Jiri, look at me," Zane ordered.

"I can't find them, Zane," Jiri said. He turned to look at Zane. "Have you seen them?"

Zane crossed over to Jiri and grabbed his hands. "I said you don't need them, Jiri."

"But...I want to go outside, Zane. You said we could go for a walk."

Zane smiled. "And we will, little one, but you don't need the collar and leash anymore. I got rid of them."

"What? Why? You said I couldn't leave the room unless I was wearing them." Jiri looked totally confused.

"I also said that pets only wear collars and leashes until they get a permanent claiming mark from their masters." Zane brushed his hand over the tattoo mark on Jiri's throat. "You're wearing my tattoo, Jiri. That's all you need."

Jiri raised his hand and stroked his fingers lightly over the tattoo. His face flushed as he began to grin, looking more beautiful than Zane had ever seen him.

Zane kissed him gently on the lips. "I'm keeping you, Jiri, for always."

THE END

WWW.STORMYGLENN.COM

SIREN PUBLISHING *Classic*

DREAM MATE

Sequel to
The Katzman's Mate

Stormy Glenn

DREAM MATE
Sequel to The Katzman's Mate

STORMY GLENN
Copyright © 2010

Chapter 1

2374 AD, The Planet Katzmann,

"*I refuse to give birth without a doctor from my home world*," Demyan shouted telepathically to his mate, Commander Chellak Rai, High Ruler of the planet Katzmann.

"Demyan, I don't think you have a choice. Our baby will come whether you want it to or not," Chellak replied. He took a deep breath and let it out slowly, trying to rein in his frustration with his mate.

Demyan, by Chellak's estimations, would give birth to their child in a couple of weeks. Chellak looked forward to the prospect of holding his son or daughter. He was not so thrilled with the rapid mood swings that his mate bounced through. He resisted rolling his eyes as Demyan crossed his arms over his chest and glared across their bedroom at him. From experience, Chellak knew that this defiant stance would be immediately followed by tears. Chellak could handle the little bouts of anger. The sadness ripped great big caverns in his heart.

"*You don't want me to have a doctor from my home world?*" Demyan asked quietly.

Oh gods, here it comes, Chellak thought as he saw the tears begin to form in Demyan's sea blue eyes. Hoping to prevent Demyan's imminent breakdown, Chellak hurried across the floor and wrapped his arms around his smaller mate.

"Demyan, if a doctor from your home world is what you want, that's what you'll get. I'll send Trajan Varl tomorrow, okay?"

"Today?"

Chellak smiled. "Okay, my own, I'll send Trajan today." Chellak reached down and tilted Demyan's head back. He brushed his thumb across Demyan's face to wipe away his tears. "Now, let's dry up these tears, and we'll go find something to eat? I'm sure you're hungry."

"I am hungry, but what I want can't be found in the kitchen."

Chellak's eyebrows rose in surprise at the soft flush on Demyan's face. Another facet of his mate's pregnancy, one that Chellak didn't mind in the least, Demyan's constant arousal. Chellak couldn't remember having so much sex in his entire life.

He felt grateful that a brüter's pregnancy only lasted five months. Any longer than that and Chellak wasn't sure he would survive it. *Of course, it wasn't a bad way to go,* Chellak thought as he followed his mate down onto the bed.

* * * *

Saris Chattan rushed across the stone floor of the palace, hurrying after the two royal guards that escorted him. It wasn't often that he received a summons to the royal palace. Hell, he had never been ordered to the royal palace. He was too low down in rank.

Which made him wonder why a summons had been sent for him now. He tried to think of any reason why he would be summoned to the palace, any transgression he might have made that would have brought him to the notice of the High Ruler. Nothing came to mind.

Coming to two large doors, Saris took a deep breath. This was it. Beyond these doors sat the ruler of his planet. Saris knew he would either be walking out of here happy or with his head detached. The High Ruler of Elquone had never been known for his benevolence.

Saris nodded to the guards. His heart almost skipped a beat when they opened the large doors and he walked in. Saris looked around in amazement. He had heard stories of the royal throne room, but he had never seen it himself.

It looked amazing. A long red carpet went up the center of the room all the way to the throne across the room where the High Ruler sat. All along the walls people dressed in their finest clothes twittered here and there, deep in conversation.

Ornate and colorful tapestries graced the walls. Vases filled with imported moonflowers sat on nearly every surface that wasn't covered by food or drink. The pure gold of the food platters shinned in the highly lit room. Saris knew that one plate alone could feed an entire family for a month.

The furnishings and decorations seemed to become more opulent the closer to the High Ruler's dais that he walked. Saris tried to keep his disgust off his face. The High Ruler of Elquone liked the finer things in life and he didn't seem to care if his people suffered because of it.

Coming to stand at the bottom of the dais, Saris bowed respectfully. "Saris Chattan, as requested, High Ruler."

"Ah, yes, the good doctor," the High Ruler replied.

Saris nodded. He tried to ignore the dribble of red wine falling down the man's chin. "Yes, High Ruler."

"I have heard of your skills in aiding the brüter during birth. Your superiors have nothing but good things to say about you."

"Thank you, High Ruler," Saris replied. He swallowed past the lump in his throat. Okay, so the king had heard of his healing skills. So what? That didn't explain why he had been summoned to the royal palace. The High Ruler had his own physicians.

"It seems that I am not the only one who has heard of your skills," the High Ruler said. He waved his hand, gesturing for someone to come forward.

The breath that Saris tried to keep steady in his chest flew out in one aroused whoosh when he turned to see the man that stepped up beside him. In all of his years of learning different species and training to care for them, Saris had never encountered one so magnificent.

The man's features looked neither cat nor man, but both. A layer of fur covered what skin Saris could see. Most of his body seemed to be covered by black leather, from the tight, leather pants that hugged his long legs to the black, leather vest-type shirt that covered his muscular chest.

Beautiful blond hair hung down to his shoulders, but not sunlight blond, more the color of a reddish sunset. Small pointed ears came out the top of his head and he had a small protruding nose like a cat. Saris would just bet that he had a pink tongue and long canines to match.

Saris felt his face flush when he looked up to encounter deep black eyes. They seemed to be assessing him just as much. Trying to hide his reaction to the man, Saris turned back to the High Ruler.

"You have been requested to assist in the birth of Demyan Rai, mate to the High Ruler of Katzmann," the High Ruler said. As much as that surprised Saris, the gleam in the Hugh Ruler's eyes made him nervous.

"I would be happy to assist in any way that I can, High Ruler."

"Yes, I thought you might say that." The High Ruler sat up straighter in his chair. He waved his hand and another man stepped forward, his chief adviser, Toc Jerell, a man hated by the population of Elquone nearly as much as the High Ruler.

The man leaned over close to the High Ruler's ear, listening as the High Ruler spoke to him. His eyes kept coming back up to Saris, time and time again, as he nodded. Finally, the man stood. The smirk on his face sent a cold shiver down Saris's back.

"Saris Chattan, it is my understanding that you were chosen as a brüter? Is this correct?" the High Ruler asked.

Saris nodded. It was true. He had been chosen to be a brüter due to his genetics, something that drove Saris crazy. Just because he had delicate-looking features, long limbs, and blond hair he had been chosen out of the many on his planet and considered more desirable.

Personally, Saris thought it all a load of crap. He wasn't any better or any worse than anyone else. Thoughts like those had gotten him kicked out of the brüter program.

"It is also my understanding your superiors removed you before your training could be completed."

"Not officially removed, High Ruler. My superiors decided that my talents could be used in a better manner," Saris replied.

"As a doctor to the brüter?"

"Yes, High Ruler."

The High Ruler stared at Saris so long, Saris started to get nervous. He wondered what the High Ruler intended with all of his questions and why the interest in Saris's brüter training.

And he wondered about the man who stood next to him. Saris could still see him out of the corner of his eye. The man had an impressive bearing. He would dominate any room he stood in. He certainly seemed to be the center of attention in this room.

"So, it is my understanding from your words that you have never been officially removed from the Brüter Caste? Is that correct, Chattan?"

Saris nodded. "Yes, High Ruler, even though I am not officially a brüter, I am still part of the caste. I'm just on the medical side of things."

The High Ruler nodded. "Very good, very good."

Saris watched with curiosity as the chief advisor leaned over and whispered in the High Ruler's ear. The High Ruler nodded a few times then waved the chief advisor away. His eyes turned back to Saris.

"High Ruler Chellak Rai has made a request of Elquone, one that I cannot in good conscience ignore. Therefore, as Trajan Varl is the representative of High Ruler Chellak Rai, I am signing over your brüter contract to him."

Saris felt his blood run cold at the High Ruler's words. Having his contract sold was one of Saris's biggest fears. Having learned to be a doctor for the brüter, he had thought he would be safe. Guess he was wrong.

"Henceforth, Saris Chattan, you will be the property of Trajan Varl until such time as he releases you from your contract, or you have completed your duties," the High Ruler decreed. "Is this understood?"

Saris nodded when he really wanted to yell at the High Ruler for being such a prick. He hadn't been able to complete his brüter training because of this very thing. He didn't want to be someone's property.

Saris nearly jumped when the man beside him stepped forward. "High Ruler, if I may," he said. When the High Ruler nodded, the man continued. "I am unable to take possession of the doctor's contract. It is against the laws of Katzmann for anyone to own another person."

"Is this so?" the High Ruler asked curiously. "How odd."

"It is a requirement for being part of the Federation, High Ruler," Trajan said.

"You do understand that I am unable to release the doctor without a contract being in place, don't you?" The High Ruler asked. "He is of the Brüter Caste, and it is against our laws for someone of that caste to leave our world without a contract."

Saris could see the tension in the body next to him. Trajan Varl didn't seem happy. Saris couldn't say the same. Delight filled him at the prospect of not being obligated to fulfill a contract he didn't believe in. No man or woman should be forced to provide services if they chose not to.

"Could we not amend the contract, High Ruler?" Saris asked.

The High Ruler jumped to his feet, his fist shaking angrily at Saris. "No, we cannot amend the contract. A brüter contract is a brüter contract. It must be followed to the letter of our laws. You know as well as I do that no one of the Brüter Caste can leave our world without a contract."

"Yes, High Ruler," Saris said.

The High Ruler glanced at Trajan Varl, giving him a sugar-filled smile that Saris knew to be false. "Please give my apologies to your commander. Under the circumstances, I am unable to fulfill your request. I hope you understand."

Saris looked over at Trajan Varl to get his reaction. It wasn't long in coming. Trajan's hands tightened into fists, his lips thinned. The fire that lit up his black eyes that fascinated Saris. It almost looked real.

"I will certainly pass your words on to my commander," Trajan said. He cast a long look at Saris before clicking his heels together. He nodded his head, turned, and walked down the long red carpet and through the double doors.

Saris glanced back at the High Ruler in shock. He thought for sure the High Ruler would see providing a doctor for Demyan Rai as a way to get into the good graces of Chellak Rai. To deny his request, especially when it came to his mate, was akin to political suicide.

The rumor mill ran amok with stories concerning Commander Chellak Rai and his brüter mate, Demyan. Rumor said that the big Katzman doted on his little mate and would do almost anything for him.

While Saris tried to comprehend the huge mistake that he believed the High Ruler was making, he noticed Toc Jerell watching him intently. The lust blazing in the chief advisor's eyes made Saris's skin crawl.

Saris had never liked the man. He had spent too much time giving medical assistance to the men and women who had caught the chief advisor's eye. He wasn't a pleasant man, even worse to those he chose to subject his desires upon.

"Saris Chattan, as your contract has been rejected by Trajan Varl, I feel that you are unsuited for the Brüter Caste. As such, I am officially removing you from your caste. Henceforth, you will be of the Vergnügen Caste."

Saris's mouth dropped open. He was being removed from his position just because someone he had never met before rejected his contract? A contract Saris didn't want in the first place?

"High Ruler, I—" Saris began only to be interrupted by the High Ruler.

"You will leave from here and immediately present yourself at the Vergnügen Caste where you will be trained in the skills of that caste." The High Ruler glared over at Saris, giving him a stern look. "Do I make myself clear?"

"Yes, of course, High Ruler, but my patients. I have—"

"You will do as you are told, or you will find yourself in my dungeon," The High Ruler shouted. "Now, go!"

Saris suddenly understood what had just happened. Instead of being given to Trajan Varl to assist in the birth of Demyan Rai, he would be to be retrained as a pleasure slave. Saris knew his life had just gone to hell.

Being of the Brüter Caste gave Saris some control over his life, especially since he was a doctor educated in cross-species breeding. His skills were greatly needed. Because he had to have a contract to leave the planet, he had felt relatively safe right here at home.

The Vergnügen Caste was different. Pleasure slaves had no rights whatsoever. The owner of their contracts could do whatever they wanted to them, including rent them out for money, force them sexually, anything.

"High Ruler, I have no training in the Vergnügen Caste. I have a lot of training and experience as a doctor. I can be of such more use there," Saris reasoned. He knew he grasped at straws, but he couldn't think of much he wouldn't do to keep from being trained as a pleasure slave.

"Guards!" The High Ruler shouted. "Escort Saris Chattan to the Vergnügen Center. See that his training is begun immediately."

Saris backed away from the dais and the High Ruler. "No, no, you can't do this," he sputtered. "I'm a doctor. I have patients that I need to see to, people who need me."

He turned to find two very large armed guards standing behind him. They grabbed Saris by his arms and pulled him, kicking and screaming, down the long red carpet. Saris gave up protesting by the time they got to the steps leading out of the palace.

A few more minutes and a transport had him delivered to the Vergnügen Center. Saris didn't struggle as he walked up the center's hard stone steps and through the large ornate doors colored in gold.

What would be the point? Everything he knew in this life would end the moment he got inside those doors. Saris wasn't sure he would retain his medical knowledge. He had heard stories of people being totally mind wiped when being retrained.

That scared him more than anything. People of the Vergnügen Caste provided pleasure like mindless drones, their only thought in life to pleasure to others. Saris liked what he did, and he was damn good at it. He didn't want to give it up.

Saris considered struggling as the two guards led him down a long, white hallway, but years of being taught to hide his emotions, even ones of terror, held him. He didn't want to do this. He needed to run, to get away. He could hear people crying out as they passed door after door until they came to the end of the hallway.

The guards led him into a small, white, walled room with a single reclining chair sitting in the middle of it. A large one way mirror sat high on the far wall. Saris knew that beyond that mirror sat the technicians that would provide his training.

The two guards lifted Saris onto the chair and clamped large bands around his arms, legs, and head. The door he had come through just moments before opened, and a middle-aged man dressed in white walked in carrying a holopad. He clicked the buttons on it several times, then looked up at Saris.

"Ah, is this the trainee, Saris Chattan?"

One of the guards nodded.

"Very well, you may leave." The man didn't acknowledge Saris or the guards as they left. He walked to the wall and pressed a button, and the wall swung open to reveal a hidden cabinet. He grabbed several items and turned back to Saris.

"Now, Saris," the man said as he began connecting electrodes to the side of Saris's head and to his chest. "A full retraining has been ordered for you, but I don't want you to worry. You should sleep through this fairly well. By the time you wake, you'll be a fully-functioning Vergnügen."

Saris opened his mouth to speak, only to have the man shove a clear plastic bite piece in the opening. He tried to spit it out, tried to tell the man he didn't want to be retrained. He could only whimper.

"Not to worry, Saris, this is just to keep you from choking in case you have a seizure. In rare cases, the retraining is harder for some than others." The man held up a large, metal object that looked like a gun filled with blue liquid. "Now, this should help you sleep."

Before Saris could protest, the man put the gun to his arm and pulled the trigger. Saris screamed over the plastic mouth piece as searing hot pain shot up his arm, then down through his entire body.

Not hurt, my ass! Saris thought as his eyelids began to grow heavy. The room became fuzzy until he could only make out faint blurs moving about the room. He couldn't even hear anything except a loud rush, like wind blowing through a canyon.

Saris thought of the tall lion man, Trajan Varl. That man who intrigued him. He would have liked to have gotten to know Trajan Varl a little more. Saris's last thought was of the tall lion man, wondering where he would find a doctor.

As reality began to fade, Saris felt one lone tear of sorrow and regret fall down his face.

* * * *

Trajan waited outside of the palace doors for the doctor to come out. He wanted to speak to him. Hell, he needed to speak to him. Something about the man that called out to him, and as a Katzman, he couldn't ignore it.

He suspected that the man might be his mate, but he couldn't be sure, not until he had a chance to talk to him, to smell him. The scent of a mate aroused a Katzman so much, Trajan would almost be unable to resist the good doctor.

Trajan glanced at the gathering darkness and wondered why the doctor hadn't appeared. He should have left the palace by now. Worried about the time, Trajan hurried back inside the palace and tracked own the nearest guard.

"I'm trying to locate Doctor Saris Chattan. I'm hoping that he can help me find a doctor for my High Ruler's mate."

"Sorry, sir, Doctor Chattan has already left."

Damn! Trajan thought. He thanked the guard and walked back out of the palace. He stopped at the bottom of the stone steps and glanced up and down the small, cobblestone road before him. There wasn't a sign of anyone anywhere.

Determined to find the doctor, Trajan headed back to his ship. He needed to check in with Chellak and then figure out how to find the doctor. He wasn't going to leave Elquone until he did.

Chapter 2

Trajan Varl shook his head at the grimace he could see on Commander Chellak Rai's face through the vidlink. "I'm telling you, Chellak, it was like being inside of an ancient society. As long as I agreed to accept the doctor as my slave I could have him, but the moment I said no, all bets were off."

"You did tell him that because of Federation Regulations that it is against the law to own slaves, right?" Chellak asked.

Trajan chuckled. "Oh yeah, I told him. He told me to tell you that he sends his regards, but he is unable to assist us. Seems the good doctor is considered one of the Brüter Caste, and as such, he's not allowed to leave the planet without a contract."

"So, amend the contract to be a temporary use of services."

"The doctor suggested that himself," Trajan replied. "The High Ruler still wouldn't go for it. He said it went against the laws of Elquone or some such crap like that."

"Any chance that the good doctor would be willing to go against the High Ruler?" Chellak asked.

Trajan shrugged. "I don't know. I mean, he seemed to really care about his patients and all, but how can you ever tell what someone else is thinking? Not all of us have mental telepathy, you know."

"So, track him down and ask him. See if he would be willing to come anyway," Chellak demanded. "Demyan could go into labor any day now, and he insists on having a doctor from his home world."

"I'll see what I can do, but I'm not making any promises. I don't even know where to start looking for this guy," Trajan said.

Chellak remained silent for a moment as if he listened to someone else talking. Trajan knew that he was. One of the benefits of being mated with a Katzman, Chellak could talk mentally with Demyan. "Demyan says to start at the Brüter Center. He also says that if the High Ruler has already said no, that you need to be extra careful. Not many people want to go against the High Ruler. Apparently, he's not the forgiving sort."

Trajan nodded. He had kind of gotten that idea when he had met the man. High Ruler Shek Tavia did not strike Trajan as a man who would accept dissention in the ranks, let alone from an offworlder.

"All right, I'll see what I can do," Trajan said. "I'll check back in same time tomorrow. If you don't hear from me by then, something has gone wrong. You need to send in the troops and get my ass off this damn planet."

Chellak chuckled. "Agreed."

Trajan turned off the vidlink and sat back in his chair. He wondered if he would be able to get the doctor to agree to go with him, even if he could find him. He still needed to figure out how to smuggle him offworld without anyone being the wiser.

He needed some shuteye before anything else. He hadn't had a wink of sleep since leaving Katzmann. Something told him he would need all of his faculties when he did find the good doctor.

Trajan turned on the security mode, locking the air hatch on his small ship and surrounding it with a small invisible bubble. The moment someone stepped within a foot of his ship, alarms would sound, alerting Trajan. It was a handy little system.

Leaving the bridge, he went down the hallway to his personal quarters and pulled his clothes off. A long groan fell from his lips as he lay back on the bed pad of his bed. He hadn't realized how tired he felt until now.

He could feel every muscle in his body tense, then relax as he took a deep cleansing breath and let it out. Wiggling around a bit until he got into a comfortable spot, Trajan closed his eyes and let his mind wander to the good doctor.

Demyan had suggested he start looking at the Brüter Center, whatever in the hell that was. He'd have to ask around a bit to find it. Maybe he could use the excuse that since the doctor couldn't go back to Katzmann with him, Trajan needed to look for another doctor.

On the other hand, he could just go visit a bar and ask a few questions there. He could get a drink and maybe find a little company, too. It had been so long since he'd laid, he wondered if he would even remember how.

It wasn't for lack of volunteers or enthusiasm on his part. Training and the invasion of Katzmann had been all he had done for the last…forever, it seemed. But that was what one did for one's pridemate, and Chellak Rai was Trajan's pridemate.

They had been put together as young children, soon after Chellak's parents were killed by Vortigern Vedek. Chellak displayed a lot of anger as a child. He had wanted revenge. Trajan couldn't blame him. He would have wanted the same thing.

Still, being grouped in a pride with Chellak had given Trajan a chance to get to know him and come to respect him more than any man he had ever met. Trajan would do anything for Chellak Rai, even find a doctor for his little mate.

As Trajan started to fade off to sleep, his last thought was of the hot little doctor that he wanted to take home with him, not for Demyan's benefit, but for his own.

* * * *

Wet, hot lips wrapped around Trajan's aching cock making him tremble. Nimble fingers gently massaged his nut sac. Lithe legs rubbed against his. Soft, silky hair tickled his hips and thighs.

Passion radiated from Trajan's core as flames licked their way up his body. He could feel each movement the man in his arms made, hear each groan that fell from his honeyed lips. Trajan's body quaked as desire raced through him.

"Sari," he groaned, "harder, Sari. Gods, please, Sari."

A soft giggle came in response, a small lick over the triangle shaped birthmark on his left thigh, a tender nip on his hip. Trajan reached for the body between his legs out of desperation. If he didn't sink his hard cock into Sari's welcoming body in the next second, Trajan just knew he would die.

"Sari, need you, Sari," Trajan whispered as way of apology as he roughly pulled the man farther up into his arms. Grasping the hips settling over his, Trajan thrust home, feeling Sari's warmth swallow him down to the root.

Trajan opened his eyes at the soft whimpers coming from above him. The sight that met his eyes nearly brought him to tears as it always did when he looked upon his mate. He had never seen anyone as breathtaking as his Sari. Not in all of his years.

His beautiful features, so delicate in nature, yet so strong. The long, golden hair of the Elquone people not lost on Sari, even if it just barely reaching his collar. It still shone bright as the twin suns of Katzmann.

Unlike most of the inhabitants of Elquone, Trajan's mate had deep sea green eyes rather than blue. It always reminded Trajan of the grassy fields of his home world. He could look into those eyes forever and die a happy man.

They expressed every emotion, showing everything Sari felt for Trajan, something Trajan would forever be grateful for. He just had to look into his mate's eye to know that he was loved.

"Sari," Trajan whispered, awed by the man above him. He never dreamed that simple hands could feel so hot against his skin, or that a body could welcome him so much. A deep feeling of peace surrounded him. He was home.

"Come for me," Sari whispered.

Trajan could feel the heat of Sari's body course down his entire length. "I am coming for you, my own," Trajan replied as the heat at the center of his universe began to ignite.

"No," Sari replied, shaking his head, "come for me before they hurt me. Please, Trajan."

Trajan's eyes widened at his mate's words, not fully understanding them. Before he could reply, a hot tide of passion swept him away, taking his ability to think, to feel anything except for Sari, and then it took Sari.

Groaning at the intensity of his orgasm, Trajan opened his eyes expecting to see his mate, Sari, above him. His heart plummeted as he realized that it all been a dream, a fantasy. *Well, part of it anyway*, Trajan thought as he noticed the seed covering his chest and abdomen.

He dropped his head back onto the pillows. Punching his fists into the bed, he let out a loud growl. He hated wet dreams. Besides being messy, they made him want for more.

And right now, he wanted the doctor with every bit of his being, which scared the crap out of Trajan. He had never had a wet dream that had seemed so real, so right. He felt even more disturbed by how right it felt to have the doctor in his arms.

If he added that to the doctor's parting words, Trajan was pretty sure he had lost his mind. He didn't know if he dreamed that or what. If he had, why would he create a wet dream where the doctor needed his help?

Trajan shook his head. He had to be losing his mind. Maybe it was this planet, these people. Maybe he worked too hard. Whatever it was, Trajan knew that he had to forget it and get on with the job Chellak had assigned him.

Trajan grabbed his shirt off the floor and wiped the seed off of his stomach before tossing it across the room. Closing his eyes, he tried to put the images of Saris Chattan out of his head so he could sleep. It wasn't going to be easy.

As sleep started to claim him, images of those deep green eyes once again assailed Trajan. Only this time, instead of glowing with love for him, they begged for help. Trajan heard the words again, more desperate this time.

"Come for me, Trajan, before they hurt me, please. Come before it's too late."

Trajan jerked awake. He sat up and swung his legs over the side of his bed. Wiping a weary hand down his face, he tried to make sense of the desperate words he had heard, not once, but twice.

He knew that the images belonged to the doctor just as much as he knew deep down inside that Saris Chattan was his Sari. He didn't know how he knew, but he did. Doctor Saris Chattan was his mate.

Knowing he wasn't going to get any sleep, Trajan got up and dressed, taking special care to grab his many weapons and hide them in the different hidden pockets of his clothing, as he usually did when going into a fight. He didn't know why, but he knew he needed to get ready for battle.

He wanted to call Chellak and ask him if he had indeed lost his mind. Telepathy between mates didn't happen until the mating cycle began. Even though he had a wet dream about the doctor, they had in no way mated.

So, why did he have dreams about a man he had met for a brief few minutes, and how did he know that the same man was his mate? Wishful thinking or had he finally cracked after one too many battles?

Trajan chuckled. Maybe both. He had either been training or fighting for most of his life. His body had the physical scars to prove it. His soul had the emotional scars. Neither would ever go away.

That still didn't explain how he knew that the doctor was his mate. It also didn't tell Trajan how he would find him or get him back to Katzmann, two things that would not happen unless Trajan started moving.

With that thought in mind, Trajan stepped out of his ship, turned the security seal back on, and started walking toward the center of town. From personal experience, if he wanted information about something, a bar was the best place to find it, and preferably not an upscale one. The seedier the better.

Such a place wasn't hard to find. Every town had one or two. The alcohol usually came watered down and cheap, the patrons rough and ready to fight over the slightest insult. The establishment itself would be run down and rank.

Trajan found one easily enough. He walked in, instantly feeling every head in the place turn to watch him cross the room. He moved up close to the bar and ordered a mug of ale.

Grabbing the mug the barkeep set on the bar, Trajan tossed down a coin and moved off to sit at a table near to the door but far enough in the corner that he could sit with his back to the wall.

It wasn't long before he heard the information he sought. A couple of tables over, two men sat talking, their heads pressed close together as if they didn't want anyone to overhear them.

Luckily for Trajan, Katzman had superior hearing and could pick up every word that they spoke.

"Did you hear about the doc?" asked the older man with gray hair.

The redhead shook his head. "Doc Chattan?"

The old man nodded. "Seems he got himself into a bit of a mess."

"Oh? How so?"

Yes, how so?

The old man looked around the room. Trajan quickly glanced out the window as if he waited for someone. He took a sip of his ale, grimacing at the stale, bitter taste. He had seen a lot of horrible places, but he wasn't sure he had ever tasted ale this bad.

"Toc Jerell had his highness send the doc to the Vergnügen Center for retraining."

"Vergnügen? Seriously?" the younger man asked. "But he's such a good doctor. Why would they retrain him as a pleasure slave?"

Trajan's mind froze on the words pleasure slave. Saris was being retrained as a pleasure slave? He felt a deep growl begin to grow in his chest at the very thought of his mate pleasuring anyone but him. It was not acceptable.

"I think Toc Jerell did it," the older man replied, catching Trajan's interest. Toc Jerell, the chief advisor to the High Ruler? "That man's always had a thing for the fair-haired doctor, even if the man was oblivious to it. You've seen how he stares at him during assembly."

The younger man nodded. "Yeah, it's too bad. Doc is a great guy. I doubt he'll even remember his own name once they get done with him."

Trajan felt his muscles tense. The way the men talked, Saris wouldn't even be the same person once he finished with his retraining. Trajan couldn't let that happen. Saris belonged to him.

Getting up to his feet, Trajan began making his way back to the bar, making sure that his steps seemed unsteady. As he stepped past the two men, he purposely pushed into the younger one, causing him to spill his drink.

"Hey!" the man exclaimed.

"Oh, I'm so sorry. I guess I had a little more to drink than I thought." Trajan laughed. "But I do love to drink. Nothing like a good ale to cure what 'ales' you. Get it, 'ales' you?"

"You're drunk," the older man sputtered, pushing Trajan away.

"Well on my way." Trajan plastered a look of surprise on his face. "Hey, why don't you drink with me? Then we can all be cured. I'm buying."

Trajan sat down in a chair between the two men and waved to the barkeep. "Barkeep, another round for me and my two friends." He looked back over at the two men, eyeing him doubtfully and held out his hand. "I'm Varl."

* * * *

It took everything in Trajan could do not to puke his guts out the moment he left the bar. It had taken longer than he had anticipated getting the two men to loosen their tongues. But, in the end, Trajan had gotten the information he needed.

Saris was being held in the Vergnügen Center for retraining. He had been taken there the day before, right after Trajan had left the royal palace. Trajan hoped that he would be able to get to Saris before too much retraining took place.

Trajan knew the location of the Vergnügen Center, and he knew when the shift change happened. He also knew the most likely location inside the center where Saris might be held, the deep retraining labs.

If Trajan could believe his two drinking buddies, by the time Saris finished his retraining, the only thing he would ever want out of life was to please his master.

Saris would forgo food and bathing, gladly accept torture and abuse, and have sex with anyone instructed to pleasure, anything to please his master. Sex would be the driving force in his life. He would be unable to think of anything else. He would be in physical pain if he didn't have sex on a regular basis.

Trajan liked sex as much as the next guy, but he felt horrified that a center like this even existed. He had been pretty appalled when he had learned about Demyan. Not because Demyan could give birth to a child, but because the genetic manipulation needed for that had been forced upon Demyan.

To know that this world had a center that trained people to be mindless sex slaves sickened Trajan. No one should be forced to do anything that they didn't want to. Trajan finally understood why the Federation had denied Elquone's request for membership.

Chellak fought against just that type of tyranny. As pridemate, Trajan had gladly joined in Chellak's fight to reclaim his home world. However, for the first time, that fight felt more personal. The fight involved Trajan's mate.

Trajan slowly made his way through the dark alleys and side streets until he came to a large building, several stories tall. He watched from the shadows across the street as a few people came and went until he knew the shift change was about to take place.

As quietly as he could, Trajan made his way to the side of the building where the workers entered. He crouched down behind a large planter, knife in hand, and waited until just the right moment.

He held his breath, his muscles poised to attack, as two workers walked by. He ignored their chitchat and concentrated on sneaking in the door behind them without being heard or seen. As soon as he got through the door, he quickly made his way around the corner and waited.

It took Trajan a moment to get his bearing and figure out where in the building he stood. He didn't know how much of the information his two drunk friends had given him was truthful and how much they made up in their ale-soaked minds.

After a moment, Trajan began making his way down the hallway. He could hear people moaning with each door he passed. Trajan had an idea of what went on behind those doors, but he was almost afraid to look.

Besides, he came here for one person, and one person only. After he got his mate safely away and home to Katzmann, Trajan had every intention of encouraging Chellak and the Federation into sanctioning Elquone or something. There had to be a way to stop this madness.

Hearing someone down the hallway, Trajan quickly opened the nearest door and went through, shutting the door behind him. He listened at the door until he couldn't hear anyone anymore then turned to see the room.

Shock filled Trajan at what he saw. A young man, no more than eighteen or nineteen years old, lay strapped naked to a reclining chair. He had wires imbedded in his head and chest. A strange blue liquid pumped into his arm from a long tube attached to the wall.

The man's eyes looked glazed over as if he were drugged. His limbs lay listlessly at his sides in metal restraints. He almost looked dead. The raging hard on jutting up from a small patch of golden hair seemed to be the only sign of life in the young man.

Trajan walked over to the young man's side. He reached up and brushed the soft, blond curls back from his face. The man didn't even flinch. He didn't move a muscle except one. His cock jumped. Knowing he couldn't leave the young man to this terrible fate, but not knowing what to do about it, Trajan leaned down to whisper in the man's ear. "I'll be back for you. Hold on until then."

With a great deal of regret, Trajan turned and headed back toward the door. He leaned his ear against the door and listened carefully for any sounds. When none came, Trajan eased the door open a crack. Peaking out, he checked for signs of life.

Not seeing anyone, Trajan made his way back into the hallway, shutting the door behind him. Deciding that Saris could be anywhere, Trajan began to cautiously open each door, peaking into each room.

He saw men and women of various ages but no Saris, not until he opened the last door in the hallway. So intent on finding Saris, he nearly didn't recognize him as the man on the bed.

Much like the young man down the hallway, Saris had wires attached to his head and chest. A long tube from the wall shot blue liquid into his arm. Metal clamps held him naked to the reclining chair beneath him.

Trajan's breath caught in his throat when he spied Saris's hard cock. He wished that he had more time to study it, watch it, taste it. It truly was a thing of beauty. He really would like to get an up-close introduction.

Shaking his head regretfully, Trajan ignored the hard cock and instead went for the wires imbedded in Saris's head and chest. As carefully as he could, Trajan disconnected the wires and then moved on to the tube with blue liquid.

That one was a little harder to disconnect. It took a little maneuvering on Trajan's part, but after a few minutes, Saris came free. Trajan searched around for something for Saris to wear, but he could only find a sheet.

Wrapping it around Saris, he picked him up. At the door, Trajan once again listened for any sounds. When he didn't hear any, he opened the door and walked out, moving quickly down the hallway to the young man's room.

Trajan knew he couldn't save everyone. Hell, he might not even be able to save Saris, but he had to try and save the young man, too. Opening the door that led to the man's room, Trajan quickly walked in and shut it behind him.

He carefully lowered Saris onto the floor then went to unhook the young man. Having done it once already, the second time went fairly quickly. Trajan wrapped him in a sheet, much as he had Saris, then lifted him up and carried him across the room.

Lifting the man to his shoulder, Trajan reached down and picked Saris up with the other arm. He grunted as he lifted Saris, grateful the man didn't weigh more than he did. Otherwise, he never would have been able to lift them both at the same time.

With an unconscious man on each shoulder, Trajan again pulled his blade weapons, one in each hand, and went back the way he came in. Moving slowly due to the weight of the two men he held, it took Trajan just a bit longer to get out than it did to get in.

Once outside of the Vergnügen Center, Trajan hurried to the opposite side of the building. He waited in the shadows for several moments to see if he had raised any alarms. When none sounded, Trajan hoped for the best and headed for his ship.

Carrying two bodies through several blocks of city would be hard on the best of days. Doing it while trying to hide and not be caught could prove to be even harder. By the time Trajan disconnected the security seal around his ship, he felt like his arms might fall off.

Once inside, he reconnected the security seal, then carried the young man to a lone bedroom and laid him down. Saris would, hopefully, be staying in his quarters. Deciding that caution would be best, Trajan locked the young man in, then carried Saris down the corridor to his room.

Laying Saris down on the bed, Trajan took just a moment to lean in and sniff his mate. He instantly felt his cock harden as the sweet scent of moonflowers and danga fruit enveloped his senses. His mate smelled luscious.

Trajan couldn't wait to get a taste of him, but first, he had to have him conscious. He lifted Saris up and pulled the blankets down before laying him back down. He pulled the blankets back up, tucking Saris in.

Getting a wet wash cloth and a glass of danga juice, Trajan sat down on the side of the bed. He wiped down Saris's face and his neck, trying to revive him. When that didn't work, Trajan shook him. Still, Saris didn't stir.

Figuring nothing else would wake Saris until his body told him it was time, Trajan leaned over and softly kissed him on the lips. "Wake soon, Sari. I want to see those beautiful green eyes of yours."

As Trajan started to lean away, intent on going to the bridge and getting the ship ready for takeoff, Saris's eyes suddenly popped open. The feverish look in them scared Trajan right down to the bottoms of his boots.

But when Saris wrapped his arms around Trajan's neck and pressed his lips against him, Trajan couldn't resist, taking what Saris offered even when he knew he shouldn't.

"You came for me."

Chapter 3

Saris felt so hot that his very skinned burned. He ached. He just knew that the man leaning over him could dampen the lava flowing through his veins. Saris knew that the gorgeous man was the answer to every prayer he had ever uttered.

A sense of urgency drove Saris. He wanted the man's hands on him. He needed to feel Trajan's hands move over his flaming skin. Saris wiggled, trying to get his body closer to Trajan's.

He pushed the blanket down to free his legs and wrapped one around Trajan's hips. His hands pulled at the black leather fabric separating him from the body he needed to be close to. He groaned in frustration when he didn't immediately feel naked skin.

"Sari," Trajan whispered huskily, sending shivers of delight racing through him. He felt his pulse beat wildly in his throat as Trajan stared intently down at him. Trajan's large hands framed Saris's face and held it gently.

"Sari, we can't."

What? No! Saris shook his head frantically. He pulled Trajan roughly, almost violently, to him. Grabbing at Trajan with his arms and arching his body, he tried to get closer to him, desperate for the feel of Trajan's muscular body pressed against his.

"Please!" Saris begged.

Saris felt Trajan's arms encircle him, holding him snuggly. He could feel the pressure of the body he wanted so much, but not in the way he wanted. Trajan had his arms pinned to his sides. His long legs were thrown over Saris's, pushing him into the bed. Saris couldn't move.

"Please, oh please," Saris pleaded. "I need—"

"Shh, Sari," Trajan crooned. "I know you're in pain right now, and as much as I would like to accommodate you, I can't. Your system is full of drugs. You don't know what you're doing."

Saris shook his head. "No, I do know. I swear. If you'd just let me—"

Saris almost lost his mind when he felt Trajan's hands move down his back and over his hip. He knew he had never felt anything so good in his entire life. He tried to push his body closer to the hand moving over him.

"Trajan, please."

Soft lips pressed against his forehead. Saris quickly tilted his head back, trying to capture those lips with his. He could feel the heat in his body moving faster, almost as if he spiraled toward an explosion. His heart raced. His body trembled.

Saris felt desperate. "Touch me, please, just touch me," he begged. "I won't ask for anything else. I promise."

The black eyes gazing down at him told Saris that Trajan felt that same intense attraction that he did. His broad shoulders heaved. Then, amazingly, Trajan nodded. Large hands moved over Saris's skin. His body tingled at the contact.

Any contact was welcome. The mere whisper of Trajan's breath on his cheek sent a shiver through Saris. The brush of his long reddish blond hair along his neck made Saris crave more. It tantalized him, erotic and pure pleasure, and it drove Saris crazy.

Saris couldn't help crying out, his body bucking, when Trajan's fingers wrapped around his aching cock. His touch, firm and persuasive, almost instantly had Saris begging for more as his senses reeled.

He lay panting, his chest heaving as the pressure in his body built. Saris gasped at the sweet agony as waves of ecstasy throbbed through him. His world spun and careened on its axis, spinning until he couldn't see or feel anything but the man pleasuring him.

"Shh, Sari," Trajan whispered. "Just close your eyes and rest."

Saris didn't have the energy to do anything else. He let his eyes drift close, savoring the euphoric lethargy that seemed to sweep through his body. He felt Trajan settle him back against the bed, blankets coming up to cover him from neck to toe.

He smiled, one lone hand coming up to brush against Trajan's chest. "Thank you," he whispered as he faded off to sleep, the soft swish of the door opening and closing the last thing he heard before his dreams took him away.

* * * *

Trajan heard the door close behind him as he leaned his head back against the bulkhead. His hands fisted. He took several deep breaths, trying to gain some semblance of control. He could barely stand there and restrain himself. He really wanted to go right back to Saris and take what was his.

Trajan had never seen a more beautiful man than Saris. The very sight of him made Trajan's teeth ache. He wanted nothing more than to claim him, to mark Saris as his mate. But until the drugs had left Saris's system, Trajan felt honor bound to care for his mate, not claim him.

Still, the feel of Saris's naked body pressed against his, the way Saris pleaded with him, Trajan didn't know if he would have the control not to take Saris if the situation came up again. A man could be expected to say no only so many times.

Feeling a small shiver pass through his body, Trajan stood straight and walked down the corridor to the bridge. If nothing else, preparing the ship to leave and taking off should keep his mind off the man sleeping in his bed.

Trajan entered the bridge and immediately readied the ship for takeoff. He logged his flight plan with the docking authorities, relaying his disappointment that he hadn't been able to find a doctor as ordered by his commander.

Once the ship was ready, Trajan carefully maneuvered out of the docking bay, holding his breath as he moved beyond the docking bay doors. Until he maneuvered the ship out of the planet's atmosphere, he could be caught by the tractor beam and forced to return.

Once in open space, Trajan let out a long relieved breath. So far, so good. He still wouldn't be completely comfortable until he was safe back on Katzmann, his precious cargo with him.

Typing in the coordinates, Trajan called Chellak up on the vidlink. He tapped his fingers impatiently as he waited for Chellak to appear on the screen. He was bringing an Elquone doctor back as ordered. He just hoped that Chellak understood that said doctor was also his mate.

"Trajan," Chellak said as soon as he appeared. "Any news? Did you find a doctor?"

"Uh, yes," Trajan replied.

Chellak looked confused. "You don't sound so sure. Is there a problem?"

"Yes and no." Trajan grimaced. "I have Doctor Chattan onboard, plus one extra passenger. However, I'm not sure how much help the doctor is going to be."

"Why? Is he upset about the High Ruler denying you the contract?"

Trajan chuckled. "No." If only things could be that easy.

"Is he upset that the contract was offered in the first place?"

"I don't think so."

"Trajan, stop beating around the bush and tell me what in the hell is going on," Chellak demanded.

Trajan dragged his hand over his face then looked at Chellak. "Doctor Saris Chattan is my mate."

Chellak's eyes widened and then a huge grin broke out over his face. "Congratulations."

"Maybe, maybe not."

"What seems to be the problem?" Chellak asked. "Is he resistant to mating a Katzman?"

Trajan thought of the hand job he had given his mate before taking off. He couldn't exactly say that Saris was resistant. But Trajan still didn't think he had any idea what was going on, either.

"No, not exactly."

"Trajan—"

Trajan chuckled, holding up his hand at Chellak's exasperated growl. "After I left the palace in search of another doctor, the High Ruler reclassified Saris from the Brüter Caste to the Vergnügen Caste."

"The Vergnügen Caste? I've never heard of that caste."

Trajan nodded. He wasn't surprised. He imagined that the High Ruler took great pains to keep that little training program under wraps. Not many planets in the system agreed with forced slavery anymore.

"Members of the Vergnügen Caste are pleasure slaves. They are trained, or programmed, much like the Brüter Caste. By the time the training is complete, they think of nothing except pleasing their master. And in Saris's case, he didn't agree to the training."

"Pleasure slaves?" Chellak shouted. "He really has a training program for pleasure slaves? Demyan's mentioned stuff like that, but I never thought it was really true."

"Yeah, it's true, and it gets worse, Chellak," Trajan admitted regretfully.

"How much worse could it get?"

"Saris underwent under intense training for nearly a day before I could free him. From what I've learned, when someone goes under intense training, everything that they know, everything that they are, can possibly be removed."

"And this means what?"

Trajan felt a cold shiver move down his spine as he thought about what he meant. It terrified him down to his very core that the man meant to be his mate might never be the man he used to be.

"I don't know how much of the old Saris remains. He's drugged out of his mind right now, sleeping. Until the drugs leave his system, I won't be able to tell how much of his personality and knowledge he retained."

Silence reigned for several moments. Trajan couldn't tell if Chellak was just thinking, or talking with his mate. As Trajan waited for Chellak, he wondered if he would develop the mating telepathy with Saris common among his people, or if they would be denied that bond.

It wasn't often that mates couldn't talk telepathically, but it did happen. It was such an intimate way of communicating, something only shared between mates. Trajan desperately hoped the bond would develop.

Considering the wet dream that Trajan experienced with Saris as the main participant, and the words he had heard in his dreams, he felt pretty sure that the bond had already begun to form. He just couldn't be positive.

"How out of it is the doctor?" Chellak finally asked.

Trajan shrugged. "It's hard to tell."

Chellak rolled his eyes. "How is he acting?"

Trajan could feel an uncomfortable flush heat his face. "He's...uh...sleeping right now." Trajan prayed with everything in him that Chellak would accept that explanation. He really didn't want to tell his commanding officer that his mate was drugged and aroused beyond control.

Chellak watched him for another moment then nodded his head. "All right, I want updates every hour until you dock. The moment the doctor comes out of his drug induced state, contact me. I want to talk to him."

Trajan nodded, letting out the breath he hadn't realized he held. "And the other passenger?"

"The other passenger?" Chellak asked curiously.

"When I rescued the doctor from the Vergnügen Center, I came across a young man under the same intense training as Saris." Trajan felt his jaw clench as he paused. "You should have seen it, Chellak. I've never seen anything so barbaric."

Chellak nodded. "Demyan has told me some of the things that happen in those training centers. It *is* barbaric. Why the Federation hasn't imposed sanctions on Elquone, I'll never know."

"I couldn't leave this man there to suffer through that, Chellak. He's so young. He has his whole life ahead of him. To be made into a pleasure slave as such an early age, I just...I couldn't—"

"I understand, Trajan, and I approve," Chellak said. A small smile graced his lips. "We'll take care of him and give him the opportunity to live the life he chooses."

"What happens if the High Ruler demands his return?" Trajan asked. "Hell, what happens if the High Ruler demands Saris's return? I won't let him go now that I have him, Chellak."

"And I wouldn't expect you to, Trajan. Once you find your mate, there is no other choice for you." Chellak shook his head. "No, for now, I think the best thing we can do is deny any knowledge of their whereabouts."

Trajan chuckled. "So we have no idea where these two could possibly be?"

"Basically. Once things settle down, Saris and this young man can petition the Federation for asylum. We'll still have to be on our guard, but it might keep the High Ruler of Elquone from storming the castle, so to speak."

Relief filled Trajan. Chellak would not only support his mating to Saris, but he would help keep Saris and the young man he rescued safe. Trajan wouldn't have to fight this battle on his own.

"I'll contact you in an hour."

Chellak nodded and signed off. Trajan turned on the auto pilot and leaned back in his chair. Things with his commander had gone pretty well. Now he just had to figure out what to do with Saris and his other passenger.

Just thinking about the good doctor aroused Trajan. He pictured the doctor in his mind as he looked earlier, naked and wanting, his soft skin flushed with desire, his plump lips begging for Trajan's touch.

Trajan groaned. He quickly reached down and unbuttoned his leather pants, freeing his cock. Wrapping his hand around his long length, Trajan leaned his head back against the chair and closed his eyes.

He imagined Saris's delicate hand held him, stroked him. The soft skin of Saris's thumb moving over the small slit at the top of his cock, the long fingers rubbing against the glands just under the head of his cock, Trajan could feel it all.

He unbuttoned his black leather vest and pushed it out of the way with his other hand before latching on to a nipple. As his hand moved faster on his cock, Trajan tugged at the brown-hued nipple.

He could feel the pleasure building in his body, the small tingle moving down his spine as he reached closer to orgasm. Trajan fantasized an even deeper ecstasy. He imagined Saris's lips on his cock, instead of his fingers.

At the first swipe of Saris's tongue against his hot skin, Trajan shattered into a million pieces, ropes of cum shooting out over his hand and abdomen. His body humping against his hands several times, Trajan cried out.

"Sari!"

Trajan stroked his cock a few more times, his movements slowing with each caress. He could feel the pulse in his neck thudding rapidly, his chest heaving. The degree of ecstasy he had just experienced stunned him.

He jerked off for years. Usually, it just released his immediate tension, leaving him wanting more. While he did want more, specifically more of Saris, he couldn't ever remember feeling this satisfied by simple masturbation.

Trajan let out a long, surrendering moan. He was hooked on the good doctor, far more than he had imagined he would be. The mating heat was always intense, but Trajan had no idea it would be this consuming.

Every thought he had, every action he took was with Saris in mind. Would he be safe? Would he be happy? Would he want Trajan as a mate? The mere thought that Saris might reject him sent Trajan's heart plummeting to his feet.

Jumping up, Trajan started for the door when he realized that he still had his spent cock in his hand, cum dripping down his abdomen. With a small roll of his eyes, Trajan walked to the bathroom off the bridge and cleaned up.

With all of his bits tucked back in place, Trajan made his way down the corridor to his private quarters. He stopped briefly to check on the man in the room across the way, finding him still asleep, before opening the door to his own room.

A small ray of light from a passing star shone through the window, illuminating the soft contours of Saris's face as he slept. He looked peaceful, almost content. His small, delicate hand curled under his cheek, his lush, rosy lips curved up at the ends.

To Trajan, he looked adorable. He couldn't describe the man any other way. Awake, Saris was breathtaking. Each movement he made seemed to be done with grace and style. Asleep, Saris looked adorable, cute even.

In both states, Trajan wanted him. He hoped and prayed that Saris would accept him because the more time he spent around the man, the more he knew that he never wanted to give him up.

Trajan started into the room when a sudden explosion rocked the ship. His eyes widened briefly until alarms blared announcing an attack on the ship. Casting one last glance at Saris, Trajan turned and ran for the bridge of the ship.

Alarms screamed and lights flashed on the control panel. He immediately ran to the console, checking to ensure the shields protecting the ship still operating properly.

Once assured of that, Trajan tried to zero in on the ship that that shot at him. It took only a moment to locate the hostile vessel. It was a Bergius Fighter ship, common in the system, easy to maneuver, and cheap to purchase. They also only allowed two people onboard due to their small size. Luckily, the small fighter was only equipped with short range pulse cannons. Trajan knew that if he could put enough distance between him and the fighter, he could get away unscathed. If not, he would have to stay and fight.

His ship was a Reran Fighter, though, better equipped with long and short range pulse cannons, laser guns, and high-powered deflector shields. It could support a crew of ten and had a cargo bay that could hold a small ship like the Bergius Fighter.

With his precious cargo onboard, Trajan wanted to avoid a fight. While his ship could take a lot of damage, one good hit could disable him enough that the other ship might be able to finish him off. Trajan couldn't allow that.

Putting his ship into overdrive, Trajan concentrated on putting as much distance between him and the hostile ship as possible. As he maneuvered in and out of a nearby asteroid belt, Trajan called up Chellak.

"It hasn't been an hour yet, Trajan. Did the doctor wake up?" Chellak asked the moment he came on screen.

"No, we're being attacked by a Bergius Fighter ship."

Chellak's eyebrows rose in surprise. "Piss someone off?"

"I'm betting that I pissed off Toc Jerell." Trajan's body jerked as another hit vibrated his ship. He glanced over quickly to see if the shields had weakened. Power was down to seventy-six percent but still holding.

"Toc Jerell?"

"The chief advisor to Shek Tavia," Trajan replied. "It seems he took a liking to Saris. I wouldn't be surprised if he arranged for Saris to be retrained as a pleasure slave just so that he could do whatever he wanted to him."

"And you think he's the one attacking you?"

Trajan shrugged. "Can't think of anyone else I pissed off lately. Besides, this is a Bergius Fighter. If the High Ruler wanted to come after me, don't you think he'd use something stronger than that?"

"Yeah, okay," Chellak agreed. "I'll send out some fighters to escort you home. Just don't get your ass shot up. Demyan is driving me crazy demanding a doctor from his home world."

Trajan chuckled as the vidlink shut off. He'd bet it was the one time in the universe that Chellak wished his mate couldn't talk telepathically to him. It wasn't something he could get away from by going into another room. It followed him everywhere he went. Trajan couldn't wait for it to happen for him and Saris.

Making another deep dive through a series of small asteroids, Trajan glanced over at the sensor array. The Bergius Fighter still followed, but dropping behind fast. In another minute or so, they should be out of firing range.

Trajan knew that the pilot of the other ship had figured out the same thing when he began to fire in rapid session. Trajan felt hit after hit land on his ship, jarring him repeatedly. By the time his sensors said he was out of firing range, his deflector shields were down to twenty-five percent.

Trajan didn't breathe a sigh of relief until he had passed through the asteroid field and the other ship had dropped off his sensors. He hoped that he could stay far enough ahead of the other ship to get home before he got attacked again.

He also hoped no more surprises awaited him between now and home. One more massive hit, and he would be without shields. And then he would be easy to pick off.

Setting the ship on auto pilot once more, Trajan ran a series of ship-wide diagnostics to assess the damage inflicted by the Bergius Fighter. Luckily, the damage to the ship seemed minimal, nothing that couldn't be repaired once he docked on Katzmann.

For the first time since the first shot hit the ship, Trajan leaned his head back and relaxed his tense muscles. He hated fighting onboard a ship. He much preferred meeting an adversary on solid ground where he could look into his face.

Fighting from a ship seemed like a dishonorable way to fight. It wasn't an indication of a fighter's abilities but rather a show of how much coinage they had sunk into the upgrades on their ship.

Trajan sent Chellak a brief message stating that he had evaded the Bergius Fighter. He also relayed the damage report on his ship, knowing that Chellak would have technicians ready and waiting when he landed.

Taking one last look at the ship's trajectory, Trajan stood up and began to turn toward the door. A flash of white caught his eyes. Trajan instantly pulled two blades out of hidden pockets in his leather pants and turned to face whoever stood behind him.

He nearly dropped the weapons in his hand when he found Saris standing behind him, a white sheet wrapped around his hips, and a bewildered look on his face.

"How did I get here?"

Chapter 4

Saris stared at the magnificent man standing before him with a bit of awe. He vaguely remembered him, but he didn't know where he remembered him from. Noting the rising bulge in the man's pants, he wondered if they were lovers.

"Do I know you?" Saris asked.

After a small hesitation the man nodded. "We've met."

"Are we lovers?" Well, he had to ask.

"Uh…no."

Damn!

"Are we going to be lovers?"

"I kind of hoped for a little more than that," the man replied, an easy grin playing across his lips.

Saris took another step into the room. "More?" Oh, he could definitely see them doing a lot more, but right now, he just wanted to get down to the lover part, plain and simple. He took another step, grinning when the man mirrored his action.

"Just what did you have in mind?" Saris asked. He could feel his pulse speed up. He had a lot of things in mind, but he wanted to be sure that the man before him thought the same thing.

Just when Saris thought the man might take hold of him, he suddenly stepped back, a stoic look dropping down over his face. Saris became confused, not quite understanding the small ache the look gave him in the pit of his stomach.

"How are you feeling?"

"Feeling?" Saris repeated absently. He couldn't explain how he felt. Too many emotions spiraled through him for him to even pick one to concentrate on. Having suppressed his emotions most of his life, the emotions filling him bewildered him.

"You've been drugged," the man supplied.

"You drugged me?" Saris gasped.

The man quickly shook his head. "No, no, I would never drug you, I swear. You were already drugged when I found you. I've just been waiting for the effects of the drugs that they gave you at the Vergnügen Center to wear off."

"The Vergnügen Center? What in the hell was I doing at the Vergnügen Center?" A spurt of hungry desire spiraled through Saris when the man's face flushed. He couldn't believe how incredibly hot that looked.

"I went to Elquone to find a doctor for my commander's mate. He's a brüter and due to give birth any day. Your High Ruler offered me your contract so that you could accompany me back to Katzmann but—"

"You bought my contract?" Saris's desire of a moment before went up in flames as he realized that he stared at his new master. His greatest fear realized. He had been sold to another, never to have a will of his own again.

"No!" The man exclaimed his objection so forcibly that Saris took a step back. A part of him was shocked at the man's denial. Another part felt almost insulted. Did he lack something that made this man not want him?

"So, if I don't belong to you," Saris asked, holding the sheet against his body with one hand, the other hand landing on his hip, "then what in the hell am I doing here?"

"I can explain."

"Then start explaining," Saris replied sharply. "And it had better be good."

"Why don't we go somewhere that we can be more comfortable while we talk," the man suggested as he edged toward the door. To Saris, he almost looked like he was preparing to run.

"I'm fine right where I am. Now talk!" With a pang, Saris suddenly realized that he stood in the middle of the bridge covered in nothing but a sheet. No wonder the man looked so edgy.

"Maybe you could find me something to wear?" Saris muttered uneasily. He bit his lip, turning away from the man's intense stare.

"Come on," the man said. "I'm sure that I have something in my quarters."

Saris followed behind the man as they made their way back down the corridor he had come through moments before. He was surprised when the man stopped before the door of the room he had woken up in, more so when the man opened the door and walked in.

"I slept in your quarters?"

"Uh, yes. This is a small ship and the other rooms are occupied." The man went to the cabinets hidden in the wall and pulled something out, handing it to Saris before closing the drawer.

Awkwardly, Saris cleared his throat as he waited for the man to leave the room so that he could dress. When he made no move to leave, Saris turned his back and started pulling the one piece black bodysuit on under the sheet.

It took some maneuvering but eventually, he got dressed and dropped the sheet back onto the bed. Running his hand over the soft black material, he realized that it was made of Jarcon fabric, a simple stretchable material that enabled people of different sizes to wear the same outfit. Saris was impressed. Jarcon-made clothing did not come cheap.

When Saris looked up, the man gestured to a nearby chair. "Please, have a seat and I will explain everything to you."

Saris moved to the chair and sat, his thin fingers tensed in his lap as he waited. He didn't understand why he was on this man's ship, but knowing that his brüter contract had been offered and rejected made him feel somewhat inadequate.

"My name is Trajan Varl," the man began. "I'm a warrior from Katzmann. My commander, Chellak Rai, is mated to a brüter who is due to give birth any day."

"You said this part. Get to the part about how I came to be onboard your ship." Uncertainty made his voice harsh and demanding. He knew it, but he felt helpless to stop it. He didn't understand what interest this man had in him.

"I'm getting to that." Trajan ran a hand quickly through his reddish blond hair. "Look, I asked for a doctor. When the High Ruler offered your contract, I couldn't accept it. It's against my laws, and frankly, I think it's nauseating to even consider owning another person."

Saris sat up straighter in amazement. He didn't often encounter people who didn't believe in owning others. It was pretty normal on his home world and something that Saris hated beyond words.

"When I refused your contract, the High Ruler said he couldn't let you leave the planet without one. I needed to find someone else."

Saris nodded. That sounded like the High Ruler. He liked getting his way. He didn't like it when he didn't. In fact, someone usually ended up losing their head if the High Ruler didn't get his way.

"I guess that after I left, the High Ruler reclassified you to the Vergnügen Caste. From what I've been able to learn, they took you to the center for deep retraining." A look of guilt crossed over Trajan's face. "I couldn't get to you until you had been there for more than a day. I don't know how much damage you suffered."

Saris swallowed with difficulty and found his voice. "That's why I was drugged?"

Trajan nodded. "They had you hooked up to these machines when I found you, Sari, two in your head and two in your chest. A tube pumped blue liquid into your arm. They had you strapped down to the table."

"What did you just call me?" Saris whispered. One word, one lone word blazed to the front of every word Trajan spoken to him. No one had ever called him Sari except the faceless man in his dreams.

"Sari." Trajan said the word tentatively as if testing it. He looked so hesitant that Saris ignored the warning bells ringing in his head.

"Why would you call me that? My name is Saris."

Trajan's face flushed, but he shook his head anyway. "No, you've always been Sari, always will be." His voice had drifted into a hushed whisper, a gleam of something Saris couldn't identify in his black eyes.

"How do I know you?"

"We met at the royal palace, remember?"

"We've met somewhere else," Saris insisted. He felt sure of it. This man seemed too familiar for them not to know each other from somewhere else. Saris bet that Trajan even had a triangle-shaped birthmark on his left thigh.

Trajan shook his head. "I've never met you before yesterday at the royal palace."

"You're lying," Saris growled, jumping to his feet to stalk across the room. "Why are you lying? Why are you denying me?"

Trajan regarded Saris quizzically for a moment, his mouth opening and closing as if he had something to say but wasn't sure if he should say it. An uncertainty crept into his expression.

"You wouldn't believe me if I told you," Trajan finally said.

"Try me."

"We've met in our dreams."

An unfamiliar image crept into Saris's mind, one of him bent over Trajan, lavishing his cock with his mouth, of Trajan begging him to suck harder. He could see the long length of Trajan's cock before him, feel the strength of his body beneath him.

Saris's mind floundered as he tried to grasp what he saw, what Trajan told him. "How—" Saris suddenly felt weak and vulnerable in the face of confusion. He stiffened, momentarily abashed.

"I am a Katzman," Trajan replied as if that explained it all.

* * * *

Trajan could see the confusion clouding Saris's green eyes. Positive that Saris would turn away from him at any moment, Trajan was shocked when his eyes suddenly filled with a fierce sparkling. He had an almost gleeful tone to his voice when he spoke.

"If we've dreamed together then that means we're mates, doesn't it?"

Trajan couldn't do anything more than nod as surprise filled him. The connection between mates was a highly kept secret known only to those that had experienced it and their close friends and family. He only knew of it because of the unusual bond between Chellak and Demyan.

"Then why are you denying me?" Saris shouted curtly.

"Sari," Trajan said quickly, grabbing him by the arms and giving him a little shake. "I'm not denying you. I would never deny you, but I just kidnapped you from a Vergnügen Training Center. I don't know how much of you is you and how much is the training that they put you through."

"I'm all me, Trajan, every last bit," Saris replied in a gentle, quite tone. "And I'm all yours for the taking."

A cry of relief broke from Trajan's lips as he wrapped his arms around Saris and buried his face in his golden hair. He breathed in the heady scent of his mate letting it wash over him. It had a calming, peaceful effect on him making him believe that life might just be perfect.

It also had another effect on him. Trajan could feel his cock harden and press against his leather pants as if demanding freedom. Trajan lifted his head to look down at Saris. He cupped his chin, searching his upturned face for any sign of anxiety.

"Why are you not upset?"

Saris shrugged. "I've been studying different life forms for many years so I could meet the needs of all of my patients. When I heard through the grapevine that a brüter had became the mate of Chellak Rai, I made it my business to study Katzmen. I learned a lot about their mating habits."

"So, you know that—"

Saris placed his finger over Trajan's mouth. "I know that if we can connect on a dream level, and both of us experience it, then we're destined to be mates. And if I'm not mistaken, you have a triangle-shaped birthmark on your left thigh. Am I correct?"

Stunned, Trajan nodded.

"Then that means the dream I had the other night wasn't something I just conjured up in my own mind. You experienced it, too."

"You remember that?" Trajan felt the soft brushing of Saris's fingers against his cheek.

"I remember a lot of things," Saris said in a low, husky voice.

"Do you...do you remember earlier?"

Saris's dark blond eyebrow shot up in surprise. "Earlier?"

Trajan felt his face flood horribly at the quizzical look on Saris's face. *Oh, this is going to be interesting*, he thought. *One wrong word and I could lose Sari forever.*

"After I brought you onboard and put you to bed you woke up. You... well," Trajan paused to swallow past the lump in his throat. "You were still under the influence of the drugs, and you started pleading with me to touch you and—"

"You had sex with me while I under the influence of drugs?"

"Gods, no!" Trajan replied sharply, maybe more so than he meant to because Saris looked slightly offended. "I wanted to, gods, did I want to, but I wanted you to want it too and not because you had been trained to want it."

Trajan had no idea why his mouth had decided to run away from him. He said things to Saris that he never would have thought to say to anyone. He just couldn't seem to help himself. His mouth had a mind of its own.

"So, what did happen?" Saris asked.

Trajan shrugged, knowing his face burned bright red again. "I kind of jerked you off until you fell asleep and then went to the bridge," Trajan murmured.

"And?"

"And nothing," Trajan replied. "I tucked you in and let you sleep."

"You didn't do anything else?"

Trajan's eyes fluttered closed. He let out a small groan. Saris would keep asking questions until Trajan told him every last detail. If the future with his mate looked like that, Trajan wondered what would be the point of being able to talk telepathically.

"I swear I didn't touch you in any other way," Trajan hedged.

"And?"

"And I went to the bridge and masturbated." Trajan opened his eyes in surprise when he felt Saris pat him on the cheek.

"There, see? That wasn't so hard, was it?" Saris said as he pushed away from Trajan and walked across the room. He stopped on the other side, turning to glance back at him. "You know, this whole mating thing is going to be a lot easier for you if you just tell me things upfront."

Trajan inclined his head in compliance, still stunned by Saris's easy acceptance of everything he told him. "You don't mind?"

Saris chuckled. "Mind that you felt so aroused you had to go jerk off? No, should I? I mean, I would have preferred that we enjoy these things together, but I can understand why you didn't, commend it even."

"So, you agree to be my mate?" That burning question ate Trajan up inside. Saris may have been accepting of everything Trajan told him, including the little bit of playing around. That didn't mean he would accept being Trajan's mate.

"I'm not adverse to it, how's that?" Saris asked. He crossed his arms over his chest and bent his head slightly forward. "I think I need to know more before I can agree to anything, the first being, where are you taking me?"

"Katzmann," Trajan replied simply.

Saris laughed. "Yeah, I should have guessed that."

"Next question?" Trajan asked eagerly.

Saris smiled. Trajan thought it a beautiful smile. It lit up Saris's face and made him seem young and carefree. Trajan vowed to himself then and there that he wanted to see that smile on Saris's face as often as possible.

"If we become mates, how does it work? I mean, what is the process and what are the effects?" Saris asked. "I've researched as much as I could, but a lot isn't known about the Katzman mating habits. I know that we can share dreams. What else?"

"If we mate, we'll be able to speak to each other in our minds."

"Can we speak mentally to others of your kind?"

Trajan shook his head. "No, it's just between mates. Demyan, my commander's mate, is unable to speak due to an old injury. He just recently learned how to read and write. Before that, they couldn't communicate at all. It's a mess. Now, they talk all of the time with their minds."

"Convenient."

Trajan leaned back against the bulkhead behind him and fit his fingers together over his abdomen. "We'll be able to talk that way, too. We'll also always be able to tell where the other one is, kind of like a homing beacon."

"Makes hide and seek kind of moot, doesn't it?"

"Hide and seek?" Trajan asked in confusion.

"Yeah, hide and seek. It's a game where one person hides and the other one tries to find him." Saris laughed again. "Haven't you ever played games like that?"

Trajan shook his head. "I've been training to be a warrior since I was a small child."

"Why?"

Trajan shrugged nonchalantly. "It was expected of us. We always knew what our pride was destined for, what we trained for. The harder we trained the better chance we had of victory."

"Victory over what?"

"Vortigern Vedek."

"Who?"

Trajan couldn't help but smile at the bewildered look on Saris's face. "Thirty years ago, Vortigern Vedek came to Katzmann on a trade mission. His forces overpowered the peaceful people there and killed the High Ruler, Chellak's father, who reigned at the time."

Sudden understanding came over Saris's face. "You were both in the same pride so his fight became your fight. That's why you trained so much, to retake Katzmann from Vortigern Vedek."

Trajan nodded. "We took Katzmann back about five months ago. Demyan was a slave to Vortigern Vedek when we arrived. Chellak, not knowing anything about brüters, claimed Demyan as reparation for the death of his father."

"He didn't know about brüters?"

Trajan chuckled. "Not a damn thing. Imagine his surprise when Demyan announced that they had a child on the way. Of course now he's thrilled about it, but at the time, well, he fell over in a dead faint right in front of the Federation Council."

Saris chuckled. "I probably would have paid to see that."

"Me, too," Trajan laughed. "I heard about it from Chellak's brother, Ciprian."

"What do *you* know about brüters?" Saris asked quietly a few moments later.

Trajan looked at Saris sharply. "I know that you belong to the Brüter Caste, but at some point you couldn't complete your training so you became a doctor."

Saris nodded. "That's true. I had a hard time adjusting to some of the requirements of being a brüter. I'm much better suited to being a doctor."

"What requirements?" Trajan asked, suddenly worried for his pridemate, Chellak.

"When someone becomes a brüter, he is required to follow a set of rules. One of those rules states that any child that you give birth to does not belong to you but the sire of that child. We have no rights to it. The child can be taken away from us, given to someone else, even sold, and there is nothing we can do to stop it."

Trajan felt his heart ache at the agony in Saris's voice. "Did that— has that happened to you?"

Saris shook his head. "No, but it happened to my twin brother, Karis. He gave birth to a little boy four years ago. The child was taken away by the sire, and he never saw it again. Since he had fulfilled his contract, he was returned to our family. He just wasn't the same after that."

Trajan walked over and laid his hand down on Saris's shoulder, giving it a small squeeze. He wanted desperately to reassure his mate that he would never be so callous as to return him to his family and give away a child.

"I'm sorry, Sari, but you know that would never happen with a Katzman. We mate for life. There would be no returning you to your family even if you had completed the training and I had accepted your contract. And we cherish our children, every one of them. We would never give them up."

Saris lifted his head to look up at Trajan. A small smile played across his lips. "I hope so, for me and for Demyan."

"Chellak would no more hurt Demyan in that way than he would return control of Katzmann to Vortigern Vedek. Demyan is his world. Any child that they have will be treasured just as much."

Saris nodded.

"Where's your brother now? Has he been contracted again?"

"No, the emotional effects of losing his son made him unsuitable for another contract. They terminated him from the program and returned him home in shame."

"In shame?" Trajan exclaimed, causing Saris to jump. "How can he be ashamed of loving his child?"

"You don't understand how things are done on Elquone," Saris bellowed right back. He pushed himself away from Trajan and began pacing around the room. Trajan watched in confusion as Saris seemed to unravel right before his eyes.

"Once we're in a caste like the Brüter Caste, we have no rights beyond what we're given by the owner of our contract. We are required to fulfill our contract under penalty of death. We don't even get to choose what caste we enter into. It's chosen for us when we hit puberty."

"Hasn't anyone ever objected before?"

"Sure, many people. They're just sent to deep training, usually in whatever caste they avoid in the first place."

"But I saw a lot of people coming and going like normal people. Are they all in castes?"

"Everyone on Elquone that is of the lower class is in a caste of one sort or another. The only way that you can get out of your caste is to die, be reeducated, marry up in ranking, or have a contract owner set you free. Most don't, they just send us home to be contracted out again."

Trajan blew out a long breath. No wonder Saris had fought his training so hard. Being a citizen of Elquone sounded like a nightmare. If Trajan had anything to do with it, Saris would never be returned to Elquone again.

"How did Demyan's contract state that he became the lawful dependent of the sire if he could be returned to his caste?" Trajan asked as the thought suddenly came to him.

"Well, if his family is well off, they could have bought a special dispensation to add to his contract. It happens but not often. Those of the Brüter Caste are chosen because of our superior genetics."

"Superior genetics?" Trajan asked in confusion.

Saris grimaced. "We make pretty babies."

"Oh." He chuckled, a little uncomfortably.

"Once we have completed our training, we become good little money makers, producing child after child for whoever pays our High Ruler the most amount of money. The better our genetics, the more money we make."

Trajan shook head. He knew he hadn't kept the disgust off of his face when Saris nodded at him. "A slave is a slave, Sari, and on Katzmann slavery is outlawed. Chellak saw to that himself."

"I want to believe what you are saying, Trajan, really, I do, but I've heard pretty little stories too many times. I don't know how much I can believe without seeing it for myself."

"I understand, and I don't expect you to take me at my word without proof." Trajan smiled, suddenly filled with confidence. "You'll see that I'm telling you the truth once we reach Katzmann."

A sudden blast rocked the ship, knocking Saris down, but Trajan jumped over and grabbed Saris before he could hit the floor. Saris's face filled with alarm as he looked up at Trajan.

"*If* we reach Katzmann, you mean?"

Chapter 5

Saris followed Trajan quickly down the corridor to the bridge. Trajan seemed worried but not any more than Saris. The shock waves that had hit the ship weren't from any passing debris. They had been fired upon.

Saris watched as Trajan sat down in the captain's chair and began searching the sensors for signs of what had hit them. He was shocked when Trajan started laughing.

"That sorry ass bastard."

"Uh, want to let me in on the joke?" Saris asked.

"Someone is trying very hard to keep me from returning you to Katzmann. I suspect that it is Toc Jerell," Trajan replied as he began maneuvering the ship through a series of evasive moves.

"Toc Jerell? The chief advisor?" Saris asked totally bewildered. "Why would he care about me? How does he even know who I am?"

Trajan chuckled, glancing over his shoulder at him. "Guess it's because you're just that darn cute."

Saris went to deny Trajan's words until he remembered the look of lust Toc Jerell had given him in the royal palace. It had given him the creeps then and it gave him the creeps now. That man was sick.

"Uh, I'd really prefer not to go back to Elquone if you can arrange it."

"I have no intentions of returning you to Elquone, Sari. You said that you wanted to explore our relationship a little more. That can't happen if we're worlds apart. Now get over to that vidlink and contact Chellak. He has fighters coming to meet us."

Saris quickly moved to do as Trajan ordered, hitting the buttons on the vidlink, blinking at the man who almost instantly appeared. "Uh, are you Chellak Rai?"

"I am," the lion man replied. "You must be Saris."

"Sari, please."

"No!" Trajan shouted from beside Saris, never taking his eyes of the console in front of him. "Sari is just for me."

Saris grinned. "Please, call me Saris."

"Saris it is, then," Chellak chuckled. "Now, what seems to be the problem?"

Saris grimaced. "We're under attack."

"Again," Trajan added.

"Again?" Saris asked in surprise. "We've been attacked before?"

"Yep, only this time, he's brought a friend."

"He?" Saris asked as he turned around to look at Trajan. "How badly did you piss Toc Jerell off?"

Saris looked back at the vidlink when Chellak chuckled. "He so has your number, Trajan."

"I told you I think Toc Jerell sent these fighters after us to get you back," Trajan explained.

"Then why in the hell is he shooting at us?" Saris shouted. "Doesn't he realize that it could get me killed?"

"I think he's hoping to disable us enough that he can board us."

"Board us?" Saris gulped fearfully.

"Not going to happen, Sari," Trajan replied with a lot more confidence than Saris felt. "I won't let him take you away from me now that I've found you. However…"

Trajan stopped speaking as he made a particularly difficult maneuver, swinging the ship around and driving it through a series of zigzag moves, then down through a cluster of asteroids surrounding a nearby planet.

"However?" Saris encouraged, wanting Trajan to finish his sentence.

"It wouldn't be a bad idea for you to get to the escape pod," Trajan replied. "And don't forget the young man sleeping in the room across from you. I rescued him from the Vergnügen Center along with you. I think he's still drugged."

"What about you?" Saris whispered. A flicker of apprehension coursed through him at the solemn expression on Trajan's face. "You're coming, too, aren't you?"

"I'll be right behind you, Sari."

Saris knew that Trajan lied. He also knew that Trajan could tell that Saris knew it. Still, Trajan had to say the words, and Saris could understand that. That didn't mean that he wasn't going to give Trajan a reason to fight.

Saris stepped over to Trajan, grabbing his face in his hands and capturing his lips. He put all of the chaotic emotions he felt into his kiss, the wonder and excitement, the attraction and growing bond. His tired and lonely soul melted into it.

When he finally lifted his head, Saris's eyes clung to Trajan's, analyzing his reaction. The expression in Trajan's black eyes seemed to plead for Saris's understanding, to not make their separation anymore difficult then it had to be.

Saris nodded that he understood the unspoken message Trajan gave him. Trajan would stay with the ship and do what he had to do to keep his mate safe. Saris's duty was to keep himself safe, even if it meant Trajan's death.

When Saris spoke again, his voice sounded tender, almost a murmur. "I'll be waiting for you in the escape pod, Trajan."

"I'll be there, my own."

Saris gazed at Trajan for another moment then turned and ran from the bridge toward the escape pod. He stopped at the room across from Trajan's quarters, surprised when he found the young man still unconscious on the bed.

With all of the noise from the other ship shooting at them, Saris would have thought the young man would be awake, even afraid. He seemed to be sleeping like a baby. Saris surmised that the man had to have had more drugs in his system than Saris had. It was the only explanation.

Picking up a spare bodysuit, Saris grabbed the man by his arms and dragged him down the corridor to the escape pod at the end of the walkway. It took a bit of maneuvering on his part, especially with all of the explosions rocking the ship, but he finally got the man inside the escape pod and buckled in.

Saris took just a moment longer to assure himself that the escape pod had adequate food and medical supplies. He had an idea that they might need them. He had no idea where they were going or how soon it would take for help to arrive, but he wanted to be prepared.

The next explosion that hit the ship sent Saris careening to the floor. He caught himself right before he would have hit his head on the side of the escape pod bench seats. Saris took a moment to steady himself, then pushed himself to his feet.

An automated voice requested evacuation of the ship, counting down the minutes until life support would be deactivated. Saris knew he only had moments before the escape pod would deploy with or without passengers.

He leaned out of the escape pod door and looked down the corridor for any sign of Trajan. Red lights blared as sparks and smoke filled the corridor. The damage to Trajan's ship was massive.

Saris glanced back at the sleeping man behind him. He was still unconscious but safely strapped in. If the escape pod left without Saris and Trajan, the young man would still be safe until help arrived—hopefully.

Still, Saris had to take the chance. He couldn't leave Trajan behind, no matter how much Trajan argued about it. Determined not to leave his newly found mate behind, Saris left the escape pod and made his way down the corridor.

It was slow going. He had to dodge falling debris and try to stay on his feet as the ship continued to shake from explosions. Saris picked up his pace. He knew that he had to hurry before the ship blew apart.

Stepping over a ceiling beam that had fallen to the floor, Saris stepped onto the bridge. It took him just a glance around the room to understand that he and Trajan were in more danger than he thought.

No one piloted the ship. A large ceiling beam pinned Trajan to the floor. He had blood covering his forehead, and he didn't seem to be moving. Saris ran across the floor, falling to his knees beside Trajan. He quickly searched Trajan over for injuries, finding a small lump under the blood on his head.

Wiping the blood away, Saris surmised that it wasn't a life-threatening injury, but it explained his unconscious state. From the location of the beam pinning Trajan to the floor, Saris knew it was most likely the cause of the injury.

Saris looked around the room and considered his predicament. He had to get Trajan free of the beam he lay under and get them both to the escape pod before it detached from the ship *and* the ship exploded. He didn't have much time.

Saris ran to the vidlink and sent a quick message to Chellak summing up their situation, giving the coordinates where they were presently and to the planet Saris hoped they were headed for. He also listed that Trajan's injuries.

Grabbing a long, steel rod off of the floor, Saris used it as leverage to lift the bigger beam off of his mate. It took a few tries, but eventually, his hard work paid off. The beam lifted up just enough for Saris to move it to the side of Trajan.

Saris jumped when the heavy beam hit the floor, making a large clanking noise against the steel floor tiles. He stopped to take a deep breath, then grabbed Trajan under his arms, dragging him down to the corridor as he had the young man.

Pulling Trajan into the small escape pod, Saris just had time to close the hatch and lock it before the automated voice from the computer announced that life support had been deactivated. The ship would implode in mere moments.

Saris's heart beat frantically in his chest as he pulled Trajan up onto the bench seat and secured him for the ride. He had just enough time to strap himself in before the escape pod launched into space.

Seizing Trajan's lifeless hand, Saris gazed out the window of the escape pod as Trajan's ship grew smaller and smaller. A large flash of light nearly blinded him as the Reran Fighter Ship exploded. Pieces of debris flew in every direction.

The only bright spot for Saris was seeing one of the other ships get caught by a piece of flying debris, exploding right along with Trajan's ship. The second ship had moved off to a safe distance. Saris just hoped that the explosion would hide their escape.

Saris turned his attention to the escape pod's console. The pod flew through space, programmed to land on the first inhabitable planet, one that could sustain their lives until help could arrive. By Saris's estimations, the planet three sectors away would fit that requirement. It shouldn't take more than an hour to get there and land.

In the meantime, Saris wanted to ensure that he deactivated the locator beacon attached to the escape pod. If Trajan wanted to reactivate it once he woke up, he could do so. Until then, Saris felt better if they stayed hidden. Locator beacons didn't discriminate between good guys and bad guys.

A small groan from the man beside him had Saris quickly turning to look at Trajan. He reached over and checked the wound on Trajan's head, pleased that the bleeding had stopped. It still looked nasty though. It might even need a few stitches, something Saris could take care of once they landed.

Assuming they landed in one piece. As great as escape pods were, there was always chance of damage to the pod, burning up in the atmosphere due to damage to the pod, and a hard landing. All of which could cause serious injury or death.

Saris hoped for neither as the shock waves from entering the atmosphere began rocking the small escape pod back and forth. The small vessel rocked enough that Saris began to wonder if it would hold together long enough for them to land.

His eyes strayed to the two men who shared the small space with him. Saris held on to the edge of the bench seat with one hand and held Trajan's hand with the other. The computerized voice system in the escape pod announced their rate of descent. Saris wished he had disconnected it too.

"One thousand feet."

Saris glanced one more time at Trajan, hoping that it wouldn't be the last. He really wanted the chance to get to know the man better, to find out what being the mate of a Katzman, this Katzman, was all about.

"Five hundred feet."

Saris closed his eyes tightly and held his breath, the muscles in his body tensing as he readied himself for impact.

"Please hold for landing."

Saris wanted to roll his eyes, but fear filled him. He held on for landing. He held on for dear life. A sudden jarring thud and the escape pod came to a stop. Saris grunted, feeling like his ass had just been pushed through the top of his head.

He took a moment to breathe before opening his eyes and looking around the small space inside the pod. The young man he had dragged into the pod remained unconscious. So was Trajan. Saris predicted that he would be on his own for a while.

Saris unbuckled his restraints and stood to his feet, realizing as he did so that the shaking in his body extended all of the way down to his toes. His steps were unsteady as he stepped across the pod to the window and looked out.

The view from the window surprised him. The planet they had landed on didn't seem too hostile. He could see blue sky above, trees in many different colors, and even snowcapped mountains off in the distance.

All in all, it looked pretty good. Saris probably would have chosen to come to a place like this for vacation, assuming he had ever been allowed to go on vacation. Saris just hoped that whatever life forms that inhabited this planet wouldn't consider them on the dinner menu.

Saris pushed a couple of buttons on the control console and then moved to unlock the door. When the door opened, cool air filled the escape pod. Saris took in a deep breath, smiling when he realized that if the air was bad, he was fucked already.

Saris grabbed the phase pistol out of the emergency box then stepped outside of the pod. He could see that they had landed on the edge of a large meadow covered in grass in several shades of green.

A large section of trees lined the area behind them. A sheer rock cliff could be seen just to the left side of the meadow, a small river on the right. Considering where they had landed, Saris started to feel optimistic about their situation.

Until he heard a loud roar off in the distance and realized that they were not alone. He had no idea what had made that intimidating sound, and he really didn't care to find out. It sounded large and hungry.

Saris closed the hatch behind him, locking it tightly. He turned and scanned the area around them trying to figure out the best location for them to hide. Down by the river where they would have a fresh supply of water seemed good.

Hearing another loud roar, Saris changed his mind, deciding that something up higher might be a better chance. He looked over at the cliffs to the side of the meadow. Maybe he could find a spot by the cliffs that at least would give them some semblance of security.

With that thought in mind, Saris began walking toward the cliffs. He glanced around frequently trying to see anything that might be coming in his direction. It would be just perfect to get through being rescued by Trajan, an attack on the ship, and landing on an alien world only to get himself killed before he could be rescued.

Saris heard a few more loud roars, a few quieter roars that seemed to come from different animals, and howling. Some large birds even flew overhead. But Saris made it to the cliffs unimpeded.

Once there, he wasn't really sure what he looked for. Healing was his expertise, not strategic planning. Saris wished that Trajan was here. He'd know what to do, what they would be looking for.

Realizing that until Trajan woke up he had to look out for them all, Saris began to walk along the cliffs. He looked for any outcropping or collection of large boulders, anything that they could use as cover.

Just as he spotted a small outcropping that looked like it had potential, Saris slipped. He cried out as his knee scrapped along a particularly sharp rock, cutting into the flesh of his knee. Saris tried to keep the tears of pain from spilling as he sat down on the ground and looked at the damage to his knee.

More of a scrape than a cut, it bled just a little and hurt a whole lot. Saris covered it with his hand putting pressure on the wound. He leaned his head forward and rested it on his knee, letting the strain of the situation carry him away for a moment.

He was all alone on a planet that he had never been on before. His only companions were either drugged or injured, and someone hunted him. He would ask the powers that be if things could possibly get worse but he was too afraid if he did, they would.

Trying to suck up his courage, Saris wiped the tears from his eyes and climbed to his feet. He looked up at the outcropping of rocks over his head, determined that he would reach them but unsure of how to do it.

There wasn't a set of stairs in sight. Grabbing a hold of the nearest rock, Saris climbed to the next one, then the next, and the next. Surprisingly, he had climbed to the ledge of a small cave before he knew it.

Holding the phase pistol in his hand for protection, Saris entered the cave. He hoped to find it empty. The opening itself wasn't any larger than a set of double doors on the ship. But a few steps inside and the cave opened up.

Saris stared around the cave, his mouth dropping open in shock. Inside seemed huge, massive even. It looked bigger than a cargo bay. Large stalagmites covered one side of the room. The rest seemed to be covered in sand.

From what Saris could tell, most of the cave seemed to be made of some sort of limestone. Hopefully, it would hold in the heat when it became dark outside if they had a fire. If he could transfer both men up the cliff edge, this place would be perfect.

Saris made his way back down the face of the cliff and back across the meadow to the escape pod. Both of his patients were still unconscious. At first, Saris wasn't sure how to transport the two motionless men and the supplies they would need.

Knowing that he only had the strength make a few trips, Saris went back to the pod and searched the supply box for the tarp and some rope, things that were always present in case of emergencies.

He tied the rope to two edges of the tarp, leaving a length between the two tied ends that would fit around his body. Once done, Saris unbuckled Trajan and pulled him out of the escape pod and onto the tarp.

He pulled several items out of the supply box and tucked them around Trajan, hoping that they would stay in place. Closing the door behind them, Saris began pulling Trajan toward the cave.

The distance between the pod and the cave didn't seem so far when he had walked there and back. Tied to a tarp, pulling Trajan and a few items from the supply box behind him, the cave seemed a million miles away.

Once there, Saris sat down and took a moment to catch his breath. He could already feel the muscles in his arms and legs tensing from the strain, and he hadn't even gotten Trajan inside the cave yet.

Knowing no one could do the work except him, Saris got to his feet and carried the supplies up the rocks to the cave. He came back out and repeated the process with Trajan.

Saris carefully settled Trajan on the sand, the supplies stacked across from him, before moving back outside. He still had another man to rescue and more supplies to retrieve. After that, he suspected that collecting some firewood would be a good idea.

It took Saris nearly an hour to get everything moved from the escape pod to the cave. It took another hour to cover the pod with some fallen branches and leaves. He knew that Chellak and his warriors wouldn't be able to find them if he hid the pod, but neither would the bad guys.

He spent just a little more time gathering firewood and getting water from the river on the opposite side of the meadow before heading back to the cave. By the time Saris carried the last of his load into the cave he felt like his arms might fall off.

Exhaustion overwhelmed him. He could sleep for a week if given the chance. He just wished he had the chance. Saris went around organizing their supplies, double checking what exactly they had, and seeing to the comfort of his patients. He bandaged Trajan's head wound and covered both him and the other man with a silver warming blanket.

As the darkness outside grew, Saris wanted to start a fire, but he was afraid to without Trajan telling him it was okay. Saris didn't know much about survival, but he did know that smoke could be seen from the air.

Knowing that there woube be nothing he could do until Trajan woke up, Saris settled his tired body down next to him and covered them both up with the silver warming blanket. The warmth of Trajan's body against his fought off the chill that had begun to settle in Saris's bones.

It felt nice to have someone to cuddle up with. He had never experienced it before. It made him wonder if being someone's mate had other benefits as well. He began to think that this mating thing wasn't half bad. Now if only his mate would wake up.

Chapter 6

Trajan groaned. His head felt like it had been bashed in with a hammer. He opened his eyes cautiously and glanced around, surprised to find himself inside somewhere besides the bridge of his ship. The darkness that surrounded him made it hard to tell.

Check that, surrounded them, Trajan thought when he noticed the man curled up by his side. He leaned his head out a bit so that he could peer down at the face of the man with his ass pressed back against Trajan's groin.

Trajan knew he looked at Saris even before he saw his beautiful face. The unique scent that belonged only to his mate permeated the air around them, sinking into Trajan's senses and filling his heart with joy.

The last thing he remembered was ordering Saris to the escape pod and then a large explosion rocked the ship. Hearing a noise, Trajan had looked up just as a large beam fell from the ceiling above him. After that, everything went blank.

As Trajan's eyes slowly adjusted to the darkness, he noted that they seemed to be inside of a large cavern. The young man that he had rescued along with Saris slept several feet away from them. Trajan wondered if he had woken up yet.

A stack of firewood, a couple jugs of water, and the supplies from the escape pod were stacked neatly against the far wall. Trajan knew that Saris had been responsible for that. Something about the man told Trajan his mate was a neat freak.

The scent of his mate floated up to Trajan again as Saris moved in his sleep. Trajan groaned, feeling his cock harden against Saris's tight little ass. He knew his little mate no longer felt the effects of the drugs forced into his system.

Knowing this and unable to deny himself a moment more, Trajan moved his hand down over Saris's chest, reaching for the hidden zipper to his body suit. He slipped his hand inside of the opening, delighting in the feel of Saris's smooth skin.

Trajan had been around the block a time or two. It wasn't something he felt ashamed of, just a fact. But his usual bed partners, while being temporary because they weren't his mate, had all been Katzmen. Trajan had never been with someone outside of his species.

He certainly had never been with someone that didn't have a fine covering of hair over their entire bodies. As his hand moved farther down Saris's smooth chest, Trajan decided that he much preferred the silky texture of the hairless skin beneath his fingers.

Trajan moved his hand back up Saris's chest until his fingers encountered a little nub. He gently tugged on the nipple. Saris's growing arousal filled the air around them, overwhelming Trajan's senses.

Needing to know if Saris was in fact aroused more than he needed his next breath, Trajan reached down and cupped Saris's cock in his hand. A low groan fell from his lips when he felt the cock harden through the fabric of the bodysuit.

He gave it a little squeeze, groaning again when Saris humped his hips at him. Trajan couldn't stand it anymore. He needed to claim his mate once and for all. The need overwhelmed him, consuming him until he felt nothing else.

"Sari," Trajan whispered into Saris's ear. "Wake up, my own."

Trajan gave Saris a little shake. He gritted his teeth against the agony produced when Saris simply rolled onto his side and pushed his ass back against Trajan's raging hard on. Trajan swore he could feel the tightness of Saris's ass through the thin fabric.

"Sari," he said again, this time a little louder. His eyes briefly lifted to the man sleeping several feet away to see if he still slept. He seemed to be asleep, or at least the snores that Trajan could hear coming from him said so.

Trajan scooted back out of desperation and a need to get rid of his restrictive clothing. He sat up and unbuckled his boots, pushing them down his feet and setting them aside. Then he went to work on his pants and his shirt vest.

Praying desperately that Saris had gotten all of the supplies out of the escape pod, Trajan crawled over to them and searched around. He nearly yelled in triumph when he located a small bottle of oil.

His prize in hand, Trajan crawled back over to Saris and pulled the silver warming blanket back from his naked body. Trajan was naked and horny. He had oil in hand. Now he just had to wake his mate.

"Sari," Trajan whispered into Saris's ear again. This time he followed it up with a long lick of his tongue along the pointed edge of Saris's ear. Saris responded with a small moan, a smile flittering across his lips.

So apparently Saris liked his ears licked. *Good to know*, Trajan thought as he did it again. This time he added a small nibble with his lips. He nearly jumped out of his skin when Saris purred.

It stunned Trajan so much that he was unable to move for a moment. His mate purred! Trajan knew under certain stimuli that Katzmen could purr, but he had never heard of another species making that noise.

Joy filled Trajan to bursting. He leaned down and ran his tongue along the soft shell of Saris's pointed ear, nibbling at the edge with his lips. *Yes, more purring!* Wanting more, Trajan pushed his hand inside of Saris's bodysuit and tugged on his nipple at the same time.

Soon, Saris began to move. His hands started caressing Trajan's arms. His hips pushed back against Trajan's hard cock. The little aroused purrs coming from his throat grew louder, more intense.

"Sari," Trajan growled, "wake up, my mate, wake up so I can claim you." He could feel himself coming to the end of his endurance.

His control hung on by a thread. This time when he licked the edge of Saris's ear, he used his teeth and bit down just a little.

It had the desired response. Saris's purr turned into a groan and his eyes opened. He blinked several times as if he didn't quite know where he was. For a brief moment, Trajan thought Saris had succumbed to the drugs again.

Then, long delicate fingers cupped Trajan's face and a wide grin was aimed in his direction.

"Trajan, you're awake," Saris whispered.

"So are you, my own," Trajan responded. He gave Saris just a moment to realize that they lay cuddled together before using his tongue to cares the edge of Saris's ear again. Saris groaned, a shudder moving down his body.

"Wha...what are you doing?"

The husky tone of Saris's voice sent a matching shudder through Trajan's body. His hand moved down to cup Saris's cock through the bodysuit again. His lips went back to licking and nibbling.

"I'm claiming my mate," Trajan whispered between nibbles. He paused, his teeth scraping over the edge of Saris's ear as he pulled back a little. "If you want me to stop, tell me now, but remember, if you agree, this is forever."

Saris remained silent. Trajan wondered if he had crossed some line with Saris that couldn't be uncrossed. When Saris tilted his head back to look up at him, Trajan braced himself, expecting to see anger and resentment.

What he saw instead made his heart pound in his chest for just a moment before it flew free. "Sari?"

"You promise you won't ever return me or cancel our contract?" Saris whispered.

Trajan felt tears gather in his eyes. He shook his head. "No, Sari, I won't ever return you or cancel our contract. I'll never let you go. If I have anything to say about it, you will never leave my side."

Saris's misty eyes begged Trajan not to lie to him. Trajan shook his head in response because tears clogged his throat and he couldn't speak. He leaned down and pressed a gentle kiss to Saris's lips.

Before he could lift his head, Trajan felt Saris's arms wrap around his neck, pulling him closer. The calm Trajan worked so hard to reclaim a moment ago shattered under the hunger of Saris's kiss. It sang through Trajan's veins and ignited a fire that only Saris could quench.

Giving himself up to the passion of the kiss, Trajan's tongue caressed the soft fullness of Saris's lips. He crushed Saris's body to his, delighting in the feel of it pressed against him.

Trajan's lips continued to explore the recesses of Saris's mouth. His hands pushed and pulled at the bodysuit covering the smooth skin he wanted to feel with his hands. Finally, he pushed the offending fabric down Saris's legs.

Smooth, silky skin pressed against his body. His heart jolted and his pulse pounded. His hands slipped up Saris's arms, bringing him closer. His lips moved to the soft contours of Saris's mouth, over his cheek, and back up to the edge of his ear.

He felt the occasional brush of Saris's thigh against his hip. Hands moved down his back to his hips and back up to grasp Trajan's jaw, bringing his mouth back to Saris's. Trajan's body tingled at the contact.

"Sari," Trajan groaned against Saris's lips, "I need…"

"Yes," Saris murmured back.

Trajan's heart raced. Saris opened his legs, throwing one leg over Trajan's hip and crooking it. His knee came to rest near Trajan's armpit. Trajan turned, gently easing Saris down onto their makeshift bed.

Saris buried his face against Trajan's neck. Trajan poured the oil into his hand then moved down to the soft curve of Saris's hip and beyond. He carefully moved his fingers between Saris's butt cheeks to the hidden entrance there.

He moved in, brushing his fingers over the puckered hole. Saris jerked in his arms, but a small groan escaped the lips pressed against Trajan's neck. More strokes brought more moans, then whimpers.

The purring began when Trajan pushed one oil covered finger into Saris's tight hole. Saris's body moved against his as he began pushing his finger in, then pulling it out. Trajan didn't know if he would make it long enough to feel Saris wrapped around his aching cock.

Trajan added another finger. Saris began to move wildly. Trajan felt his hands clench desperately at his shoulders. Soft bites pressed into the skin of his neck. Long limber legs wrapped around his hips.

"Are you ready for me, my own?" Trajan whispered, his breath heaving against Saris's ear. "Are you ready for me to claim you as my mate?"

Saris stilled, his head falling back, his eyes finding Trajan's in the darkness. "Yes," Saris whispered.

Trajan let his eyes briefly close in thanks to all of the powers that be for the gift granted to him the moment he met Saris. Trajan opened his eyes and gazed down at the beautiful face looking up at him.

He was fully aware of the hardness of Saris's thighs over his as he slowly pressed his way past the first ring of muscles, then farther in until he felt the soft tickle of Saris's pubic hair against him.

Once he pushed in all the way, Trajan paused. He lifted himself up onto one arm. Using the sharp claws on the other, he cut a small cut in his chest just over his heart. Reaching down to cradle the back of Saris's head with his hand, he lifted him.

"Drink, my own."

Trajan's head fell back and he closed his eyes. A long groan rushed from his lips as Saris's lips touched his skin, his tongue lapping at the blood. Saris's eager response seemed to match his.

A spurt of hungry desire shot through Trajan. He leaned over his mate and sank his sharp canines deep into the soft skin between his neck and shoulder. Trajan was totally unprepared for the sweet taste that filled him.

He began to thrust his hips, pushing his hard cock deep into Saris's tight grasp, then pulling out. The dance would almost immediately start again when Trajan thrust back in. Over and over he moved until his whole body flooded with desire.

Pulling his teeth from Saris and licking away the dripping blood, Trajan grasped Saris's face in his hands. He stared down into Saris's green eyes as he moved, stunned by the emotions he could see there. He was the glowing image of fire, passion, and love. He was mate.

Trajan roared as he yielded to the burning passion consuming him. An answering cry met his, and he felt Saris's hot seed spill between their bodies even as he filled Saris with his own. With one last thrust, Trajan felt the knot at the end of his cock extend and lock him into place within his mate. He never wanted to leave.

Trajan dropped his head forward to rest against Saris's shoulder. His chest heaved with the enormity of what had just happened to him, of what still happened to him. Soft hands caressed his back as he tried to regain some control.

"Sari?" Trajan whispered telepathically, hoping that they had been gifted with the mating bond. When Saris didn't answer him, Trajan lifted his head and looked down at him. Rapid breaths escaped Saris's slightly parted lips, his eyes closed.

"Sari?" Trajan whispered again.

His eyes widened when Saris growled at him through clenched teeth. "Move, damn it."

Trajan knew that they were still knotted together. If he moved too much he could injure Saris, but just a little shouldn't be a problem. Trajan thrust his hips forward. Saris groaned. He did it again and again until Saris cried out, a wetness filling the space between them again.

When the knot finally receded, Trajan reluctantly pulled from his mate and rolled them both to their sides, Saris's head pressed against his throat. Trajan wrapped his arms around him, holding him close.

"You okay, Sari?" Trajan asked out loud.

"I'm not sure," Saris said, chuckling.

"Do you hurt?" Trajan asked, suddenly worried that he might have injured his mate.

Saris shook his head. "No."

"Then what's wrong?" Confusion filled Trajan. Saris wasn't acting like he thought a newly bonded mate would act.

"I can't move."

Trajan instantly loosened his arms. "Am I holding you too tight?"

Saris chuckled again. "No. You're holding me just right."

Trajan got more confused by the moment. He opened his mouth to ask Saris what was really wrong when he felt a hand pat him on the chest. Surprised, considering Saris's words, Trajan glanced down only to realize that it was indeed Saris's hand.

"I'm okay," Saris said. "I'm just tired."

Trajan let out a relieved sigh thankful that he hadn't done anything to harm his mate. That would devastate him. As Trajan held Saris to him, his eyes strayed to the carefully organized stack of stuff on the opposite wall.

"Did you do all of that?" Trajan asked, gesturing to the supplies, stacked firewood, and jugs of water.

Saris turned his head to look where Trajan pointed, then glanced back. Saris shrugged, dipping his head as if embarrassed. "Yeah, it seemed like the thing to do at the time."

"I thought I was supposed to be rescuing you, not the other way around."

"Oh, you're more than welcome to take over the job, believe me," Saris said. "This emergency preparedness stuff is for the birds!"

"What happened? I thought I ordered you to the escape pod."

Saris laughed. "You did, but one thing you'll learn about me is that I have a real hard time following orders." Saris's eyes moved up to meet Trajan's. "Especially if I feel strongly about something or someone."

"So, you ignored my orders?"

"Hell yes," Saris said. "The computer read down the time before life support would be shut off and explosions went off all over the place."

"Which is exactly why I wanted you safely onboard the escape pod," Trajan reminded Saris. Inwardly, he felt pleased that his mate had risked his life to save him, even though he wasn't happy the danger Saris experienced. It showed that Saris cared for him on some level.

"Trajan, I couldn't leave you there to die, and we both know that's exactly what you planned on doing."

"Sari, I—"

Saris sat up. "You can't tell me that that's not what you planned, Trajan. You'd be lying."

Trajan didn't have a way to argue with Saris. He had known he would die onboard his ship when he had sent Saris away. Someone had to stay and steer the ship, distract their attacker until the escape pod could get away. That someone wasn't going to be his mate.

"So, what did happen?" Trajan asked as he pulled Saris back down into his arms. He chuckled when he saw Saris roll his eyes. It looked like his mate wasn't going to be a submissive type of person like Demyan. Trajan wasn't sure that was a blessing or a curse.

"You got knocked out by a falling beam. I pulled you free, got us to the escape pod, and away we went. I'm sorry, Trajan, but your ship exploded while we escaped."

Trajan nodded. He wasn't happy about losing his ship, but having his mate alive and well meant a whole lot more. Still, it had been a good little ship, getting him where he needed to go and mostly keeping his ass out of trouble.

"So how did we end up in a cave?" Trajan finally asked.

Saris groaned. "It wasn't easy, I can tell you that. You need to consider a diet because your ass is heavy when you're out cold."

Trajan chuckled. He could just imagine. Well, no he couldn't. He'd never been in this particular situation before. "Sari, how did you get me into this cave?"

Saris pointed across the room to the folded up tarp. "I loaded you on that and pulled you here. Then I went back for your little friend over there. Next, the supplies."

"And the escape pod?"

"It's outside across the meadow." Saris looked like he was contemplating something for a moment. "I disabled the locating beacon and covered the pod with branches."

Trajan frowned, surprised. "Why would you do that?"

"One of the ships attacking us was destroyed when your ship exploded, but the other one is still out there. As this is the closest habitable planet and a sure place for us to land, I didn't want us to be discovered until you had regained consciousness."

Saris leaned his head back and glanced up at Trajan. He had a worried look on his face. "I consider myself a pretty smart cookie, but I can't fight my way out of any situation, Trajan. I'm more likely to stab myself in the foot than fight off an adversary."

Trajan chuckled, patting Saris on the arm. "That's okay, Sari, you have me for that."

"Do I?" Saris asked with a bit of his uncertainty written on his face.

"We've mated now, Sari. That means you belong to me and I belong to you," Trajan assured Saris. "I'll never send you home. I'll never cancel our contract. And I'll never let you go."

"Promise?" Saris whispered.

"I promise, Sari."

"You wouldn't lie to me, would you?"

"I'll never lie to you, Sari," Trajan assured him.

"Then would you please tell me how in the hell we're going to get off of this damn planet?"

Chapter 7

"Here, Sari, I got you something to eat," Trajan said as he held a tin of food out to him. Saris sat up, grabbing the tin. He gave it a small sniff, his nose crinkling in distaste.

"What the hell is this swill?"

Trajan chuckled. "Uh, I believe it's Chicken ala King, but I could be wrong." He glanced down at the tin in his hand, eyeing the glob of cream colored goo doubtfully. "Very, very wrong."

"I don't suppose there's some fresh fruit in there?" Saris asked, nodding toward the supplies.

Trajan shook his head. "Nope. Emergency rations are compact, made to last long periods of time, and aimed toward giving us the most nutrients with the least amount of taste."

"That's reassuring."

"Isn't it?" Trajan took another bite from his tin, gulping past the bland taste. He took another few bites then set the tin down on the sand next to him. He didn't know if he could stomach another bite, no matter how hungry he felt.

"How about I go out and see if I can catch us something to cook over a fire?" Trajan asked, looking across at his mate. He chuckled at the surprised look on Saris's face.

"You can do that?"

"Sure," Trajan said as he pushed himself forward onto his knees, his face within an inch of Saris's. "They teach us all sorts of neat stuff like that at warrior training school."

"Oh yeah?" Saris asked, his voice sounding husky, filled with need.

"Yeah." Trajan leaned closer and ran his tongue along the edge of Saris's plump lips. He grinned when he heard Saris groan.

"They teach you *that* in warrior training school?" Saris asked, his voice low and seductive. It made Trajan's toes curl.

"No, I learned that all on my own."

Saris's lips thinned. "From whom?"

Trajan's eyebrows shot up. Did he detect a bit of jealousy in his mate's tone? Trajan wasn't sure he could adequately express the joy that brought him. "I don't remember."

"Been with that many people, have you?"

Trajan bit his lip, suppressing his grin. "No, but they don't matter anymore. They aren't my mate. You are."

Trajan felt the intensity of Saris's stare. He seemed to be measuring Trajan's words for their truthfulness. Trajan knew that Saris had no reason to believe him. They had only known each other for a few days. True, they had been eventful days, but still, it wasn't a lot of time to get to know someone.

After a moment, Saris nodded. "Good answer."

Trajan let out a relieved breath. "Good enough for a kiss?"

Saris laughed. "Maybe."

"What would I have to do to convince you?" Trajan liked this game. It filled him with light and joy, made him believe that all was right in the world. And all of it due to his gorgeous mate. Trajan determined that they would have many moments like this.

He was mildly surprised, and forever grateful, that his mate had such a playful personality. Besides Saris being intelligent, humorous, and downright sexy, Trajan respected the man.

Expecting a kiss, shock filled Trajan when Saris held the small tin of food out to him. "Find me something to eat that doesn't taste like kuhmucca dung."

Trajan's lips twitched. He leaned forward quickly and stole a kiss from Saris before climbing to his feet. He grinned down at Saris. "Consider that my incentive." He walked over to the supplies, grabbed the phase gun and a small length of rope then headed for the mouth of the cave. His mate wanted something to eat? Trajan could provide that.

* * * *

Saris watched Trajan walk out of the cave, still a little stunned with how quickly the man had agreed to go find him some real food. The creamy glob in the tin Trajan had given him could not be considered food. Nutrients? Yes. Food? No.

He thought over the last couple days since he had met Trajan. If nothing else, they had been eventful. Between being reclassified as a pleasure slave, being rescued by Trajan only to learn they were mates, and being shot out of space by someone hunting them, Saris wondered what would happen next.

He wasn't sure he wanted to know. Granted, he'd go through it all over again if it meant meeting Trajan. Saris had never met a man like him. Trajan seemed easy going, funny, and loving. He also seemed totally committed to trying to make their unusual relationship work.

The tingle that shot down his spine when he thought of Trajan and the things they had done together earlier didn't surprise Saris. Trajan was gorgeous and sexy and totally drool worthy.

Saris hadn't expected to feel the connection to Trajan that he did. He worried about him being outside all on his own. He worried that something would happen and he would never see Trajan again. He worried that Trajan would be injured and Saris wouldn't know. Hell, he just plain worried.

Could he really make Trajan happy? Could he fulfill the needs of a Katzman? He knew from his research that Katzmen naturally had very active libidos. The sum of Saris's sexual experience could be counted on one hand. He didn't know if he could satisfy Trajan.

The whole mating thing just topped off the last couple of days. According to Trajan, as mates, they had a special connection, one that only they would share between them. It went soul-deep.

It made Saris wonder why they couldn't speak mentally as Chellak and Demyan could. They had mated, they had exchanged blood as the mating ritual required. Saris had even felt Trajan's knot lodge inside of him. In fact, he delighted in it. Were they truly mates?

Trajan said he wouldn't lie to Saris. He would always tell the truth. Saris hoped so. If this all turned out to be some sick joke or just Trajan's way of getting down his bodysuit, Saris wasn't sure he would be able to live through it.

Shaking his head at the morose direction his thoughts had taken, Saris got to his feet and walked over to the young man still sleeping across the way. The man remained unconscious. It concerned Saris.

He couldn't find any signs of trauma other than the injection spot for the blue liquid. It looked a little red, but nothing more than Saris expected from an injection tube. Other than that, nothing explained the young man's condition.

Until he had access to more modern technologies, Saris could only make him comfortable. Saris wet a rag and squeezed a few small drops onto the man's lips then wiped down his face and neck. With nothing else to do, he covered him back up and walked to the mouth of the cave.

From where he stood on the edge of the small rock ledge, Saris could see across the meadow to the river and the tress beyond. Off to one side he saw the escape pod, still covered with branches and leaves.

It looked to be midday, the sun from above shining down as a soft wind blew through the tall green grass. Trees gently swayed in the breeze. All in all, it looked like the perfect setting. Except that Trajan was out there somewhere all alone.

Saris would give anything to be with Trajan. He knew he wouldn't be much help, but at least they would be together. And if something happened to Trajan, Saris could be there to help him, give him medical attention.

Saris disliked not knowing where Trajan, if he had been hurt or worse. He knew somewhere out there, Trajan hunted for food. He could at least feel that. Saris attributed it to the mating bond. He just wished that they had developed the telepathy part. Then Saris could contact Trajan and assure himself that nothing had happened to his mate.

With nothing to do but wait, Saris decided to gather more firewood and refill the water jugs. Granted, they had yet to use any of the firewood and only a bit of the water, but it never hurt to be prepared.

It took Saris less than thirty minutes to complete his task. Standing on the edge of the rocks again, Saris cast one more look out over the meadow for Trajan. This waiting thing sucked big time.

As he started to turn and head back into the cave a flash of something moving through the edge of trees on the far side of the meadow caught his eye. Saris paused, squinting for a better look. His heart hammered in his chest when he recognized Trajan.

A delighted bounce in his step, Saris jumped down from the rocks he stood on and ran across the field toward his mate. He could see the wide grin that crossed Trajan's face when he spotted Saris running in his direction.

Trajan had just enough time to drop his catch on the ground before Saris threw himself into his arms. Saris heard him chuckle, his strong arms wrapping around him.

"More welcome homes like that and I might have to leave every day."

"Leave again and you won't be welcomed home again," Saris responded with a small snarl. He pushed himself away from Trajan trying to pretend that he wasn't relieved that the warrior had come back safe.

"What did you get me to eat?" Saris asked, quickly changing the subject.

"Do I get a kiss?" Trajan asked, one eyebrow raised in a way that irritated Saris to no end. It made him feel like Trajan could see right through him and tell how emotional he felt despite his calm demeanor.

Saris crossed his arms over his chest and glared up at Trajan. He ignored the grin on Trajan's face. "Do I get dinner?"

Trajan countered. "Do I get a kiss?"

Saris knew he acted childish, but he couldn't help it. He had been so worried about Trajan and he felt like Trajan made light of his concern. He stomped his foot on the ground.

"Oh!" he growled, "go soak your head."

Saris turned on his heel and started back toward the cave only to be stopped by two powerful arms wrapping around him from behind. He felt Trajan's body press against his, his soft breath on his neck.

"What's wrong, Sari?" Trajan asked softly.

Saris leaned his head back against Trajan's shoulder. He took several deep breaths, blinking to clear the tears that had gathered in his eyes. He didn't like this new emotional turmoil he felt. His emotions seemed to be out of control, nearly raging.

He felt like it unmanned him, made him less than what he was. But he couldn't seem to stop them. He felt anxious and confused. At the same time he felt desperate and needy. And all of it narrowed down to one gorgeous man, the one that held Saris in his arms.

"Sari?"

"Nothing," Saris replied quietly. "Nothing is wrong, Trajan, I'm just hungry."

Saris wasn't sure that Trajan would buy his explanation, but he wasn't ready to discuss his chaotic emotions just yet. Hell, he wasn't sure he would ever be ready to discuss them. He had been taught from an early age not to have them or, at least not to express them.

It sucked, but it was the way things were done on Elquone. Those of the Brüter Caste weren't allowed to show emotion at any cost. Emotions meant attachment, want, need.

Emotions meant that when the brüter returned to Elquone after his contract had been fulfilled he would be unfit to be contracted out again. Saris had watched it happen with his brother, Karis, and he never wanted to experience it for himself. It destroyed people.

"Well, luckily, I found a couple of rabbits running around," Trajan said. He reached down and picked up the catch he dropped earlier. He held them up in the air for Saris to see.

"There's not much to them, but there should be enough for us to have a good dinner tonight and maybe breakfast tomorrow morning."

"You think we're going to be here that long?"

"What?" Trajan asked looking away from the dead rabbits to look at Saris. "No. At least, I hope not. Chellak should be looking for us even now. But it never hurts to be prepared just in case."

Saris nodded. He had that very thought several times. "So, do you know how to cook these things?" he asked, pointing to the two dead rabbits.

Trajan nodded, grinning. "Just another skill from warrior training school."

"You seem to have learned a lot of things from warrior training school," Saris replied as they started making their way back across the meadow. "What else did you learn?"

"Well, I'm pretty good in a fight, although Chellak has handed me my head a time or two."

"Seriously?" Saris asked. He wasn't sure he liked the idea of anyone touching Trajan in any way. His little spout of jealousy earlier had surprised him. The thought of Chellak Rai fighting with Trajan in fun or for real just made him angry.

"Most of it was all for fun," Trajan said quickly.

"Most of it?"

Trajan shrugged. "We did get into it a couple of times when we had a difference of opinion. Katzmen can be a stubborn lot."

"No!" Saris exclaimed in mock shock. "Really?"

Trajan's lips twitched. "Brat!"

Saris chuckled. "You did walk into that one, Trajan."

"You didn't have to walk away with it," Trajan complained, but Saris could tell he wasn't really offended. The grin on his face told him that much.

"Yeah, I did."

* * * *

Trajan sat across the fire from Saris watching him lick his fingers clean. They had just finished eating the rabbit Trajan caught and cooked. Watching Saris lick his fingers made Trajan wish Saris would lick something else.

He doubted Saris had a clue how sexy he really looked, or how aroused Trajan felt just watching him eat. It was stupid to be turned on from watching Saris eat. But each stroke of Saris's tongue made Trajan ache.

Even the damn firelight seemed to be against him at the moment. The soft red glow of the flames cast just enough light to make Saris seem almost ethereal. The delicate contours of Saris's face, the lean muscles of his chest, the soft curve of his hips, all designed to drive Trajan crazy. He just knew it.

Trajan wanted nothing more than to cross the room, take his mate in his arms, and claim him again. But something had happened to Saris while he had gone hunting. Trajan didn't know what exactly, but something felt different.

Saris would converse with him, even laugh and joke, but the moment Trajan crossed some invisible line between them, Saris backed off faster than Trajan could blink. It felt as if he couldn't stand to be intimate with Trajan.

And it made Trajan's heart ache. Saris had agreed to be his mate the night before. Trajan hadn't forced him. He had even given him several opportunities to decline. Saris hadn't declined. He had accepted being Trajan's mate and even seemed enthusiastic about it.

He dropped his eyes from the tantalizing sight of his mate to look down at the sand beneath his feet, anything not to look at Saris. He knew that if he continued to look at him, he wouldn't be able to keep himself from claiming him.

Trajan just didn't understand. Maybe this explained why they couldn't communicate telepathically. Maybe Saris didn't really want to be his mate. Trajan guessed it could always be a possibility.

As big and as strong as Trajan appeared, he knew it would be a natural reaction for someone like Saris to look to him for protection. He just hoped that Saris knew that that protection didn't come at a price. He'd protect Saris no matter what. That's what warriors did.

If Saris agreed to be his mate because he thought he had to in order for Trajan to protect him, Trajan felt pretty sure his heart would break. He wanted Saris to want him for him and not because his strength meant he could protect the man.

"Sari," Trajan said, lifting his head to look across the fire at him. "You know I would protect you and take care of you even if you weren't my mate, don't you?"

Surprised eyes looked up at him. "Yeah, I know that."

Okay, so that wasn't it, Trajan thought as he looked back down at the sand. He picked up a small stick and made doodle lines in the sand as his thoughts moved about in his head.

Had he done something to cause Saris to not want to be with him anymore? Trajan racked his brain and tried to think of anything he might have done to make Saris angry or upset. The only thing he could think of was when he had asked for a kiss. Saris had looked pissed.

Trajan felt like someone squeezed his heart in his chest as he realized that Saris might be angry at him for asking for a kiss. Did

Saris not like kissing? Had Trajan done it wrong? Had he done it too much? Was asking for a kiss wrong where Saris came from? Had he insulted Saris by asking?

Question after question flew through Trajan's mind and doubts began to fill him. Just because he felt the mating bond between them didn't mean Saris did, too. He said he had studied the Katzman race and knew of the bond. He had readily accepted it.

Trajan wondered if Saris ever really wanted to be his mate in the first place or if he had just accepted it. Or had he? Maybe that was the problem. Maybe Saris hadn't accepted their mating. That would explain why they weren't able to speak telepathically.

Even if they had mated, if they didn't truly accept each other then they wouldn't be able to speak to each other in such an intimate way. The more Trajan thought about it, the more that it made sense, and the more it made his heart hurt.

Trajan blinked several times to clear away the tears forming in his eyes. He stood up and started toward the mouth of the cave before Saris spotted the wetness in his eyes that threatened to spill down his face.

There was no point in Saris knowing how much agony filled him. Besides the fact that Trajan wasn't sure Saris would even care, he didn't want Saris to feel pressured into being nice to him. Or, gods forbid, pretend.

"Where are you going?" Saris called out just as Trajan reached the entrance to the cave.

Trajan paused. He turned his head just a little to acknowledge Saris, but not enough for his face to show. "I need to scout around just a little before it gets too dark outside. I want to make sure we're still hidden."

He waited for a response from Saris, any response. When none came, Trajan walked out into the cold air that had settled in the small valley. He got as far as the edge of the cliff before he had to sit down before he fell down.

His misery felt like a physical pain as it filled him. His eyes burned from holding the tears in. His head pounded. Trajan covered his mouth with his hand as a raw, primitive grief overwhelmed him.

Trajan knew he felt things strongly. He always had. Chellak had often accused him of being too emotional. Right now, he almost wished he felt nothing at all. That would be much better than this all-consuming heartache.

Trajan almost cried out at his sense of loss as he thought about Saris. He couldn't keep Saris if he truly didn't want to be together, and Trajan would never force him. That meant giving Saris his freedom.

Trajan wasn't sure he would survive it. He wasn't sure he wanted to. Being without his mate after bonding with him would be akin to a death sentence. Trajan had seen it happen before with other Katzmen who had lost their mates. They slowly lost their minds.

Katzmen were very possessive of their mates. They needed to know that they were safe and happy at all times. It became a driving force in their lives once they found their mates. To be separated and not able to protect or care for their mates was more than most Katzmen could handle.

Trajan suspected from the misery he felt just thinking about it that he would be one of the ones that totally lost it. He knew without Saris, he would grow more and more careless with his safety, not caring what happened to him.

He might even look forward to his own death, anything to get away from the loss. That knowledge twisted and turned inside of him because he knew it would come. His heart still squeezed with anguish as he realized that he would do anything to make Saris happy, even give him up.

"Trajan?" murmured a sweet voice behind him. "Are you coming to bed soon?"

Chapter 8

Saris didn't know how he knew that Trajan was upset, but he did know. He could feel the anguish flowing from him. Trajan's emotions swirled around and twisted together with Saris's until he didn't know who felt what.

Saris felt overwhelmed. The emotions inside of him, the emotions he felt coming from Trajan, confused him. He needed something to keep him grounded, to keep him from going crazy. He needed Trajan.

"Trajan?" Saris asked again.

"Yeah, I'll be right there," Trajan answered, but he didn't turn around to look at Saris, and he didn't sound happy about being disturbed.

Saris knew that he was being overly emotional again, and he should probably be ashamed of himself, but right now he didn't really care. He needed to feel Trajan's hands on his skin, feel their bodies pressed together.

Taking the few steps that separated them, Saris wrapped his arms around Trajan's neck and pressed his body against him. He felt a shudder pass through Trajan's body. Before he could wonder about it, two arms grabbed him and pulled him around to sit in Trajan's lap.

Saris inhaled deeply when he glanced up and saw Trajan's face. Tears glistened on his eyelids, his face filled with misery. He heard a low, choking sob and suddenly Trajan wrapped his arms around Saris's body, almost crushing him.

"I'll do anything for you to stay with me," Trajan whispered against Saris's hair. "We can go wherever you want, do whatever you want. I'll even sign a contract for you if that's what you want."

Saris was stunned. "You…you don't sign contracts," he said quickly. "It's against your laws to own slaves."

"I don't care," Trajan snarled as he lifted his head to stare down at Saris. The tears on his eyelashes slid slowly down his cheeks. "If that's what you need, I'll break the law. Or we can go somewhere that it's not against the law, someplace outside of the Federation."

"You'd leave Katzmann for me?"

Trajan's brows drew together in a frown. "I'd do anything for you, Sari."

Saris swallowed hard and bit back his own tears. "Trajan, I would never ask you to do something like that."

"You're not asking me, Sari," Trajan insisted. "If that's what you need to stay, we'll do it. I can make arrangements for us as soon as we get back to Katzmann. I don't have a lot of money, but it should be enough to set us up somewhere else."

Saris's eyes widened. He couldn't think of anything immediately to say to Trajan. What could he say? Trajan was offering to give everything in his life, his people, his home world, his very belief system, just for him.

Even as he thought over Trajan's words Saris knew that he couldn't let that happen. If he took everything away from Trajan, he wouldn't be Trajan. Being a Katzman warrior for Chellak wasn't just a job for Trajan. It filled every fiber of his being.

Besides, Saris could be a doctor anywhere as long as that anywhere included Trajan. Saris reached up and cradled Trajan's face with his hands. He pulled his face down for a small kiss.

"Then you agree? You'll stay with me?" Trajan asked the moment that Saris released his lips.

Saris could see the apprehension in Trajan's eyes. He could feel the tension in his body. He sensed the feelings of rejection pouring off of him. He just didn't understand why. They had mated. There shouldn't be any question of Saris leaving.

"Trajan, where do you think I'm going?"

Saris watched, confused, as Trajan squeezed his eyes closed. His body seemed to stiffen even more. When he opened them a moment later they filled with the misery Saris had felt earlier.

"I know you don't want to be with me, that you're only here because you think you have no other option," Trajan murmured quietly. "I know you don't want me, not really."

"Have you lost your mind?" Saris said harshly as he pushed himself away from Trajan. He felt Trajan's hands grasp at him, but he felt too angry to care, too angry to give in to the small whimper he heard come from Trajan.

"I thought we were mates. You told me we were!" Saris shouted. "Did you lie to me?" Saris's hands spread wide as if taking in the entire area. "Was everything a lie?"

"No, I never lied to you, Sari."

"Then why—" Saris stopped speaking, his lips pressing together. He took a deep breath through his nose. He swallowed past the lump in his throat before trying to speak again. "Then why are you saying all of these things to me?" he asked in a much lower tone.

"I saw the way you reacted when I asked you for a kiss," Trajan challenged as he stood to his feet. "I know that you don't want to kiss me, to be with me. I told you that I would protect you no matter what, and I meant it. You don't have to pretend with me, Saris."

Saris had no way of expressing how much it hurt to hear Trajan call him *Saris* instead of *Sari*. Trajan had never called him anything except Sari. It felt like an endearment. He wrapped his arms around himself to ward off the chill that suddenly started to set into his tired body.

"You were making fun of me," Saris murmured as he stared down at the ground. He kicked at the pebbles beneath his feet. "You laughed at me, at my concern for your safety. How did you expect me to act?"

"What are you talking about?" Trajan asked. "I never laughed at you."

"You did," Saris insisted. "You had your eyebrow raised, and you laughed as if what I felt wasn't important. I know I'm supposed to keep my emotions at bay, but I can't seem to do that when I'm around you."

"Keep your emotions at bay?" Saris looked up at the astonished sound ringing in Trajan's voice. "When have I ever asked you to keep your emotions at bay?" Trajan asked.

"Isn't that…well, don't you…but you—" Saris suddenly sat down. He ground the heels of his hand against his eyes as he tried to make sense of his confusion.

"Saris."

Saris dropped his hands to see Trajan squatting down in front of him. He looked concerned and just a little confused himself.

"Saris, if you need to express your emotions, either verbally or physically, then do so. I would never deny you that." Trajan's voice sounded so soft that Saris nearly didn't hear him. "I just want you to be happy."

"I am happy, I mean, I have been happy these last two days with you."

Trajan smiled, but Saris could see that sadness still filled him. He reached over and caressed the side of Trajan's face, then leaned in, and kissed him. "I like kissing you."

Trajan's hand covered Saris's, holding it against his cheek. "I like kissing you, too."

"I don't want to leave you, Trajan," Saris said. "I don't want either of us to leave Katzmann. That's where you belong, where you're needed. I'm just hoping that you want me there with you."

Saris tried to wait patiently for Trajan's reaction. He felt as though he stood on the edge of a very high cliff waiting to either be rescued or fall over the edge to his death. The waiting almost killed him.

"You're my mate," Trajan replied. "Of course I want you with me."

"Of course," Saris said. He pulled his hand from beneath Trajan's and stood to his feet. It surprised him that he could hide his emotions behind a cool smile when inside his heart crumbled into a million pieces at Trajan's words. *Of course.* "We should go in before it gets too cold."

He had only taken a few steps when Trajan stopped him. "Saris, what's going on?"

"What do you mean?"

"A second ago you said you wanted nothing more than to be with me and now you can't get away from me fast enough." Saris jumped when he felt Trajan's hand land on his shoulder. "I want to know what in the hell is going on with you."

"Nothing is going on," Saris said. "I just think we should go inside."

Saris yelped when two large hands picked him up, swung him around, and pinned him to the rock face. He could see the anger burning in Trajan's eyes but, strangely enough, he wasn't afraid of him. Trajan would never hurt him.

"Don't fucking say *nothing*!" Trajan yelled. "I won't play these hot and cold games with you, Saris."

"Hot and cold games?" Saris exclaimed, suddenly just as angry as Trajan looked. "Then stop playing them with me. First you say I'm your mate and you start calling me Sari like it's some sort of endearment, then you start calling me Saris all of a sudden?"

"What do you want me to call you?" Trajan shouted, shaking Saris by his arms. "What do you want from me?"

"I want you to want me and not because of some fucked pheromone shit," Saris shouted right back. "I want you to want me for me. I want you to want to be with me and only me. I want you to love me."

The words came out of Saris's mouth before he could stop them and there wasn't any way he could take them back. They hung in the air between him and Trajan like a razor sharp pendulum getting closer and closer to both of them.

He slowly lowered Saris to his feet but kept him pinned against the hard rock. His hands tangled in Saris's blond hair, tilting his head back. "What do you think this is all about, Sari?" Trajan asked in a low voice.

Saris didn't know what to think. Once again the emotions running rampant through his system seemed to be a mix of his emotions and Trajan's. And they slammed him so hard and so fast that he had trouble processing them.

"I don't know," he finally whispered.

"Well, I don't know what books you studied or who you talked to, but, clearly, you haven't learned the real truth about Katzmen and their mates."

"Then explain it to me."

Trajan was silent for a moment as if he considered what exactly to tell Saris. "Katzmen, me in this instance, wait our entire lives to find our mates. It's something we look forward to with great anticipation and not because of some so-called 'fucked pheromone shit.'"

Saris tried to drop his eyes from Trajan's intense gaze but Trajan wouldn't allow it. "Uh uh, I want you looking into my eyes when I explain this to you so that you will see that I am telling you the truth."

"Trajan," Saris said, but Trajan placed his finger over Saris's lips to stop him.

"When a Katzman finds his mate, it's a time of great celebration for us. We've found our other half, the one person in the entire universe that the gods fated just for us. Our mates make us whole. They give us back a part of ourselves that we don't know is missing until it's returned."

Little by little, with each word that Trajan spoke, warmth began to return to Saris's body. Trajan said everything right, but he had yet to say the most important thing. Saris was afraid that he wouldn't.

"It's not a matter of will we love our mates but how long we have to wait before we can love our mates." Trajan gave him a smile, the first real smile Saris had seen since the whole conversation had started. "My fucked up pheromones made me want you, Sari. They didn't make me love you."

Saris's heart fractured.

"You did that all on your own," Trajan said softly, "with your intelligence and courage, even when you're afraid, your smile and your laughter. Even your anger. That's what made me love you, nothing else."

Saris's heart started to heal. "You love me?"

"I wouldn't have mated you if I didn't love you, Sari."

"You can do that?" Saris asked in confusion. "I thought you had to mate, well, your mate."

Trajan shook his head. "Not exactly. You have to understand, Sari, when we find our mates we have a nearly uncontrollable urge to claim them—"

"But you just said—"

"I said *nearly*, not totally," Trajan said. "If we really cannot love our mates, we are able to keep from mating them. Luckily, when the fates choose our mates for us, they choose the most perfect person for us."

Trajan's hand caressed the side of Saris's face. His look was tender, loving, as he gazed down at Saris. "I know that for me, the fates chose the perfect mate. I couldn't imagine being with anyone else, ever."

Saris felt suddenly overwhelmed with emotions. His mind reeled with confusion. He felt a panic like he had never known well up inside of him. His eyes filled with tears of frustration. He couldn't make sense of the emotions blasting through him.

"Shh, Sari, it's okay," Trajan murmured. He wrapped his arms around Saris. "I didn't tell you all of this to make you feel obligated to me. I just wanted you to understand. If you don't want to be mated to me, you don't have to be."

Saris shook his head frantically. He wasn't upset because of what Trajan told him. In fact, he was thrilled. He just didn't know how to process all of the emotions that bombarded him.

Saris tilted his head back and looked up at Trajan. "I want to be your mate. Don't ever think differently. And I want all of it with you, the mating, the kissing, even the crazy things that have happened to us in the last two days. I just—"

"Just what, my own?"

"We're taught from a very early age to suppress all of our emotions, especially our need for love and acceptance. An emotional brüter is not one best suited to contracting out." Saris shook his head, his mouth opening and closing rapidly as he tried to form the words jumbled in his head. "The emotions I've been feeling since I met you, the emotions I feel coming from you, I can't…I can't—"

"Now see," Trajan said, joy filling his voice and making it lighter, "that's why you're so perfect for me. Chellak always says I'm too emotional. I feel things too much. And you've been taught not to show emotions."

Saris chuckled. He sniffled, wiping the tears from his eyes. "I guess I balance you out."

"You do," Trajan replied. "Remember what I said earlier? When we find our other half we become whole."

Saris sniffled again. "Does that mean you don't mind me falling apart?"

"Not in the least, Sari." Trajan gripped Saris's chin and lifted it. "I think it would be easier on both of us if we were honest about what we felt, though."

"I'm not exactly sure what I'm feeling."

"Then tell me what you're feeling, and I'll help you work them out. I have a lot of experience being emotional."

Saris laughed for a moment then grew somber as he tried to sift through his emotions enough to explain them to Trajan.

"I know I want to be with you. I don't like it when you're gone. I can't tell if you're hurt or if you need me or anything. I can't be there to take care of you if something happens to you and that upsets me."

"So, I guess that means you'll be going with me the next time I go hunting, huh?"

"I feel funny being concerned. You're a warrior. Who's better to take care of you than you?"

Trajan shook his head. "My being a warrior has nothing to do with it, Sari. We worry about the ones we love. What? You think I don't worry about you every second that I'm away from you?"

"I guess."

"No guessing about it. You've already proven that you can handle yourself in a dangerous situation. You took care of me, found us shelter, and transferred all of our stuff while I was unconscious. You even patched me up. I'd say that makes you pretty courageous. Now, what else is confusing you?"

"What if I can't satisfy you?"

"You satisfy me just by breathing. Yes, sex is great, wonderful in fact, but it is not the be all end all of our relationship. Right now, I'd like nothing more than to fuck you where you stand, but I'd be just as happy cuddling with you for the rest of the night."

"Seriously?" Saris asked in surprise.

"Of course. Sex is not mandatory between us, Sari. It's highly encouraged, mind you, but it's not—"

"No, I'm talking about the fucking me part," Saris complained. "You want to fuck me right now?"

"There are a lot of things I'd like to do with you right now, Sari," Trajan replied. "Fucking you is just one of them."

Saris licked his lips. "Like what?"

* * * *

All of the blood in Trajan's head seemed to drain down and pool in his groin at Saris's husky words. While his cock seemed to always be hard around Saris, now it ached, needing his mate.

"Sari," Trajan groaned.

He knew this conversation with Saris was important, that they had a lot of things that they needed to work out. He just couldn't quite remember exactly what they were. The only thought that made sense to him at that moment was feeling Saris's naked body pressed against his.

Trajan's hands went to the hidden zipper on Saris's bodysuit. He worked the zipper down slowly until his knuckles brushed against Saris's abdomen. He chuckled when he heard Saris moan, glad that he wasn't the only one aroused.

He placed one hand on each of Saris's shoulders and pushed the bodysuit off his shoulders and down his body, baring Saris's naked skin inch by glorious inch. With the bodysuit down around Saris's waist, his arms still trapped in the sleeves, Trajan knelt on the ground in front of him.

"This is where the fun begins," he said just before he pushed the bodysuit down enough to free Saris's cock. Impressed, Trajan growled as it bounced up and nearly hit him on the chin. It was a beautiful cock.

Trajan leaned forward and blew across the purplish head, feeling the long shudder that passed through Saris's body. He glanced up. Saris had his lips caught between his teeth, his eyes closed tight.

"You ever have someone take your cock into their mouth before?" When Saris rapidly shook his head, Trajan chuckled. "Then you're going to love this."

Trajan leaned forward again and licked the drop of pre-cum gathering on the head of Saris's cock. He wasn't surprised the delicious taste of Saris mirrored his sweet scent. He licked again and again, savoring each taste.

Finally, he wrapped his lips around the tip and swallowed all of Saris's cock. His hands gripped Saris's hips as he began moving his head back and forth, lavishing Saris's length with his tongue.

He could hear Saris above him whimpering and crying out every time he moved up or down. It spurred him on to do more. As he continued to suck the cock in his mouth he grabbed the bottle of oil he began carrying this morning out of his pocket.

Quickly lubing his fingers, Trajan moved his hand between Saris's legs. He pushed against him with his shoulder, encouraging Saris to spread his legs. It worked. Saris spread his legs enough for Trajan to reach between them and find his hole.

He sucked Saris's cock into his mouth at the same moment he pushed his finger into Saris's puckered hole. Saris cried out above him. Trajan began a slow rhythm of moving his finger in and out of Saris at the same time he sucked his cock up and down.

Trajan wanted Saris so far gone that he would be thinking of nothing but Trajan fucking him. After a few minutes, Trajan added another finger. Saris started bucking his hips. Trajan moved faster.

A third finger made Saris's legs tremble. His cries had turned into one long continuous whine. Needing to feel Saris wrapped around him immediately, Trajan pulled his fingers from him and grabbed the edges of his bodysuit with both hands, ripping it down his body.

Trajan didn't care if it tore. He'd replace it. Right now, having Saris naked was more important. Getting to his feet, Trajan lifted Saris up in his arms. He pulled on Saris's legs until he got the idea and wrapped them around Trajan's waist.

"You ready for me, Sari?" Trajan asked, his voice sounding unsteady even to him.

"Yes, gods yes, I need to feel you in me," Saris groaned. "I need you to claim me."

Trajan didn't need to hear more. Grabbing Saris's ass cheeks, Trajan pulled them apart and guided his cock in. His long groan matched Saris's as he sank home. Trajan paused just a moment to savor the feeling of being deep inside his mate. He doubted anything felt so good.

"Trajan," Saris whispered against the soft skin of Trajan's neck, reminding him of the gorgeous man he held in his arms. Saris's hands kneaded Trajan's shoulders. His hips moved frantically against Trajan's.

Trajan chuckled at Saris's impatience. He used a sharp claw to cut a small line in his chest just over his heart. "Drink, my own, drink and be mine."

Trajan's heart fractured into a million glowing pieces when Saris leaned forward and began to lap at the small trail of blood on his chest without a hint of hesitation. He felt blissfully happy, alive.

Pulling Saris away from his chest, Trajan pushed him back enough that he could lean in and sink his teeth into the soft flesh of Saris's neck. Power and strength filled him, and his heart sang with delight as Saris's sweet blood swept over his tongue.

A buzzing began in Trajan's head. It grew louder and louder until it began to distract Trajan from loving his mate. Trajan lifted his head, giving it a small shake, but the buzzing grew even louder.

Trajan opened his mouth to say something to Saris when the sweetest sound in the world filled his mind and nearly brought him to his knees.

"Tra, Tra, Tra," Saris cried out over and over again like a silent mantra, and Trajan could hear it all in his mind.

"Sari," Trajan whispered back through their newly developed mind link. He felt Saris jerk, then his head fell back against his shoulders, and he stared up at Trajan in shocked amazement.

"Trajan," Saris said, "I just—"

Trajan nodded. *"Just heard me in your mind?"*

Saris nodded.

Trajan grinned, delighting in the shared moment between them. "It's called the mating link, my own. It means that we have finally accepted our mating."

"Trajan—"

Trajan thrust his hips forward at the same time that he pulled Saris's hips down. He showered kisses around Saris's lips and jaw.

"Love you, my own, my Sari," Trajan whispered. Between each word, he planted kisses on his shoulders, neck, and face. His hands caressed the gentle curve of Saris's hips, his ass. His cock burrowed into Saris's tight grasp over and over again.

His breath came in deep, soul-drenching drafts as he exploded in a downpour of fiery sensations. Waves of ecstasy throbbed through him. Saris cried out, filling the space between them with his hot seed, his inner muscles gripping Trajan until he couldn't move.

"Sari," Trajan roared as he yielded to the searing need building inside of him. His release came in a great rush that consumed him until the only thing that mattered in his world was the man in his arms.

Trajan leaned Saris against the rock face behind him. He rested his head on Saris's as the knot inside of him took hold, locking them together. Saris's exhausted eyes sparkled up at him.

"I like this," Sari said.

"What?"

"You not being able to leave me immediately." Saris tightened his hips emphasizing the way the knot connected them.

Trajan chuckled. "I like it, too. It gives me a good excuse to cuddle with you afterwards without seeming too needy."

Saris wrapped his arms around Trajan's neck. "You can be needy anytime that you want to." He grinned, his eyes dropping down to Trajan's lips. "I'm feeling needy myself, so you'd better kiss me."

Chapter 9

Saris groaned, rolling toward the warm body next to him. It didn't seem to relieve the persistent ache in his side. He wiggled a bit trying to get away from whatever pressed against his side.

Rolling onto his back and opening his eyes, Saris gasped, realizing a fear of panic when he saw the man standing over him.

"Well, well, well," Toc Jerell smirked, "it's about time you joined us."

Saris's eyes batted around the cave frantically as he took in the scene around him. Toc stood over him and Trajan, the phase pistol in his hand aimed directly at them. Two more men stood at the entrance to the cave, the phase pistols in their hands aimed in the same direction.

"Trajan," Saris whispered hoping that their mental bond still connected them. Sheer, black fright swept through him when Trajan didn't move, didn't respond to him in any manner. He wanted to turn his head and look at his mate, to assure himself that he remained uninjured, but Saris was afraid to.

"Trajan!" Saris exclaimed through their bond, nearly shouting this time.

"Shh, Sari, I'm awake."

Saris closed his eyes in relief only to open them a second later when a hard boot connected with his rib cage. He grunted, suppressing his gasp of pain. He wouldn't give Toc Jerell the satisfaction of knowing he had hurt him.

His mind worked overtime as he tried to develop a plan to get out of the dangerous situation he and Trajan found themselves in, but nothing came immediately to mind. Keeping Trajan safe overshadowed every other thought racing through Saris's head.

"What do you want, Jerell?" Saris asked.

Toc Jerell brought the gun in his hand up to his lips, tapping it there several times. "What do I want?" he asked. "What do I want? What the hell do you think I want?" he shouted, pointing the pistol back at Saris.

The devious gleam in his eyes that told Saris that Toc Jerell had lost his ever-loving mind. He absently wondered if Toc Jerell was on some type of drugs. He didn't seem to be in touch with reality.

Toc kicked him again. "Get up!"

"Trajan?"

"Go ahead, Sari, do what he says."

Saris rolled to his side and climbed to his knees, all the while keeping his eyes on the gun Toc Jerell held in his hand. He grabbed the edge of the silver warming blanket and pulled it up with him as he stood, trying his best to cover all of his manly parts.

He realized a moment later that it didn't matter when he saw the lustful glint in Toc's eyes. It sent a cold shiver of fear up his spine.

"Drop it." Toc waved the gun at the blanket.

Saris could feel the heat of embarrassment building up in his body as he dropped the blanket, revealing his naked body to Toc's interested gaze. After Trajan had ripped his body suit last night, Saris hadn't bothered to find something else to wear when he went to sleep. Now he wished he had.

"Oh, you'll do nicely," Toc chortled. "You'll do very nicely indeed."

Saris had absolutely no plans to ask Toc what he would do nicely for. He didn't want to know. Shock filled Saris a moment later when Trajan spoke from below him. Apparently he had no qualms about asking.

"Why do you want Saris so bad?"

"Ah, the big warrior is awake," Toc said, his grin big and toothy. A wave of apprehension swept through Saris when Toc waved his pistol at Trajan. "You can get up, as well."

Saris glanced over his shoulder and watched Trajan get to his feet. He desperately wanted to throw himself into Trajan's arms and pretend that they both weren't standing naked before a crazy man with a gun.

Toc whistled low under his breath, bringing Saris's attention back to him. "Well, Saris, if you're going to be unfaithful to me at least you chose a spectacular specimen. I had no idea that Katzmen were so well made. I just might have to try him out before we leave."

Fear, stark and vivid, filled Saris. Toc Jerell talked about forcing his mate. Saris knew he couldn't let that happen, even if it meant sacrificing himself. With the single blinding thought of saving Trajan in his mind, Saris stepped forward.

"You never answered Trajan, advisor" Saris said, refusing to refer to the man by his name. "What do you want with me? I've never even met you before a few days ago."

Toc's head tilted to one side as if he considered Saris's words. "But I know you, Saris. I've been watching you for ages, waiting until the time came to claim you."

"Claim me for what?"

"To give birth to the next Elquone Dynasty, my dynasty," Toc replied as if Saris should already know this.

"I never completed the brüter training program. I can't give birth." And for that, Saris would be forever grateful. It wasn't that he didn't dream of having children now that he had found Trajan. He just didn't want to have children with Toc Jerell.

"So innocent, so naive," Toc drawled. "So very wrong."

Icy fear twisted around Saris. "What do you mean?"

Toc's hand moved out to caress the side of Saris's face. Saris quickly jerked away, not wanting Toc to touch him. A moment later, he felt a sharp pain in his face as Toc backhanded him.

"Don't ever pull away from me," Toc shouted, anger making his face red and muddled. "You belong to me. You've always belonged to me, you and your brother."

"Karis?" Saris whispered in shock. "What does Karis have to do with this?"

"You both entered the Brüter Caste at the same time. You were both meant to be mine, but Karis became too emotional, too high strung. Even after he gave birth to my son he resisted the things I wanted from him."

"You?" Saris whispered in horror. "You held Karis's contract? You sent him home?"

"I had to," Toc insisted. "He kept asking about the child, always the child. He didn't understand that the boy needed special training, an environment meant to educate him for his future as the next High Ruler of Elquone."

"What?"

Toc smirked. "Didn't I mention that? How rude of me." Toc began slowly pacing around the cavern. "The beauty and intelligence of your genetic makeup, of Karis's genetic makeup, make both of you ideal candidates to unite with mine. Together, we will create the next ruler of Elquone. He will be a god!"

"I can't give birth!" Saris shouted. "I'm not a brüter."

Saris felt the earth beneath him shift and start to fall away when Toc grinned over at him. "Oh, but you can, my dear, you can."

"I never finished the program," Saris insisted.

"No, you didn't, but even if you had it wouldn't have mattered. I chose you to be my brüter because you were born with the ability to be a breeder. All brüters are. That's why they are chosen as brüters."

Toc laughed. It sounded sinister and twisted and chilled Saris to the very bone. "You don't think you're chosen because you're pretty to look at, do you? While that is a plus in your case, I chose you to be a brüter because you can breed. You were born that way."

"But I thought we underwent some sort of genetic manipulation that turned us into breeders."

Toc shook his head. "No, that's just the story that they feed you so that you won't fight your training. Like I said, you were born a breeder."

"Trajan," Saris cried out silently as Toc's words began to make sense to him. If what Toc said was true, then Saris could even now be carrying Trajan's child. Brüters only needed to eat meat to be fertile, and Saris had eaten rabbit for dinner right before they had made love.

"I know, Sari," Trajan whispered back. *"While I am overjoyed with the prospect, right now we need to concentrate on freeing ourselves from this mad man. We will explore the possibility of a child once this is over."*

"But how do we get away from him? He's crazy."

"I'm working on it." Trajan chuckled silently.

"Work faster, damn it," Saris demanded.

"Yes, my own."

Assured that Trajan had a plan to free them, Saris returned his attention to the man pacing in front of him. Toc looked a little too confident for Saris's liking, as if he knew something Saris didn't.

"Why are you doing this?" Saris asked. "Elquone already has a High Ruler."

Toc shook his head. "Not for very much longer. I've been slowly feeding him whistle weed over the last five years. Yes, it's time consuming and a slow way to die, but just a little amount can drive a man crazy."

"You're poisoning him with whistle weed? Why?"

"A ruler that is removed from his position because he is crazy is much better than one that is assassinated. By poisoning him slowly, I am also assured that he will die soon after being removed from his throne, thereby, not causing issue when I take over."

Saris couldn't fault Toc's logic. It did make sense. No one would look into the death of a ruler removed from his throne because he was crazy. If he was assassinated, however, there would be a huge investigation.

"What makes you think that you will be chosen as his successor?"

"I've already made arrangements for that. It seems that the High Ruler has a certain taste for bedroom games. I made myself available to play those games with him, thus, earning his everlasting love and esteem." Toc gave a little shrug. "Once the drugs had entered his system, he looked to his lover, me, for guidance. It was easy to convince him to make me his heir."

It seemed that Toc had thought of everything.

"And what about me?" Trajan asked from behind Saris. "What do you plan on doing with me because you know I will never let you take Saris."

"You?" Toc laughed. "Why, you were killed in a horrible accident while using your escape pod." He waved his hand in a dismissive gesture. "Oh, it will all be very tragic. My sensors picked up a distress beacon. When I came to investigate, I found poor Saris alive, beside himself because his big strong protector got killed in the landing. I may even let him attend your funeral."

Saris growled, taking a threatening step toward Toc. No one threatened his mate. He took another step toward Toc, intent on attacking him and hopefully getting the phase pistol away from him, when strong arms suddenly pushed him to the side.

As he fell to the ground, Saris saw Trajan leap at Toc, taking him unaware. The men began to grapple for the upper hand. Saris wanted to help, but the two men standing by the door rushed in, and he knew he needed to stop them.

Grabbing two handfuls of sand from the floor, Saris jumped to his feet and leapt toward them, tossing sand at their faces. He knew he had distracted them for a mere moment. That's all he needed.

Bending low, Saris dove for the knees of the closest man, knocking him to the ground. He heard the man grunt, then go still.

Saris glanced up to see blood welling on his forehead and dripping down his face.

One down, one to go. Saris glanced over his shoulder to the other man, his heart sinking when he found himself looking down the barrel of a phase pistol. The man gestured with the pistol for Saris to get to his feet.

His hands held out to his sides, Saris slowly climbed to his feet. A glance beyond the man's shoulder drove the breath from Saris's lungs. Toc, an almost exact match to Trajan in height and weight, had his arm around Trajan's throat. He slowly choked the life from him.

Saris's eyes met Trajan's for just a moment, but the whole world passed between them in that time. Saris could read Trajan's love for him, his sorrow that he wouldn't be there to see the birth of their child, even his regret that he wasn't able to protect Saris.

Saris shook his head in a silent gasp. His anger became a scalding fury. He didn't care if he died. He didn't care that he might never see Trajan again. He didn't care that emotions overwhelmed him. He didn't care about anything but saving Trajan.

"No!" He shouted as he dove at the man holding him at gun point. Saris felt a searing pain in his shoulder, but thoughts of Trajan spurred him on. He clawed at the man's face. He used his teeth to rip into soft flesh. He pounded on the man's body with his hands.

Saris's rage was ferocious, blinding him to anything but the need to get to Trajan. He didn't realize that the man he had attacked lay dead and bleeding on the floor until a low groan across from him soaked through his fury.

Saris looked up at the two men standing a few feet away from him. Toc had a look on his face of utter horror. Trajan looked proud and just a little worried. Saris could understand why. Toc stood behind Trajan, an arm held tightly around his throat. His other hand held the phase pistol pointed at Trajan's temple.

Saris took a step closer. Toc jerked the pistol in his hand, jabbing it closer to Trajan's temple.

"Not another step," he ordered.

"Hurt my mate and I will kill you," Saris growled.

"Your mate?" Toc asked in astonishment. "Your mate? You mated this Katzman?"

"I did."

Toc suddenly began to laugh. Confusion filled Saris until he spoke. "I may have a better use for you than I thought," Toc said as he looked down at Trajan. "I'm sure you'll be very helpful in keeping Saris in line."

"You let him go and I'll do anything you want."

"Sari!" Trajan yelled through their bond. Saris gave him a regretful look.

"I'm sorry, love, but I can't let you be harmed," Saris replied. He looked back up at Toc. "Will you let him go?" he asked out loud. "I swear I'll do whatever you want."

Toc watched him for several long tense moments then shook his head. "No, I don't think so. If I let him go, then you have no reason to follow through on your words. No, I think we'll keep him. Maybe we'll send him to the Vergnügen Caste and then we can both enjoy him."

The very thought of Trajan being some mindless pleasure slave sent waves of horror and disgust spiraling through him. Sent to the Vergnügen Caste, everything that Trajan was, everything that he knew, would be gone. He wouldn't be Trajan anymore.

Saris tensed his body, ready to attack Toc and free his mate, when Toc suddenly got a strange look on his face. Saris watched in shock as Toc crumbled to the floor, the phase pistol falling from his limp fingers.

Trajan fell to the floor beside him, the stunned look on his face matching Saris's. He pushed himself up to a sitting position, both he and Saris looking to the young man that stood there, a large rock in his hand.

"Got anything to eat?" the young man said as if he had not just knocked a man out with a rock. "I'm starved."

* * * *

Saris sat on the floor next to Trajan as he doctored his injuries. There weren't many, a few scratches and abrasions, nothing life threatening, but he'd be hurting for a few days. Still, Saris wished he had access to his own medical supplies.

The young man that had saved them both, Anjali, sat across from them eating the cream colored goo from the emergency rations like it was food fit for a king.

Saris would be forever grateful to Anjali for his timely rescue. He had saved both him and Trajan. Toc and the second man now sat against the far wall of the cavern, tied up, and ready to be transported.

"You know we're going to have to talk about this, Sari," Trajan said.

Saris nodded. "I know, but I'm not ready to talk yet. I just need a while longer to process all that happened, all that we learned. Then we'll talk."

"You know I love you, right?"

Saris nodded again, this time giving Trajan a smile. "I know, Trajan. I love you, too."

Trajan's hand covered Saris's abdomen. "I won't be upset if you do have our child."

Saris placed his hand over Trajan's. "I think a little warrior just like his father would be a wonderful thing, a little boy with your strength and—"

"And your courage?"

Saris chuckled. "That wasn't courage, Trajan. That was abject terror."

"Don't fool yourself, Sari." Trajan chuckled. He wrapped his arms around Saris and pulled him down to rest at his side. "That was courage, and I am very proud of you. A little in awe, but proud nonetheless."

Saris's breath hitched in his throat when he felt Trajan's hand caress his hip. A small yelp escaped his mouth when Trajan smacked him on the ass. "Still, I may have to punish you for being so reckless with my heart."

"Trajan," Saris groaned. He leaned up to kiss his mate when a chuckle sounded behind him. Knowing that Anjali sat across the fire from them, Saris turned to face whatever new adversary stood behind them.

"Only you, Trajan, could kidnap someone, escape undetected, get shot down, and still come out of it with a mate."

Chapter 10

"Okay, Demyan, just one more small push," Saris directed as he stood over the small Elquone, assisting in the birth of his child. "That's it, that's it. Oh, here he comes."

Saris gently grasped the small shoulders pushing through the natural birthing slit in Demyan's abdomen. He cradled the infant's head in his hand as he guided him out. Suddenly, the baby slid free, and Saris held a wet, squalling infant in his hands.

"Oh, he is a beautiful little boy, Demyan," Saris said as he placed the small infant farther up on Demyan's chest. He carefully cleaned the infant's mouth of mucus, ensuring his clear airway.

As Chellak repeatedly kissed Demyan's face, murmuring soothing words of praise to his mate, the infant let out one lone cry, then stuck his fist in his mouth, fading back to sleep. Chellak quickly looked up at Saris in panic.

"Demyan wants to know if he's okay. He's not making any more noises. Shouldn't he be crying or something?"

"No," Saris replied, "that's an old wives' tale. He's just sleeping. It takes a lot of energy for a little baby to be born, both from the baby and the one giving birth." Saris nodded his head to where Demyan lay, his eyes closed.

The more Saris watched, however, the more concerned he grew. Demyan didn't look like he slept. He looked to be in pain. Saris quickly cut the umbilical cord and lifted the baby. He wrapped him in a small blanket and handed him to Chellak before turning back to Demyan.

"What's wrong?" Chellak shouted. "Why is Demyan still in pain?"

Saris shook his head. "I don't know." Saris quickly checked Demyan's heart rate. It beat way to fast. Further examination of Demyan had Saris grinning. Chellak looked at him like he had lost his mind.

"What?" Chellak shouted.

Saris reached into the small birthing opening in Demyan's abdomen and guided another infant out of his womb. He heard a small gasp from Chellak as he laid the infant on Demyan's chest. He quickly cleared the baby's airway and cut the umbilical cord.

Wrapping the infant in another small blanket, he held the child out to the High Ruler. "Chellak Rai, I'd like to introduce you to your daughter."

"Twins?" Chellak whispered as he took the small bundle in his other arm. He looked stunned.

"Apparently so," Saris replied, a wide grin on his face. "It seems your little mate is full of surprises."

Chellak laughed quietly. "He always has been."

Saris leaned down over Demyan and assured himself that no more surprise babies would pop out. Once he knew all the babies had made their appearances, he covered the small birthing incision with mucca cream.

Saris had discovered mucca cream quite by accident and now used it in all of the births he assisted in. Mucca cream would encourage the healing and closing of the birthing incision. Once the incision healed, there would be no sign of it until the next child came along.

One last check of Demyan found him sleeping peacefully. Saris knew he had to be exhausted. It took a lot of work to give birth to one child, let alone two. Demyan should sleep for the next few hours. Chellak seemed to be quite content to sit in a chair next to Demyan holding his twin children in his arms.

Saris patted Chellak on the shoulder. "I'm going to step outside for a little while and get cleaned up. I'll be right outside if you need me."

Chellak didn't even look up from the faces of his children as he nodded his head. "Thank you, Saris, for everything."

"That's what I'm here for, Chellak. Now get some rest." Saris stepped out of the room and quietly closed the door behind him. He leaned back against it, taking a deep breath, then chuckling to himself. Giving birth was hard on the doctor as well.

"How's Demyan?"

Saris glanced over to find Anjali standing by the window watching him. The young man intrigued him. Not because he looked drop dead gorgeous, and he did, but because he had an unusual personality.

Ever since Anjali hit Toc Jerell over the head, Saris tried to thank the young man. Anjali wouldn't hear of it. He insisted that he was just helping out, that he hadn't done anything that anyone else wouldn't have done.

"He's fine, sleeping right now." Saris grinned. "Chellak is currently being dazzled by his son and his daughter."

"Twins?" Anjali asked, surprised.

Saris nodded. "I can only assume the little girl hid behind her brother because I didn't see her. She's healthy, though, and a good weight even if she is a little small. I suspect she will take after Demyan in size. The boy, however, is definitely Chellak Rai's son. He's huge."

Anjali giggled, another thing that intrigued Saris. Anjali giggled, he didn't chuckle or laugh, he giggled. His mannerisms were often feminine as well. With his blond hair, unbelievably long eyelashes, and his delicate features, Saris wouldn't have even known he was a man if he hadn't seen him naked.

"Where's your shadow?" Saris asked, referring to Bogden Wuher, one of Chellak's warriors. Since the moment he had arrived with

Chellak to rescue them and took a single look at Anjali, Saris had yet to see Bogden leave his side.

Anjali rolled his eyes. "I sent him to get me something to eat. I swear that man won't let me breathe on my own."

Saris chuckled. "He likes you."

Anjali's face flushed as silence filled the room for a moment. "I like him, too. I just wish he'd give me a little space."

"Be careful what you wish for, Anjali, you just might get it."

Saris turned to see Yerik standing in the doorway. His mate, Ciprian, Chellak Rai's brother and right hand, stood beside him, an arm thrown around Yerik's shoulders.

"And that cryptic response would mean what?" Anjali asked.

"Chellak once wished Demyan would give him space, leave him alone. So Demyan left. Chellak almost lost him. If it wasn't due to their mating bond and Demyan feeling Chellak's pain, he might never have come back. You don't have that bond with Bogden. You won't feel his pain."

Anjali stayed quiet. After a moment, he nodded and turned back to the window. Saris glanced over at Yerik, an eyebrow raised in query. Yerik just shrugged.

"So, how are my niece and nephew?" Yerik asked as he walked over to stand next to Saris.

"You knew?"

"I had an idea," Yerik said. "Nothing I could put my finger on exactly, but you have to admit, he looked huge."

Saris nodded. "He had reason to be."

"Don't laugh, Saris, you'll be just as big," Yerik chuckled.

"I'll be just as bi—" Saris stuttered. "What are you saying?"

Yerik laid his hand over Saris's abdomen. He rubbed his hand in a small circle then grinned. "Twins tend to do that to you."

"Twins!" exclaimed a voice from the doorway. Saris looked up to see Trajan standing in the doorway where Ciprian and Yerik had stood moments before. His mouth hung open in stunned amazement.

Saris hesitated, apprehensive of Trajan's response. They had discussed the possibility of having children but at a later date, much later. Seemed they didn't have the choice now. Their baby, or babies, were on the way.

Saris had eaten nothing but fruit and vegetables since their rescue, just to be safe. Eating meat made him fertile. Considering that they had made love right after Saris ate the rabbit Trajan had caught, Saris now knew that he had been fertile then, and Trajan's seed had taken root.

"You do like to do things in a big way, don't you?" Trajan drawled as he walked across the room. He wrapped his arms around Saris. "Guess that rigid control you have on your emotions is going right out the window then."

"You don't mind?" Saris said mentally as he buried his head between Trajan's neck and shoulder. *"I suspect that my emotions are going to be totally out of control. I haven't figured out how to deal with them now and I haven't even hit the pregnancy mood swings yet."*

"We'll deal with it as it comes, my own," Trajan replied. *"As long as you and our children are safe, there isn't anything we can't deal with."*

"Thank you, Trajan, for everything."

"That reminds me," Trajan said as he wrapped one arm around Saris's shoulders and pointed the other one toward the doorway. "I have a little surprise for you."

Saris looked to the doorway and let out a cry. He ran across the room and threw himself into the arms of the blond-haired man standing there. "Karis!"

"Hey, brother," Karis replied. "I see Trajan wasn't lying to me when he told me that he had made it his mission in life to make you happy." His hand stroked the hair on the back of Saris's head. "I'm glad for you, Saris."

Saris pushed himself back from Karis, looking him up and down. "How did you get here?" His eyebrows drew together in a frown. "What are you doing here? I thought you were back on Elquone with our parents."

"I was," Karis replied. He looked past Saris to Trajan who stood across the room with a grin on his face. "But it seems your mate over there decided that you needed here. He kidnapped me."

Saris laughed, turning toward Trajan. "He does that a lot." Saris dropped his arms from around Karis and crossed over to Trajan to wrap them around his waist. "He does a lot of things that he really shouldn't, but each one of them makes me happy."

"Then this should make you ecstatic," Karis said. He stepped to one side and gestured to someone right outside the door. "When he came for me, Trajan told me that he had something he wanted to return to me, something that I had lost."

Saris's mouth dropped open as a small boy stepped into the room and reached for Karis's hand. Karis had the world's widest grin on his face, tears in his eyes. "Saris, I'd like you to meet Torin, my son and your nephew."

Saris felt tears well up in his eyes. He couldn't remember being so overwhelmed with emotion, not even when he fought off Toc Jerell and his goons. The joy and happiness inside of him threatened to spill over and flood him.

Saris turned to Trajan, his mate, his safety from the world, and buried his face in his neck. He knew Trajan could feel his hot tears slipping down his neck. Trajan didn't say anything. He just tightened his arms around Saris and let him cry.

"I know I've said this before, Trajan, but thank you. You've given me so much and I have given you so little. Why do you put up with me?" Saris whispered.

"You give me everything, Sari. Without you, remember, I am only half of what I could be. Half my soul, half my heart, half of everything that I am," Trajan replied out loud for everyone to hear. "I don't put up with you, my own, I need you. You're my dream mate."

THE END

WWW.STORMYGLENN.COM

ABOUT THE AUTHOR

Stormy believes the only thing sexier than a man in cowboy boots is two, or three men in cowboy boots. She also believes in love at first sight, soul mates, true love, and happy endings.

Stormy lives in the great Northwest region of the USA, with her gorgeous husband and soul mate, six very active teenagers, two boxer/collie puppies, two old biddy cats, and three fish.

When she's not being a mother to her six teenagers or cleaning up after her two 70 pound lap puppies, you can usually find her cuddled in bed with a book in her hand and a puppy in her lap, or on her laptop, creating the next sexy man for one of her stories. Stormy welcomes comments from readers. You can find her website at www.stormyglenn.com.

Also by Stormy Glenn

Wolf Creek Pack 1: *Full Moon Mating*
Wolf Creek Pack 2: *Just A Taste Of Me*
Wolf Creek Pack 3: *Tasty Treats: Volume 3, Man to Man*
Wolf Creek Pack 4: *Blood Prince*
Wolf Creek Pack 5: *Love, Always, Promise*
Tri-Omega Mates 1: *Secret Desires*
Tri-Omega Mates 2: *Forbidden Desires*
Tri-Omega Mates 3: *Hidden Desires*
Tri-Omega Mates 4: *Stolen Desires*
Tri-Omega Mates 5: *Unspoken Desires*
Lover's of Alpha Squad 1: *Mari's Men*
Lover's of Alpha Squad 2: *The Doctor's Patience*
Lover's of Alpha Squad 3: *Julia's Knight*
Lover's of Alpha Squad 4: *Three of a Kind*
Love's Legacy 1: *Cowboy Legacy*
Love's Legacy 2: *Cowboy Dreams*
Sweet Treats
Mr. Wonderful
The Katzman's Mate
Sequel to *The Katzman's Mate: Dream Mate*
My Lupine Lover
Wolf Queen
The Master's Pet
His Gentle Touch
Available at

BOOKSTRAND.COM

Siren Publishing, Inc.
www.SirenPublishing.com

Breinigsville, PA USA
06 July 2010
241245BV00003B/88/P